MRS. JEFFRIES
and the
Alms of the Angel

Berkley Prime Crime titles by Emily Brightwell

THE INSPECTOR AND MRS. JEFFRIES
MRS. JEFFRIES DUSTS FOR CLUES
THE GHOST AND MRS. JEFFRIES
MRS. JEFFRIES TAKES STOCK
MRS. JEFFRIES ON THE BALL
MRS. JEFFRIES ON THE TRAIL
MRS. JEFFRIES PLAYS THE COOK
MRS. JEFFRIES AND THE MISSING ALIBI
MRS. JEFFRIES STANDS CORRECTED
MRS. JEFFRIES TAKES THE STAGE
MRS. JEFFRIES QUESTIONS THE ANSWER
MRS. JEFFRIES REVEALS HER ART
MRS. JEFFRIES TAKES THE CAKE
MRS. JEFFRIES ROCKS THE BOAT
MRS. JEFFRIES WEEDS THE PLOT
MRS. JEFFRIES PINCHES THE POST
MRS. JEFFRIES PLEADS HER CASE
MRS. JEFFRIES SWEEPS THE CHIMNEY
MRS. JEFFRIES STALKS THE HUNTER
MRS. JEFFRIES AND THE SILENT KNIGHT
MRS. JEFFRIES APPEALS THE VERDICT
MRS. JEFFRIES AND THE BEST LAID PLANS
MRS. JEFFRIES AND THE FEAST OF ST. STEPHEN
MRS. JEFFRIES HOLDS THE TRUMP
MRS. JEFFRIES IN THE NICK OF TIME
MRS. JEFFRIES AND THE YULETIDE WEDDINGS
MRS. JEFFRIES SPEAKS HER MIND
MRS. JEFFRIES FORGES AHEAD
MRS. JEFFRIES AND THE MISTLETOE MIX-UP
MRS. JEFFRIES DEFENDS HER OWN
MRS. JEFFRIES TURNS THE TIDE
MRS. JEFFRIES AND THE MERRY GENTLEMEN
MRS. JEFFRIES AND THE ONE WHO GOT AWAY
MRS. JEFFRIES WINS THE PRIZE
MRS. JEFFRIES RIGHTS A WRONG
MRS. JEFFRIES AND THE THREE WISE WOMEN
MRS. JEFFRIES AND THE ALMS OF THE ANGEL

Anthologies

MRS. JEFFRIES LEARNS THE TRADE
MRS. JEFFRIES TAKES A SECOND LOOK
MRS. JEFFRIES TAKES TEA AT THREE
MRS. JEFFRIES SALLIES FORTH
MRS. JEFFRIES PLEADS THE FIFTH
MRS. JEFFRIES SERVES AT SIX

MRS. JEFFRIES
and the
Alms of the Angel

Emily Brightwell

BERKLEY PRIME CRIME

NEW YORK

BERKLEY PRIME CRIME
Published by Berkley
An imprint of Penguin Random House LLC
penguinrandomhouse.com

Copyright © 2019 by Cheryl A. Arguile
Penguin Random House supports copyright. Copyright fuels creativity,
encourages diverse voices, promotes free speech, and creates a vibrant culture.
Thank you for buying an authorized edition of this book and for complying with
copyright laws by not reproducing, scanning, or distributing any part of it
in any form without permission. You are supporting writers and allowing
Penguin Random House to continue to publish books for every reader.

BERKLEY and the BERKLEY & B colophon are registered trademarks and
BERKLEY PRIME CRIME is a trademark of Penguin Random House LLC.

Library of Congress Cataloging-in-Publication Data

Names: Brightwell, Emily, author.
Title: Mrs. Jeffries and the Alms of the angel / Emily Brightwell.
Description: First Edition. | New York : Berkley Prime Crime, 2019. |
Series: A Victorian mystery; book 38
Identifiers: LCCN 2019022556 (print) | LCCN 2019022557 (ebook) |
ISBN 9780451492241 (hardcover) | ISBN 9780451492258 (ebook)
Subjects: LCSH: Murder—Investigation—Fiction. | GSAFD: Mystery fiction.
Classification: LCC PS3552.R46443 M623 2019 (print) |
LCC PS3552.R46443 (ebook) | DDC 813/.54—dc23
LC record available at https://lccn.loc.gov/2019022556
LC ebook record available at https://lccn.loc.gov/2019022557

First Edition: September 2019

Printed in Canada
1   3   5   7   9   10   8   6   4   2

Cover art by Mark Fredrickson

For Julia, Lady Higgs, a delightful person and a wonderful traveling companion, even on the Loneliest Highway in the World.

CHAPTER 1

Darkness could conceal numerous sins, but on this December night the killer needed it to hide only one. The traffic from the busy street outside the five-story house would cover any noise the victim might make, and she was the only one to worry about; the servants were gone. She was alone and that wasn't just luck, either. It was good planning.

The assailant glanced to the right, confirming that the house next door had already closed the curtains for the evening. Again, good planning.

Moving faster now, the murderer hurried down the cobblestone walkway and into the garden proper. It was black as sin, but that was of no concern. The slayer had been here many times before.

The garden was huge, especially for a London house. It was separated from its neighbor by a hedge of now barren gooseberry bushes. A strip of grass stood between the shrubbery and an old uneven cobblestone path that ended at the edge of the small kitchen terrace. Across the lawn were two huge oak trees, now bare and stripped of their leaves, and a seven-foot-tall statue of an angel with outstretched arms. Rose-bushes, cut back for the winter, stood sentinel at the far end of the property next to a garden shed. Stopping at the edge of the terrace, the killer put down the sack.

Giving the burlap a well-placed kick, the murderer laughed as an enraged series of shrieks and screeches came from the depths of the bag. Good. That should get the old witch outside. The air had turned colder and it was well past time to deal with the matter at hand.

The cat would be released when it was finished. It was important that "Gladstone" be alive in the days to come—not that the murderer cared whether the foul-tempered feline lived or died, but it wouldn't do to have anyone notice the animal had gone missing only this morning. The police weren't complete fools, and the plan could go awry if they managed to connect Gladstone's disappearance with tonight's task.

Catching the creature had been easy: The kitchen door was always held open with a brick. The miserable cow didn't care that her servants might freeze, but she did want her ill-mannered cat to come and go as he pleased. Only minutes after the scullery maid had propped open the door early this morning, a few ounces of fresh fish on the side of the terrace had done the trick.

Gladstone loved to eat—loved it so much, it barely registered when he was scruffed, picked up, and tossed into a heavy burlap potato bag. The catnapping had been done early enough to avoid anyone on the street noticing a wiggling sack or hearing Gladstone's furious screams.

The trespasser stared at the kitchen door and, when it didn't open, leaned to one side and administered another kick, this time hard enough so that the yowls of the enraged tom could be heard halfway to Westminister.

Light appeared in the kitchen door window, and the intruder picked up the sack and raced across the dead winter grass to the statue, dumped it onto the ground, and then ran to the other side of the garden shed, where a heavy shovel was propped up and waiting. Grabbing the handle, the attacker hurried back to the statue, stood behind the wide base, and waited for the victim.

"Gladstone? Gladstone, is that you?" Margaret Starling stepped out the kitchen door holding an oil lamp. "Gladstone! Come on, darling. Mama's been worried. Where are you?"

There was a pathetic meow as the cat heard her voice.

"Oh, my goodness, Gladstone, where are you?" Holding the lamp high, Margaret crossed the terrace and stepped onto the lawn, moving as fast as her arthritic old legs could carry her. "Please, sweetie, Mama's been so worried. Where are you?"

Gladstone meowed again piteously.

Margaret, whose ears were still sharp, stopped across from the tree. "Gladstone?"

"Meow."

Come on, come on, get closer. The visitor gripped the handle tightly before moving farther out of her immediate line of sight.

"Meow, meow!" The cries turned into a wail. Margaret squinted and stepped onto the lawn. "Oh, my gracious, Gladstone, are you in there?" She hurried toward the burlap sack, which was now shaking, twisting, and wiggling as the animal responded to his mistress.

"Who could have done this?" she muttered as she knelt down on the cold ground, wincing as her sensitive knees settled into the dirt. She put the lamp down and reached for the rope holding the top of the bag shut. "I'll bet it was that disgusting Mrs. Huxton. It's the sort of petty nastiness she'd indulge in just because you chased that stupid spaniel of hers out of the yard." But the rope wasn't tied—it was threaded through the top of the material—and her hands, like her knees and ankles, were riddled with arthritic inflammation.

Gladstone meowed once more, this time less loudly but equally piteously.

"Don't worry, my darling, it won't be much longer. Mama's going to the kitchen to get the scissors . . ." She started to get up. But suddenly there was a whooshing sound cutting through the air and then a searing pain in the back of her head. Then another blow came, and another, but by this time Margaret Starling was past hearing anything. Her body slumped to one side, almost cradling the sack against her middle.

Her killer took a deep breath, hurried to the angel statue, and leaned the shovel against the cold stone base. Moving fast, the murderer stepped around the dead woman, bent down, and grabbed the top of the bag.

Gladstone started screeching again, only this was no piteous meow now: The animal was righteously enraged, kicking and clawing at the burlap and shrieking at the top of his lungs. Ignoring the cat's complaints, the assailant picked up the moving sack and hurried to the back door. As expected, it was unlocked. Opening it, the killer knelt down and tugged at the ends of the rope, untying the knot quickly. The top of the bag drooped to the ground, and Gladstone, ears back and teeth bared, leapt out and flew at his captor.

The murderer tried to protect his face by jerking the arm up, but Gladstone, obviously out for revenge, wasn't deterred in the least. He clasped all four paws around the flailing appendage and held tight. The attack was sudden, vicious, and so strong that the surprised killer scrambled backward. But the cat was relentless, digging his claws into the thin material of the catnapper's coat as the killer frantically flung his arm in a circle in a futile attempt to dislodge the furious beast.

The murderer had picked the garment because it was working-class and ordinary, and would be easily overlooked when the escape was made. But that had been a terrible mistake. The threadbare material was no protection against sharp claws or teeth. For one long, eerie moment the assailant wondered if the cat was wreaking havoc to take revenge for the death of his mistress, but that was impossible—this wasn't a dog protecting its master; it was a damned cat. It should be running by now.

But Gladstone wasn't going anywhere. He worked his way down the assailant's arm until he could sink his teeth into the flesh. Gasping now in pain, the killer banged against the partially open kitchen door, finally dislodging the animal. But Gladstone wasn't finished. He stood there for a second, ears flattened backward, hissing, and then gave a mighty leap toward the assailant, landing on a shoulder but close enough to deliver a stinging attack to the killer's exposed neck and dig his claws in deep enough to draw blood.

The visitor twisted hard to one side, trying desperately to

move the cat while at the same time keeping fingers, arms, and hands away from the piercing claws and bared pointed teeth.

Gladstone took one more swipe, aiming for the assailants chin but missing before he leapt off and disappeared through the kitchen door.

The killer got up and debated pursuing the animal and beating it to death, but suddenly a light went on in the house next door.

Taking care of Gladstone would have to wait for another time.

Mrs. Goodge, the cook at Upper Edmonton Gardens, home of Inspector Gerald Witherspoon, put the pan of bread in the oven, and closed the door. "Did the inspector say what time he'd be home tonight?" she asked the housekeeper, Mrs. Jeffries.

Mrs. Jeffries looked up from the household accounts ledger. She was a woman of late middle age, with auburn hair turning to gray, freckles sprinkled across her nose, and warm brown eyes. "He said nothing one way or another, so I expect he'll be home at his usual time. Why do you ask?"

"I'm wondering whether or not to make a lamb stew or to use up that beefsteak." The cook straightened and pushed a lock of white hair back under her cook's cap before adjusting her spectacles. "I'm thinking we'll do better with the stew, I've a feeling the inspector will be late tonight."

Mrs. Jeffries glanced back at the open ledger, more to hide a smile than to return to the task at hand. "That sounds lovely."

"What sounds lovely?" Phyllis, the housemaid, asked as she carried the inspector's breakfast dishes into the kitchen.

"Mrs. Goodge is going to make a lamb stew for dinner tonight," the housekeeper said.

"Good. With this miserable weather, we need something to stick to our ribs." Phyllis put the tray on the counter by the sink and placed the dirty plates into the hot, soapy water. The few bits of food the inspector hadn't eaten had already been scraped into Samson's bowl. The cat sat on a footstool on the far side of the room, next to the pine sideboard, his attention drifting between the cook, whom he adored, and the food dish, which he wanted as full as possible. Everyone except the cook hated the cat, not because they weren't animal lovers—no, they all adored Fred, the household dog, who was currently having his morning walk with Wiggins, the footman. Samson was disliked because he had a nasty disposition with everyone except Mrs. Goodge.

"True, but that's not why I'm doin' the stew." The cook sent an irritated frown at the housekeeper.

"Then why are you cooking it?" Phyllis put the last dish into the water, picked up the dishrag, and scrubbed the wooden tray.

"Because I've had one of my feelings." Mrs. Goodge went to the table, pulled out a chair, and sat down next to the housekeeper. "We're going to get us a murder. I know it; I can feel it in my bones."

Mrs. Jeffries shut the account book. She didn't dismiss the comment out of hand because the truth was they ended up with a murder every Christmas. But she also knew that ever since Mrs. Goodge had attended that silly lecture about awakening one's psychic powers, she'd been given to ominous pronouncements and sage words of wisdom. Oh, well, the housekeeper thought, it was harmless. "You're probably right. But let's hope we don't."

Phyllis crossed to the cook's worktable and put the tray on the bottom shelf. "I don't know . . . they always make the holidays a bit more exciting."

"Yes, but this year, our little one is old enough to really enjoy herself." Mrs. Jeffries declared. "That will mean so much to the inspector and Luty."

"And to me," the cook added. "I'm a godparent as well."

They were referring the daughter of Smythe, the inspector's coachman, and Betsy, his wife, the former housemaid. Amanda Belle was the goddaughter of Inspector Witherspoon, Luty Belle Crookshank, and Mrs. Goodge.

"Of course you are," the housekeeper soothed. "But I'm being silly. I'm not going to worry about anything except enjoying Christmas."

"And even if we get a murder, we'll still be able to spend time with the little one," Phyllis said. "We always have before."

Mrs. Jeffries glanced at the maid. When Phyllis first arrived at the household, she'd been a frazzled, slope-shouldered mess of a girl, terrified of her own shadow and so afraid of losing her position and being tossed in the street that she'd refused to help on the inspector's murder cases. Now she was a vibrant, confident young woman with excellent posture, a porcelain complexion, and dark blonde hair that highlighted her sapphire-blue eyes. "Still, we mustn't wish for a human being to die just so we have a murder."

"I'd never do that, Mrs. Jeffries." Phyllis pouted as she

joined them at the table. "It's just, well, we are good at it, and we've not had a decent one since February."

"We had that one in June," the cook reminded her.

"But it was nothing; the inspector didn't need us at all. The wife confessed she'd stabbed her husband the minute he started asking questions."

Mrs. Jeffries nodded in agreement. She knew what Phyllis meant and she was quite sympathetic to her point of view. Still, she couldn't condone wanting someone to lose his or her life. On the other hand, if a homicide occurred, it was a good bet her employer would catch the case, especially if the victim was someone important.

Inspector Gerald Witherspoon had solved more murders than anyone in the history of the Metropolitan Police. What most people, including the inspector, didn't realize was that he had a great deal of help with his investigations.

Mrs. Jeffries, the widow of a Yorkshire policeman, had started it off years earlier when she'd first come to Upper Edmonton Gardens. Witherspoon had been in charge of the Records Room at Scotland Yard, but when those horrible Kensington High Street murders began, she'd encouraged him to ask a few questions in the neighborhood. Not only that, but she'd made sure the household staff was out and about, asking questions as well, her excuse at the time had been "curiosity." Naturally, Smythe and Betsy, who hadn't been married then, figured out what she was doing. It hadn't taken Wiggins or Mrs. Goodge long to suss it out, either.

Witherspoon had ended up catching the killer, saving several lives, and had been promoted out of the records room to the Ladbroke Road Police Station. Since then, they'd added several trusted friends to their small band of sleuths and took great pride in working for justice. Naturally, the inspector had no idea he was getting assistance.

The back door opened and slammed shut, and then foot-steps and the clatter of paws pounded up the corridor. Wiggins, a handsome young man in his early twenties, burst into the room. A brown, black, and white mongrel dog was at his heels. "I've just run into Constable Griffiths and he was on his way to Putney to join the inspector and Constable Barnes."

"Putney? But that's across the river, why would he go there?" Mrs. Goodge asked.

"Because it's 'appened again," Wiggins announced. "We've got us another Christmas murder."

Inspector Gerald Witherspoon's annoyance at being called out of his own district for a homicide evaporated when he saw the victim. "Poor woman. If the blow to her head didn't kill her, then lying out here for hours would have done it." He shook his head in disgust. He rose to his feet and wished he could avoid looking at both the body and the stained shovel that was probably the murder weapon. But he knew his duty. "Who found her?"

The tall young constable who'd accompanied them from the local station pointed to the back door of the house. "The scullery maid, sir. She's the first down in the mornings, and when she went into the kitchen to make the cook's tea, the cat wanted out. She said when she opened the back door, she noticed the oil lamp there"—he pointed to a spot a few feet away from the statue—"and when she opened the door wider, she saw her mistress lying here."

"She kept her wits about her," Constable Barnes added. "I've spoken to her, sir, and after she told the housekeeper, she went to the fixed-point constable on the corner and raised the alarm."

Witherspoon nodded and then glanced at the victim. "Who is this lady?"

Barnes opened his little brown notebook. "Margaret Starling. She's a widow and she lives here with her servants."

Witherspoon frowned in disbelief. "She has servants? Didn't any of them notice she wasn't in the house last night? I'm no expert on bodies, but this poor woman's flesh is almost frozen. She has to have been out here for hours."

"According to the maid, sir, none of the servants were home last night. Mrs. Starling gave all of them an evening out." He looked up as a two police constables and a middle-aged man wearing a black overcoat and a bowler and carrying a medical bag hurried toward them.

"That's Dr. Littleham, sir, the police surgeon for our district," the constable explained.

Witherspoon turned to the young constable. "Please search her pockets before the doctor begins," he instructed.

Barnes, who knelt on the other side of the victim stood up and joined the inspector. The two men headed for the doctor and introduced themselves. As soon as the introductions were over, they went to the house. Barnes knocked on the back door.

A housemaid with red eyes swollen from weeping opened up. She stared at them for a long moment.

"May we come in, miss?" Witherspoon asked politely.

"Sorry, sir." She stepped back and held the door open for them to enter. "I was told you'd be coming in to speak to us. Please come inside. Mrs. Wheaton, the housekeeper, is waiting for you in the old butler's pantry."

They stepped over the threshold and followed her to a door halfway down the dimly lighted corridor. The maid rapped once and then stuck her head inside. "The police are here, Mrs. Wheaton."

As they stepped inside, a tall, white-haired woman rose from behind a long table. "I'm Agnes Wheaton. This has been a terrible, terrible time for all of us here, I hope you'll find the person that did this quickly." She gestured at the row of straight-backed chairs opposite her. "Please, make yourselves comfortable. Would you care for tea?"

"No, thank you, ma'am. I'm Inspector Gerald Witherspoon and this is my colleague, Constable Barnes." He surveyed the long, narrow room as they took their seats. He'd often interviewed servants in the butler's pantry, and they were usually dismal places with shelves of mismatched crockery, scratched, rickety furniture, dirty windows, and stained linens. But this one was decent. The chairs all matched, an unstained white tablecloth covered the table, the two windows were clean—as was the blue cotton curtains—and the floor was polished. Apparently, Mrs. Starling wanted her servants to have their meals in a cheerful room.

Mrs. Wheaton took her own seat.

"Mrs. Wheaton, I understand how difficult this might be for you—" he began, only to be interrupted.

"I want her killer caught," Mrs. Wheaton cried. Her eyes filled with tears, but she blinked and held them back. "Forgive me, Inspector, but it has been a most upsetting day. Go ahead and ask your questions; I'll do anything I can to help catch whoever did this to Mrs. Starling."

Witherspoon nodded. It was rare to find servants who seemed on the surface to be so fond of their employers, but

Mrs. Wheaton obviously liked and cared about the victim. He wondered if the rest of the staff felt the same way. "Thank you. We appreciate your cooperation. We were told that Mrs. Starling was here alone. Is that correct?"

Mrs. Wheaton nodded. "That's right. She gave us the night off. She does it every year. It's an early Christmas present to the staff. She buys us tickets to a play or a pantomime. Last night it was *A Runaway Girl* at the Gaiety Theater."

"What time did you all leave?" Barnes asked.

"We had to get up to the West End, so Mrs. Starling let us go at a half past five. She only wanted a cold supper, so I left it on the sideboard in the dining room and off we went." Again tears flooded her eyes. "We'd no idea something so awful was going to happen to the mistress."

"Of course you didn't know," Witherspoon murmured.

"When we came home last night, we assumed Mrs. Starling was asleep in her bed. It wasn't until this morning when Martha came running in that I realized something was amiss."

"The entire staff was together last night, is that right?" Witherspoon asked.

"Yes. Mrs. Starling was a very independent woman; she wasn't the sort who would worry about being on her own in the evening."

"Would she have locked the doors?" Barnes opened his notebook and began to write.

"Of course. This is a very good neighborhood, but the front door was always kept locked," she replied. "Mrs. Starling gave me a key to use last night—" She broke off and covered her mouth with her hand. She took several long, jagged breaths and then brought herself under control. "I've just realized, if we'd used the back door, we might have found her in time to save her. Oh, my Lord, how dreadful."

"Ma'am, don't distress yourself," Witherspoon said. "At this point, we've no idea what time Mrs. Starling passed away. But as you've brought the subject up, why didn't you use the back door?" Even the most liberal of employers generally expected their servants to use a side or a back entrance.

"Normally we would have, but the back door key's been missing for over a month now, so Mrs. Starling told us to come in the front." She shook her head. "Why, just yesterday I told her we ought to get a new key made, but she wanted to wait a bit to see if the key turned up."

Barnes stopped scribbling and looked at her. "Why would it suddenly turn up?"

"Mrs. Starling thought the key had accidentally been dropped somewhere in the house and that eventually we'd find it. It happened once before: The key went missing and then it was found on the floor of the dry larder a few weeks later," she explained. "Getting a new key isn't as easy as it sounds, and it's also expensive. Mrs. Starling had modern locks put on both the front and back doors last year, the kind that you can lock and unlock from the inside without a key. She wanted to make sure that, in the event of a fire, everyone could get outside quickly. The key was only needed if you wanted to unlock it from outside."

Witherspoon nodded. "Where was the key kept?"

"On a hook by the back door."

"So anyone coming or going could have taken it," Barnes remarked.

"That's possible." Mrs. Wheaton fixed him with a cold stare. "But it's more likely one of us grabbed it, intending to run an errand or do a bit of shopping, and ended up losing it. As I said, the key has been missing since the middle of November. No one here would do anything to harm Mrs. Starling. She was a good mistress, nor would any of the tradespeople or delivery lads want to harm her."

"I didn't mean to imply otherwise," the constable soothed. "I'm merely looking at the possibilities, and a missing key always gets a policeman's attention."

Her expression softened. "Of course. Don't mind me, Constable, I'm dreadfully upset."

"Was Mrs. Starling in the habit of going outside by herself?" The inspector thought of the oil lamp.

Mrs. Wheaton shook her head. "No. As a matter of fact, I can think of no reason she might have gone out last night. But she obviously did: The lamp was outside, and it didn't walk there by itself."

"Could she have gone out because she heard something, or perhaps someone came to the door, or maybe she went to find her cat?" the inspector asked. "Any of those reasons would explain the oil lamp."

"I don't think so, Inspector," Mrs. Wheaton replied. "She might not have been nervous about being home on her own, but she wasn't foolish. She wouldn't have opened the back door and gone out just because she heard a noise, and if someone had come to the back door, she'd have definitely kept it closed. As for the cat, Gladstone was inside when we got home, and the back door was closed and locked, which means she must have let him inside."

"Nonetheless, something made her go outside," Witherspoon said. "Can you think of anyone who wished to harm Mrs. Starling?"

Mrs. Wheaton shook her head. "Not really. She was very strong-willed and free with her opinion at times, but I can't think of anyone who would do such a thing to her."

"Had she had any recent quarrels or disagreements with anyone," the inspector persisted.

"Well, as I said, she was free with her opinions." She hesitated. "Actually, recently she's quarreled with several people, but it was over silly, petty things. The only serious matter that I know of is the lawsuit."

"Lawsuit?" Witherspoon repeated.

"She was suing Mrs. Huxton. She lives next door."

"For what?" Barnes asked.

"Slander and defamation of character." Mrs. Wheaton sighed. "It's quite a sad situation, really. The two of them used to be very good friends. Then they had what I thought was a minor dispute over the property line between the two homes, and before you knew it, they weren't speaking. Then Mrs. Starling found out that Mrs. Huxton had written an anonymous nasty letter to the vicar at St. Andrew's Church. It accused her of all manner of dreadful things. Mrs. Starling decided to sue her."

"She's suing her neighbor. That's quite serious," Witherspoon murmured. "May we start from the beginning, please? This Mrs. Huxton wrote to the church?"

"It sounds ridiculous, but the vicar is on the board of the Angel Alms Society of Fulham and Putney. Mrs. Starling was sure Mrs. Huxton was trying to ruin her reputation at both places." She took another deep breath. "The alms society is domiciled in the building next to St. Andrew's Church. Mrs. Starling has been a supporter of the organization for years, both as a patron and an active member of the advisory board. Women aren't allowed on the board of governors as yet, but Mrs. Starling wants to change that rule." She paused closed her eyes. "Sorry, I keep referring to her in the present tense."

"That's quite all right, Mrs. Wheaton. We'll certainly have a word with Mrs. Huxton."

"Of course, Inspector, but, honestly, Mrs. Huxton is a lady. She'd never do such a terrible thing."

Witherspoon resisted the urge to tell her how often it was a "lady" or a "gentleman" who'd committed the most heinous of crimes. "Is there anyone else that you can think of—anyone who might have had a grudge against your mistress?"

"I don't think so, but speak with the rest of the servants. Perhaps one of them might know more."

"How many servants are there?" Barnes asked.

"All together, there are eight of us." Mrs. Wheaton replied. "This is a big house. Gretchen Terry is the upstairs maid, Fanny Herald is the tweeny, Louise Rector and Jane Prescrott do the downstairs, and Martha Horsham is the scullery. Mrs. Adkins is the cook and Arthur Gormley takes care of the garden."

Barnes added their names to his notes, not bothering to check the spelling, as he'd be having a word with all of them. "All of you live in?"

"Everyone but Mr. Gormley; he lives in Fulham and comes in six days a week."

There was a sharp knock on the door and then Martha stuck her head inside. "The police doctor wants to speak to you," she announced, directing her comment to the inspector.

"Thank you, miss. Tell him I'll be right out." Inspector Witherspoon looked at Mrs. Wheaton as he rose to his feet.

"I'll speak with you again, I'm sure. In the meantime, Constable Barnes will take statements from the servants. We'll need two rooms, one for him to use and one for me."

"This room is available and the dining room upstairs." Mrs. Wheaton got up.

"I'll stay down here, sir," Barnes offered. "If it's all the same to you, I'll start with the young lady who found Mrs. Starling."

Witherspoon nodded and hurried out.

The doctor was standing on the terrace, overseeing the removal of the body. "Be careful!" he yelled as one of the constables carrying the stretcher stumbled. "I don't want any extra bruises caused by you lot dropping that poor woman."

They disappeared down the walkway to the street where the police van waited. He turned to Inspector Witherspoon. "Sorry, but a postmortem is no good if I can't tell if the victim's bruises and wounds were caused by the assailant or a careless constable bashing the body about willy-nilly." Dr. Littleham was a portly man in early middle age with curly brown hair, heavy eyebrows, and a luxuriant mutton chop whiskers and mustache.

"I quite understand, sir. I feel the same way about people trampling all over a murder scene before I've had a chance to have a thorough look." Witherspoon had examined the area surrounding Margaret Starling's body in great detail. He'd not spotted anything that appeared to be useful, but nonetheless it was good police procedure.

"Of course you understand. Now, I don't generally speak to the investigation officer before I've done a proper postmortem, but I'll make an exception in this case. Some of her tissue was almost frozen, so I'm sure she was outside for most of last night. I'll know more after the examination. I understand you're not from this district, so where should I send the autopsy report?"

"Huh." It took a minute before Witherspoon understood the question. "Oh, sorry. Send it to the Upper Richmond Road Police Station. I'll be working from there."

"Right, then, I'll send it along as soon as possible." He started to leave and then stopped and looked back at the inspector. "Forgive my asking, but is there a reason you're on this case and not Inspector Nivens?"

Witherspoon wasn't sure how to answer, so he did what he always did when faced with an uncomfortable question: He told as much of the truth as he could. "I really don't know. The moment I walked into my station this morning, I had instructions from Scotland Yard to report here and take over."

He suspected he knew exactly why he'd been sent, but he didn't wish to add any fuel to what might become an inflamed situation. Inspector Nigel Nivens was eager to add a successful homicide investigation to his list of accomplishments. But he wasn't seen as a particularly competent officer, and someone at Scotland Yard obviously wanted this case solved quickly.

"So the orders came down from the chief superintendent." Dr. Littleham smiled broadly. "Sorry, didn't mean to be intrusive, but, well, from what I know of Inspector Nivens, he'll not take kindly to being pushed aside."

"I assure you, I've no wish to intrude in Inspector Nivens' district, but orders are orders." Though in truth he wondered how on earth someone at the Yard could have found out about the murder so quickly when it was only reported this morning.

Wiggins pulled his hat down further over his ears as he rounded the corner and spotted the small crowd in front of what he hoped was the victim's home. After his announcement that they had themselves a murder, Mrs. Jeffries had sprung into action, sending him first to Betsy and Smythe's home, where he dropped a note through their door, and then here to see what he could learn from the locals. She'd sent Phyllis to Luty Belle's so she and Hatchet could be at Upper Edmonton Gardens this afternoon for a meeting. They were friends of the household and had been helping on their cases almost from the beginning. Mrs. Jeffries had taken on the task of going across the communal gardens to Lady Cannonberry's herself. Ruth Cannonberry was also a friend and very much a part of their investigations.

He'd paid attention as he reached this neighborhood and noted that there were half a dozen pubs and two hansom cab stands within a mile of the victim's home. Good ground for learning interesting bits and pieces, like who may have had a reason to want the victim dead. It was too bad Smythe hadn't been home: Between the two of them, they could cover twice as much territory as he could on his own. He reached the edge of the group of spectators in front of the house and slipped between them until he was in the center.

Wiggins looked up and studied the façade. It was a rich person's home and was set back from the road, with a huge lawn bisected by a brick walkway leading to the front porch. The five-story redbrick house had pristine white wooden trim around all the windows. Full-grown evergreens shielded the left-hand side of the house from the street, and on the right side was a black wrought-iron gate leading to the back garden.

Wiggins stepped back as two large women, one holding a shopping basket, elbowed their way past him, blocking his view. He looked around them just as the gate opened and two policemen carrying a covered body on a stretcher emerged and moved toward the police ambulance pulled up at the curb.

"Oh, Lord, poor Mrs. Starling. I heard she laid outside all night," the shopping basket lady said to her companion, a redheaded woman dressed in a brown-and-gold-plaid overcoat and matching hat. "Nita says she heard that the girl who raised the alarm told the police constable the poor woman's skull was bashed in."

"How would Nita know that?" Redhead asked.

"Because Bobby Fallon was right there waitin' to cross the road and he heard every word the girl said. You know he runs and tells Nita everything he hears."

"Poor Mrs. Starling. What a terrible way to die." Redhead clucked her tongue.

Wiggins started to ask a question, but before he could open his mouth, Shopping Basket Lady added, "Maybe the killer knew she'd be alone; after all, it wasn't any secret that they was all getting the night off. Mr. Gormley was in the pub last Saturday braggin' to everyone who'd stand still for more than two seconds about what a generous employer he had and how they was all goin' out to see a play in the West End."

Redhead snorted. "Maybe she was generous to her servants, but there was plenty around that couldn't stand the woman. Amy Maitland, she does for that vicar at St. Andrew's—you know, the one that no one likes—and she told me that Margaret Starling and the vicar had a right old shouting match a couple of weeks ago."

Wiggins took a step back as the two women talked. He didn't want them realizing he was eavesdropping on their conversation, though in truth they were talking so loudly that half the people clustered there were listening and most of them weren't bothering to hide their curiosity.

"What was they fightin' about?" A blond-haired street lad in a green jacket and scruffy trousers asked.

"It's rude to listen to someone else's conversation," Redhead snapped.

"Oh, come on, you was talkin' loud enough to wake the dead," the boy shot back.

"Harry Linton, I'll not have you speak to me like that." Redhead raised her fist and took a swipe at young Harry, who easily evaded her, laughing as he dodged toward the crowd's edge.

"What a nasty boy," Redhead mumbled.

"We'd best watch our tongues." The lady with the shopping basket looked around her uneasily. "You never know who is listening. We'd not like people to think we're gossipmongerin'."

Well, blast a Spaniard, Wiggins thought as the crowd began to move off and disperse. The little brat's antics had put a stop to getting any more information from this bunch.

"The dining room is here, sir," Fanny Herald said as she escorted Inspector Witherspoon down the wide corridor to a set of double doors. Suddenly the front door knocker banged loud enough so that both Witherspoon and Fanny started in surprise.

"Are you expecting anyone?" Witherspoon asked.

"No, sir, but perhaps it's one of your lot, sir. I'll just nip up and see." She went to the door and opened it, and a moment later the inspector heard her say, "Mr. McConnell, what are you doing here?"

"I've come to see Mrs. Starling. I don't have an appointment but she told me to come by. Is there something wrong here? There's a number of people milling about outside on the street, and a police van."

Witherspoon hurried to the foyer, and the tweeny stepped to one side. A man with wire-rimmed spectacles, wavy brown hair riddled with gray, and a round face with a small chin stood in the doorway.

"Hello, I'm Inspector Gerald Witherspoon. And you are . . . ?"

The man's mouth opened in surprise but he caught himself. "I'm Graham McConnell. I'm the director of the Angel Alms Society and I've come to have a word with Mrs. Starling."

Witherspoon hoped this man wasn't a close friend. "I'm afraid that's impossible, Mr. McConnell. Margaret Starling was murdered last night."

McConnell gasped. "Oh, dear Lord, you can't mean that. But I just saw her yesterday. I don't understand. Margaret murdered? Surely there must be a mistake!"

"I'm afraid not, sir."

"But that's absurd. Who on earth would do such a thing? Was it a robbery?"

The inspector ignored the question and asked one of his

own. He might as well find out as much as possible about her movements on the day she was killed. "Where did you see her yesterday?"

"At church—at St. Andrew's Church. I spoke to her after the service and told her I'd be by this morning."

"What was the reason you wanted to see Mrs. Starling?"

"We needed to fix a time for her committee to sort through several bags of donated clothes. This is dreadful news, Inspector, absolutely dreadful."

"Yes, I'm sure it is a terrible shock. You knew Mrs. Starling quite well?" Witherspoon asked.

McConnell smiled sadly. "We weren't close friends, but I've known her for several years now. Despite some of the controversy she's caused, she's been a tremendous asset to the Angel Alms Society. We shall miss her terribly. Do you have any idea who might have done this dreadful thing?"

"Controversy?"

McConnell shifted awkwardly and looked down at his feet. "I shouldn't have made that comment, Inspector, I spoke without thinking. Margaret Starling was always—always—pushing the society to do better in serving those in need, and sometimes people got a bit impatient with her. That's all I meant. But can you tell me, do you have any idea who might have done this?"

Witherspoon shook his head. "Not yet, but we'll catch the killer. I'm glad to have met you, Mr. McConnell. You're on the list of people we are going to interview."

He drew back in surprise. "You want to speak to me?"

"We'll be interviewing everyone in Mrs. Starling's circle." Witherspoon nodded politely. "Now, if you'll excuse me, I must get on with the investigation."

"Of course, Inspector," McConnell stepped out onto the porch. "Good day, sir."

Downstairs in the butler's pantry, Constable Barnes smiled at the young woman sitting across from him. "What's your name, miss?"

"Martha Horsham, sir. I'm the scullery maid." She was an attractive, slender girl with brown eyes, brown hair, and a rosebud mouth.

"How long have you worked for Mrs. Starling?" he asked.

"Two years, sir."

"And she was a good mistress?"

"She was, sir. Paid our wages properly, didn't make us pay for our own tea and sugar, and gave us our afternoons out every week." She blinked hard to hold back the tears. "And she always let us have a nice evening out at Christmas. That's where we were last night."

"I understand you were the one that found Mrs. Starling, is that correct?"

"That's right, sir, I did." Her lips began to tremble. "I'm sorry . . . I've never seen a murdered body before."

"It's all right, Miss Horsham. Begin at the beginning and tell me what happened in your own words. Take your time."

She dabbed at her eyes and sat up straighter. "I'm the first one down in the mornings. I come in and get the fire started in the cooker for Mrs. Adkins; she's the cook. I'd just got the kindling lighted, when Gladstone began crying to be let out, so I went to the back door and opened it. He went running out, and as I was propping the door open so he could get back in for his breakfast, I saw the oil lamp sitting outside, so I opened the door wider and then"—she swallowed heavily, her eyes finally filling with tears—"that's when I saw Mrs. Starling."

"Take your time, miss."

She swiped at her cheeks as the tears spilled out. "It took me a second or two to realize what I was seein'; I mean it was a real shock. I ran to her, thinkin' she'd had a heart attack or something; but as I got closer, I could see she was dead."

"You knew she was dead? How? You just said you'd never seen a dead body before?"

"No, sir, I said I'd never seen a murdered body before; I've seen lots of dead bodies. My uncle is an undertaker, and my mum and I help out there when he needs us."

"My mistake, Miss Horsham." Barnes smiled at her. "Please, go on."

"I could tell right away that something dreadful had happened. I've a strong stomach, sir, but there was blood all over her clothes and the ground. So I turned and hurried back to the house. I didn't even bother bein' quiet; I just rushed up the stairs to Mrs. Wheaton's room and told her that we had to send for the police, that something terrible had happened and Mrs. Starling was laying outside. I don't think she believed me at first, but she come right down and we went outside, though, truth to tell, I stayed on the terrace. But it didn't take her more than a moment to see what had happened, so she sent me off for the constable at the corner."

Barnes studied the young woman. She was upset that her mistress was dead, but she had her wits about her. "How did you know that Mrs. Starling had been murdered?"

"Because, sir, the back of her head was bashed in, and

when I started back to the house to get help, I saw the gardener's heavy shovel propped up against the angel statue. The end of it was covered in blood. Well, sir, she didn't bash herself in the head and then walk five feet over to the statue and put the shovel against it herself, did she? Seemed to me someone else must have done it. That makes it murder, doesn't it?"

CHAPTER 2

Inspector Witherspoon put his notebook on the table and pulled out a chair. Sitting down, he surveyed the cavernous room while he waited to take a statement from Gretchen Terry, the upstairs maid.

Portraits of well-dressed men and women hung on the gold-and-white-striped walls. Opposite the dining table, which could easily accommodate twenty guests, was a marble-topped sideboard that ran the length of the room. Heavy cream-colored velvet curtains tied back with thick gold braids and topped with elaborate valances draped the two floor-to-ceiling windows. The polished parquet floors were covered in black-and-gray Persian rugs, and there were elegant filigree wall sconces placed strategically around the doors and windows. Upon arriving, the inspector had given the outside of the house only a quick glance, but now he saw the place was much bigger than he'd realized. Judging what he'd seen so far, Margaret Starling had been a very wealthy woman.

"Excuse me, sir, but Mrs. Wheaton said you wanted to speak to me."

Inspector Witherspoon turned and saw a young house-maid standing in the doorway. Her hands were clutched together and her expression apprehensive. She was a slender girl with even features and dark blonde hair beneath her maid's cap.

"I do." He smiled as he waved her over, pointing to the empty seat to his right. "Please don't be nervous. We're going to be taking statements from everyone in the house. You're Miss Terry?"

"I am, sir," she stared at the dining chair that the inspector had pointed at and hesitated briefly before sitting down. "Sorry, sir, but I've never sat in the dining room. It feels strange."

"Yes, I'm sure it must. Now, first of all, Miss Terry, how long have you worked for Mrs. Starling?" He opened the notebook and took a pencil out of his breast coat pocket.

"Three years, sir."

"I understand you and the others were gone last night."

The maid nodded. "We were, sir, it was our annual night out. Mrs. Starling did it every year, and when we got home, no one thought to have a look in to make sure Mistress was all right."

"What time did you arrive home?"

"It was eleven. I know because I heard the bell from the carriage clock in the little sitting room striking the hour."

"And you went straight up to bed, is that correct?"

"Yes, sir . . . well, all of us did but Mrs. Wheaton. She

went down to the kitchen to make sure Gladstone was safely inside. He'd been missing all day."

"Gladstone? Oh, yes, the cat."

"Right, sir. usually he has the run of the place, but he's taken to slipping out and disappearing, so Mistress ordered us to keep the downstairs window closed and make sure he was inside at night."

"And I take it he was in?"

She laughed uneasily. "Yes, sir. I overheard Mrs. Wheaton telling Cook all was well and that Gladstone was prowling the hall with his ears pinned back and his tail twitching. He gets like that sometimes when he's thwarted. Mistress spoiled him, so he's used to getting what he wants."

Witherspoon noticed she'd relaxed a bit, so he decided more direct questions were in order. "When you came home last night, did you notice anyone in the immediate vicinity?"

"Truth to tell, sir, I was crammed in the middle between Mrs. Adkins and Martha, but even if I had been able to see, Mrs. Wheaton had closed the shades on the windows because of the cold. When the carriage pulled up in front of the house, it was too dark to see anything except the two brass lamps on the front porch."

"That's understandable," he murmured. "Let's try this another way. Yesterday during the day, did you notice anyone odd or suspicious near the house?"

"I was outside only once, sir. Cook asked me to post a letter for her and I took it to the post box on the corner. But I don't remember seeing anyone except Mrs. Hinckley from across the road, and she was just getting into a hansom cab."

"To your knowledge, did Mrs. Starling have any enemies—

anyone she'd recently had a disagreement or a conflict with?"

Surprised, Gretchen's brown eyes widened. "Uh, it doesn't feel right speakin' ill of the dead, sir. Mrs. Starling was a good mistress, treated all of us decent."

"Then you should want her killer caught," he said softly. "The more we know about who may have been angry or upset with Mrs. Starling, the easier it might be for us to catch her assailant."

"I know, sir, but if I tell you, you'll think she was mean and quarrelsome, and she wasn't; it was just that lately she started acting strange."

"Strange?" he repeated. "In what way?"

"In several ways, sir."

Miles away, at the headquarters of Scotland Yard, Inspector Nigel Nivens stood rigidly at attention in front of Chief Superintendent Barrows. "Is that your final word on the matter?"

Barrows considered his answer carefully. He was Nivens' superior officer in the Metropolitan Police Force, but he wasn't a fool. He knew this inspector wasn't one of the usual rank-and-file coppers. Nivens had powerful family members and important friends who could make life miserable for a policeman, even one at his high level. "Inspector Nivens, I understand your disappointment in being taken off the case, but the instructions to hand the matter over to Inspector Witherspoon came from the very highest levels."

"May I ask who gave those orders?" Nivens struggled to bring himself under control. He could feel the heat rising on his cheeks, and his hands itched to pound the edge of the chief superintendent's desk. He sucked in a quiet, deep breath and forced his fingers to relax.

"No, you may not. I was told to keep his intervention confidential and I intend to do so. Please, Inspector Nivens, do calm yourself. I can assure you, this is no reflection upon your abilities as a police officer."

"Of course it is." Nivens couldn't stop himself. "The only reason I'm to be taken off the case is because someone very powerful thinks I'm not up to the task."

"Don't be absurd. You've a fine record," Barrows said. "It's simply that Inspector Gerald Witherspoon has solved more homicides than anyone in the history of the Metropolitan Po—"

"That's only because he has help on all his cases. Why can't you understand? I've told you time and time again, Gerald Witherspoon wouldn't have been able to solve any of those cases without assistance. His entire household and a number of other people—"

"That's ridiculous." Barrows didn't like being interrupted. "I've heard this nonsense from you before, Inspector. Frankly, it's most unbecoming. Even without Witherspoon's excellent record of homicide solutions, he'd still be considered a fine officer."

"Fine officer!" Nivens yelled. "He was in the ruddy records room before he got lucky and solved those horrible Kensington High Street murders."

"Nonetheless, since then he's become an excellent detective as well as a good officer."

"No one but a complete imbecile would have called him a good officer . . ." Nivens' voice trailed off as Barrows jerked off his spectacles and leapt to his feet, his expression furious.

"I'm sorry, sir. I didn't mean that as it may have sounded." Nivens swallowed nervously. He knew he'd gone too far. "Of course you're not an imbecile. I'm merely so distraught over losing my chance to prove that I'm just as capable as Inspector Witherspoon that I let my emotions get the best of me."

Barrows said nothing for a moment; he merely fixed the inspector with a hard stare.

Nivens could feel the beads of sweat starting to form along his hairline and silently prayed they wouldn't come rolling down his forehead. "Please accept my apologies, sir."

Barrows relaxed a fraction, put his spectacles back on, and sat back down. "Right, then. I'll pretend I didn't hear your insubordination."

"Thank you, sir. I appreciate your understanding."

Barrows ignored him and picked up a file folder from the stack on his desk. "I've a lot of work to get through, Inspector, so unless you have something else to say, I suggest you get back to Upper Richmond Road and attend to your duties. Inspector Witherspoon will handle the Starling murder and you're to assist and cooperate with him in every possible way. Is that clear?"

"Yes, sir." Nivens nodded curtly. "Good day, sir." He turned and left the office, taking care to close the door softly.

As expected, Constable Forman was waiting for him in the corridor. The tall, blond-haired constable shoved away from the wall and stood to attention. The smile that had started to form on his thin, bony face disappeared.

Nivens realized the lad had taken one look at his expression and seen that things had gone wrong. That would never do; he wasn't going to have anyone, least of all a mere constable, read him like the ruddy morning paper. Nivens unclenched his fists and put on his bowler. "I do hope there won't be too much traffic. I don't want any delay getting back to the station."

Forman's brow creased in confusion. "Uh, yes, sir."

Nivens was back in charge now. He was pleased with himself for having picked Forman out of the crowd of officers at the Upper Richmond Road Police Station. The constable didn't disappoint him. He was smart enough to keep quiet and see which way the wind might be blowing before he started asking any questions. Nivens admired that particular characteristic. He'd gotten where he was today by being able to read people correctly, and the minute he'd walked into the Upper Richmond Road Police Station he'd spotted the one constable so ambitious he could easily be used.

But Forman, for all his ambition, was no fool, and Nivens knew the man had calculated the risk he'd be taking by falling in with him. Nivens was under no illusions about his popularity with the rank and file. They were subservient and civil, of course, but he knew they loathed him. Forman, however, had his eye on moving up in the ranks, and attaching himself to someone with the Nivens family connections and power could be advantageous in the future.

It was important he make sure that Constable Forman still saw him in that light. It wouldn't do to let him see that a mere chief superintendent like Barrows could intimidate Nivens in any way, shape, or form. He didn't want Forman jumping ship now. If Nivens was going to prove that Witherspoon wasn't as capable as everyone thought he'd need help. Someone like Forman could play that part easily.

The skirmish with Barrows was unimportant; he was angry, of course, but the meeting had gone the way he'd thought it might, although he was a bit annoyed with his own reaction. He should have kept his temper. "Let's go," he said, and started down the stairs.

"Yes, sir," Forman replied as he followed him.

Nivens deliberately didn't speak until they were a good two blocks away from headquarters. "As expected, Chief Superintendent Barrows has allowed himself to be influenced by politics." That wasn't precisely the truth, but it wasn't precisely a lie, either.

"I take it things didn't go as you hoped, sir."

"Not as I'd hoped, but exactly as I predicted. As I said, the chief superintendent has allowed politics, not proper police procedures, to influence his decision."

"That's unfortunate, sir."

"Not for me, Constable." Nivens smiled. "This isn't the end of matter, and I'm going to make sure Barrows is going to regret this. I'm going to make him rue the day he pulled me off this case."

Gretchen cast a quick, furtive look toward the closed dining room door. "I don't want the others to think I'm tellin' tales," she explained to the Inspector. "But I'm the upstairs housemaid, sir, and I saw and heard things the others didn't."

"By 'others,' I take it you mean the other staff?" Witherspoon had learned from past mistakes to be specific when asking questions.

The maid nodded. "That's right, sir. Mrs. Starling was a good mistress and they'll not want to face the truth. In the last few weeks of her life, she wasn't her usual self." She paused and took a deep breath. "Like I said, sir, I'm the upstairs maid, and as well as doin' the cleanin', I'd often act as lady's maid for the mistress. You know, helping her get dressed when she had a meeting or an important social occasion."

"She went out often?"

"Not as often as some, like that Mrs. Huxton next door—she's out every night of the week—but the mistress did go out to dinner parties, and she went to the Angel Alms Society every week for her committee work or the meetings. But the point is, sir, recently, when I'd go in to help her dress, she'd be starin' off out the window, muttering to herself."

"Can you be a bit more specific? Was Mrs. Starling speaking to someone who wasn't there, or was she simply thinking out loud?"

"At first it was like she was thinking out loud, like she'd seen or heard something she couldn't understand, but a few weeks later it was more like she'd found something out and was arguin' with herself about what to do about it." Gretchen shook her head. "I know it doesn't make sense, but that's what happened; and as the weeks went on, she got worse and worse."

Witherspoon looked up from his notebook, his hand now motionless on the paper. "Can you recall exactly when Mrs. Starling began acting in such a manner?"

She thought for a few moments. "It was early last month . . . Yes, that's right. She came home from shopping and went straight up to her room. She wasn't angry or anything; it was more like she was confused about something."

"You said it got worse and worse. What did you mean?"

"Well, the next day, when she came home from her

meeting—it was her usual fortnight meeting of the alms society, and I was upstairs dustin' the second-floor landing—she was in a right old state, sir. I could tell she was upset about something, but when I asked if everything was all right, she said for me not to worry, that she'd take care of the matter."

"So she was upset," he repeated.

"Not upset; I used the wrong word. She was angry, sir. Really angry about something."

"Do you have any idea why?"

"No, sir, and it wasn't my place to press her any further."

"And you think it was about then that she began behaving in a manner unlike herself?" he asked.

"Yes, sir. Please don't misunderstand, sir. She treated us the same as always, but . . . oh, this is hard to explain. Let me give you an example. Mrs. Starling had an appointments diary, and unless she was ill, she always kept her engagements. But twice recently she's canceled appointments at the very last minute and gone off on some errand of her own. That wasn't like her, Inspector, not at all."

"Where did she go?' Witherspoon asked.

"The first time she went to Tunbridge Wells, and a few weeks later she went to Chelmsford. I know, sir, because she had me book her tickets and bring them here."

"Did she say why she'd gone to either of those places?"

"No, she just said she had something important to do"—Gretchen's eyes filled with tears—"and I can't help feeling that whatever it was she was doing is what got her murdered."

Downstairs, Constable Barnes had taken statements from Mrs. Adkins the cook and Louise Rector, one of the downstairs maids. Both of them had said more or less what Martha Horsham had stated: No one saw anything, no one heard anything, and no one had any idea who might want to kill their mistress.

Barnes hoped the dark-haired young woman who had just sat down might have something more to say than the others had. Surely someone here must have noticed something on the days leading up to the murder.

"What's your name, miss?" he asked.

"Fanny Herald, sir, I'm the tweeny."

"How long have you worked for Mrs. Starling?"

"Four years, sir, since I was sixteen." She smiled shyly, revealing a set of even white teeth.

"And you've been happy here?"

"Oh, yes, sir. It's a nice household. I can't imagine anyone wanting to hurt Mrs. Starling. I don't know what I can tell you."

"Why don't you just let me ask the questions? You might know more than you think you do," he assured her. "First of all, have you seen anyone suspicious hanging around the neighborhood recently? Someone who you'd never seen before. Someone who didn't seem as if they belonged here."

"No, sir, I've not seen anyone like that."

"Then has anything odd or unusual happened lately?"

She thought for a moment. "Not really, sir. Gladstone caused a bit of bother—he'd not come home by the time we left for the theater—but he does that all the time. He likes to sit in Mrs. Huxton's garden so he can aggravate her spaniel."

"I see." Barnes nodded. "When you were coming home from the theater last night, did you see anyone in the area?"

"It was too dark, sir." She smiled ruefully now.

Same as the others, he thought. No one saw anything, no one heard anything, and every single member of the household assumed that their mistress was safe in bed. But she wasn't—she was lying dead out in the back garden. "Yes, I'm sure it was."

"But Gladstone was back inside when we come in, sir," she added. "Mrs. Wheaton went down to make sure he was home."

He stifled a snort of disgust. The housekeeper had checked on the cat but not on her mistress. But then he caught himself; it wasn't the servants' fault that someone had murdered their employer.

"I wonder what'll happen to him now." Fanny frowned.

"Happen to who?"

"Gladstone." Her frown deepened. "Come to think of it, what'll happen to all of us? With the mistress dead, they'll not need us here."

Barnes wished he could give the girl some assurance that it would be all right, but he couldn't. If Mrs. Starling had been as good a mistress as the servants claimed, she might have made provisions for them, but then again she might not have. "I'm sure that's worrying for you and the others," he said, "but right now let's just concentrate on the matter at hand. Has Mrs. Starling had any conflicts recently?"

"Conflicts?"

"Disagreements, arguments, anything of that nature," Barnes explained.

Fanny's brows drew together. "Well, I'm not sure if you'd call it an argument, but I know she had a disagreement with Mr. Redstone."

"Who is Mr. Redstone?"

"He was married to Mrs. Starling's niece, but she's passed away now. Mr. Redstone was here last week and he had words with the mistress. I wasn't eavesdropping, but when he was here, he was shouting so loudly when they were in Mrs. Starling's study, I couldn't help but hear what he said." She looked down at the tablecloth.

"What did you hear?" Barnes demanded. When she looked up, her eyes filled with tears, and he knew he'd used the worst possible tactic to get the girl to talk. "I'm sorry, miss. I don't mean to upset you, but this is a murder investigation, and every small bit of information might help us find her killer. So please stop thinking you're protecting her memory by being discreet about what you overheard."

Fanny sucked in a deep breath and nodded. "You're right, sir. Mr. Redstone was shouting that Mrs. Starling had robbed him."

"Robbed him of what?"

Shaking her head and biting her lip, she said, "I don't know, sir. Honestly, at that point Mrs. Wheaton came into the room and told me to go downstairs to help with laundry."

A constable stuck his head inside. "Excuse me, sir, Constable Barnes, if you've finished, the inspector would like you to join him in the dining room."

"I'll be there in just a moment." Barnes looked at Fanny. "Is there anything else you can tell me? Anything odd or strange that happened in the days leading to Mrs. Starling's death?"

"No, sir." Fanny shook her head, her eyes filling with tears again. "If there was, I'd tell you, because Mrs. Starling was the first mistress I've ever had that was decent to me."

*   *   *

"Should we wait for Wiggins?" Mrs. Goodge glanced toward the back door, her expression anxious. "He's been gone for hours."

"Now, stop fretting, Mrs. Goodge. Wiggins is probably learning something useful or he'd be here. He can take care of himself," Betsy, a blonde, blue-eyed young matron, reached across the table and patted the cook's hand. "Don't worry, he's fine."

The cook looked doubtful. "Let's hope so, but I'm beginning to get one of my feelings."

"He's fine," Mrs. Jeffries assured her. "And I don't think you're having a 'feeling.' You're hungry. You were so busy sending off notes to your sources at lunchtime that you didn't eat more than two bites."

"I only sent out three of them," the cook retorted, "and the ones to Janice Miller and Lester Halliday had to be mailed so I needed to get them done for the early afternoon post."

Mrs. Goodge did her share of their sleuthing from the kitchen. She'd worked in some of the finest, most aristocratic houses in England before ending up at Upper Edmonton Gardens, and she had dozens of former colleagues whom she could count on for useful information. Add to that, there was a small army of tradespeople, delivery boys, and street lads who came into her kitchen. She plied them with tea, treats, and in some cases sympathy to loosen their tongues and find out what she needed to know.

"I was hoping he'd get here before we started." Phyllis put the teapot on the table next to the plate of jam tarts and then took her own seat. "I wish I could have gone with him. I'm curious as to what he's found out."

"He'll git here in his own good time," Luty Belle Crookshank declared. The elderly American was tiny, white-haired, and rich. She'd been involved in one of their first cases and had noticed the inspector's servants asking questions. After that case was solved, Luty had come to the household with a problem of her own, one that she wasn't certain the police would take seriously. Since then, she and her devoted butler, Hatchet, insisted on helping with the inspector's cases. Luty knew everyone who was anyone in London. She was as much at ease with an aristocratic cousin of the queen as she was with a beggar.

"I don't see how we can have much of a meetin' without him," Mrs. Goodge muttered. She was a bit annoyed to be told that her "feeling" was nothing more than hunger, although in this particular instance it was probably true. She helped herself to a tart. "We don't know anything."

"But of course we do." Mrs. Jeffries took her seat at the head of the table. "We know that the Inspector and Constable Barnes were sent to Putney this morning. And I've a feeling that Wiggins will get here before too long. You do realize you're all here very early. It's only just gone half three."

"It seemed later with it getting dark so early." Smythe took the seat next to his wife. He was a tall, muscular man with harsh, heavy features and enough gray in his dark brown hair to make the fifteen-year age difference between him and his Betsy noticeable.

"I agree with Mrs. Goodge, we don't have much information." Hatchet put his old-fashioned top hat on the coatrack, crossed the room, and sat down next to Luty. Tall, with a poker-straight spine, the bearing of an emperor, and a headful of thick, white hair, he and Luty were more than just employee and employer. They had a history together and were devoted to each other.

"It won't hurt us to wait a few more minutes before we begin," Ruth, Lady Cannonberry, said as she accepted a cup of tea from Phyllis. She was an attractive woman of late middle age, with only a few strands of gray in her dark blonde hair. The widow of a peer as well as a country vicar's daughter, she took seriously Christ's admonition to love thy neighbor as thyself and firmly believed that all souls were equal in the sight of God. She was also the inspector's "special" friend, and that occasionally caused problems, as she was as devoted to the cause of women's suffrage as she was to the inspector. There were times when she knew her activities might cause him embarrassment, although out of deference for his feelings she had refrained from chaining herself to the railings at Parliament.

Suddenly, Fred got up from his spot by the cooker. Wagging his tail, he scrambled to the back hall, his nails clicking hard against the wood floor.

"Oh, good, Wiggins is home now," the cook sighed happily.

"'Ello, old fellow," they heard the footman say. "You 'ad a good day, then? Come on, let's go inside."

"Thank goodness you're here!" Betsy exclaimed as he came into the room.

"We want to know what happened."

Wiggins shed his coat and hat as he went to the coat tree. Mrs. Goodge poured him a cup of tea while they waited for him to hang up his things.

"Right, then." He nodded his thanks to the cook as he

took his seat. "This murder is pretty ugly—not that there's such a thing as a pretty murder. Sorry, it bothered me a bit when I 'eard about it. The lady was killed by gettin' 'er 'ead smashed with a gardening shovel." He paused to take a quick sip of the hot brew. "'er name was Margaret Starling and she lived in this enormous 'ouse right near the river."

"She lives in Putney, right?" Luty's brows drew together. "So the inspector got called out of his district again."

"'E got sent there by Chief Superintendent Barrows, but you'll never guess who else is there: Inspector Nigel Nivens."

There was a collective groan around the table. None of them liked Inspector Nivens, and there were several people present who positively loathed the fellow.

"What's more, I overheard two of the local constables, and they was sayin' that Nivens is bloomin' angry that our inspector was brought in to take care of this murder."

"He's going to try and hobble our inspector," Betsy said. "You know how much he hates him."

"This isn't good," Hatchet murmured.

"Not good!" Luty snorted. "It's a calamity! I don't trust Nivens further than I could pick him up and throw him."

"Let's not jump to conclusions," Mrs. Jeffries warned them—although, in truth, she was one of those who loathed Nivens. She, more than the others, realized how much of a threat Nivens might become. The man wasn't getting any younger, and the key to success and moving up the ranks of the Metropolitan Police Force was directly linked to the number of murders one solved and the number of times your name was mentioned in the press. The only reason Inspector Witherspoon hadn't been promoted was that he had let the powers that be know he had no interest in doing anything except being an inspector. After inheriting a fortune from his late aunt, Euphemia Witherspoon, he didn't need the money, and he was such a modest man, the trappings of power meant nothing to him. "Perhaps Nivens will realize that our inspector was sent into his district by his superiors at Scotland Yard."

Smythe shook his head dismissively at the thought of Nivens. "Don't count on it, Mrs. Jeffries, 'e's so jealous of our inspector it would take the home secretary himself to keep 'im in line."

"I'm right worried about this, Mrs. Jeffries," Wiggins admitted. "When I was eavesdroppin' on the constables, it was clear that none of the lads at the station wanted to work under Nivens. Except for one fellow, a constable named Forman. 'e's not well liked, either; as a matter of fact, 'e's a bootlicker." That wasn't precisely the word the constables had used, but he couldn't repeat what had actually been said—not in front of the ladies.

"Let's hope for the best, shall we?" Mrs. Jeffries said.

"Come on, don't keep us in suspense. What did ya find out?" Luty said to Wiggins.

He took a quick sip. "As I already said, the victim is named Margaret Starling, and accordin' to what I overheard from the constables, she was probably killed sometime last night." He told them what he'd heard from the two women when he'd first arrived at the Starling home. "I 'ad to be careful when I was there, because I didn't want our inspector or Constable Griffiths to see me, so 'angin' about the murder scene was 'ard. I did find out a few other bits and pieces when I went to the local pub."

"What did you hear?" Mrs. Jeffries took a sip of tea.

"First of all, the victim was 'avin' some sort of spat with her next-door neighbor, a lady named Olivia Huxton. She's a widow lady, too, and I expect she's rich as well. Her house is as big as the Starling place."

"Excellent. Perhaps tomorrow someone here can find out a few more details about this spat."

"I'll give it a go," Betsy offered. "Too bad the weather has been so cold; if it wasn't, I could take Amanda with me. She's wonderful for getting people to chat."

"That's because she's such a smart, sweet-natured little one." Luty looked at Betsy. "And much as I miss our baby not bein' here now, you were right not to bring her out in this cold. You sure the woman who's watchin' her is reliable?"

"Mrs. Packard takes good care of Amanda, otherwise I wouldn't leave her," Betsy assured her.

"Tomorrow I'll see what I can suss out with the local cabmen. From what I know of Putney, there's two hansom shelters in the neighborhood," Smythe offered quickly. He wanted to get the focus of the conversation back to the matter at hand. Too much discussion about his family could lead to some awkward revelations—mainly, that he and Betsy paid a pretty penny to the woman looking after their daughter. She did a great deal more than just taking care of Amanda; she was their housekeeper as well, but that wasn't a fact he was ready to share.

"The house is in good order, and if I give the downstairs a good dusting this evening, I can spend tomorrow seeing what the local shopkeepers can tell me about Mrs. Huxton as well as the victim," Phyllis said.

"Don't worry about the dusting," Mrs. Jeffries told her. "I'll take care of that tomorrow. We don't want the inspector coming home this evening and seeing you wielding a feather duster." She looked at Luty. "Can you tap a few of your sources and see what you can learn about Mrs. Starling's finances?"

"That should be easy if the victim was as rich as Wiggins thinks. I'll see if I can find out anything about Olivia Huxton as well."

"I'll see if any of my sources know anything about either of these individuals," Hatchet offered.

Wiggins swallowed the last bite of the tart he'd just put in his mouth. "After Mrs. Jeffries has her chat with our inspector tonight, we might 'ave a few more names to add to our list."

"And we'll have whatever bits and pieces we can get from Constable Barnes," the cook reminded them. "Who knows: we may have half a dozen more suspects by our morning meeting tomorrow."

Barnes held the empty tea mug by the handle as he headed for the kitchen. The interviews had taken longer than he'd hoped, but they still had time to do a proper search of the victim's study and her bedroom. Reaching the doorway, he hesitated, not wanting to be rude and interrupt the two women who were having a lively chat.

"Fanny seems het up about something." The cook, Mrs. Adkins, put a slab of beef roast on the counter.

"Her nose is out of joint because Mr. McConnell didn't so much as give her a glance when he came to the front door," Martha Horsham said.

"She didn't really think the fellow had any interest in her, did she?" Mrs. Adkins picked up a butcher knife and attacked the fat cap on the meat. "He was just bein' kind. In any case, he's way too old for her. Goodness, he's fifty if he's a day. She's a lovely young woman, and when she wants to marry, she can find a nice young man."

"Well, Mr. McConnell did walk her home from Evensong service three or four times." Martha dried the roasting pan and put it down next to the cook.

"He's a decent man, and for all we know, he might have escorted her home hoping she'd say something nice about him to the mistress. Them charity people are always on the lookout for a bit more money in the coffers . . . Oh, blast!" The cook's voice broke. "I keep forgetting she's gone and we'll never see her again. We've no idea what's going to happen to any of us. I don't know if I should even be cooking this roast when she's not here to eat it."

"It was on the menu for today, and if you don't cook it, it'll go bad. Don't you worry, now, Mrs. Adkins. You're a wonderful cook and you'll find another position." Martha stepped closer to the woman and spotted Barnes. "Did you need something, Constable?"

"I was just returning my tea mug." He held it up as he advanced into the room. "Is Inspector Witherspoon still in the dining room?"

"As far as we know," Martha replied. "Shall I go see?"

"No, that's all right. I'll go. We also need to speak to Mrs. Wheaton so we can get some details about Mrs. Starling's family."

"She's in the downstairs linen closet, sir. It's just at the top of the stairs."

Barnes climbed the staircase, wincing as his bad knee

began to throb. Reaching the top, he saw Inspector Witherspoon standing in the open door of the closet with the housekeeper.

"Ah, Constable. Mrs. Wheaton has very kindly provided the names and addresses of Mrs. Starling's next of kin as well as her solicitor."

"I took the liberty of sending telegrams to her relatives," the housekeeper explained. "All she had left when Mrs. Redstone passed away were two elderly cousins in St. Ives."

"That's fine," Witherspoon replied. "We need to search Mrs. Starling's room now, and then we'll search her study."

"Her bedroom is on the first floor up the front staircase. It's the first door on the left. Her study is just across from the dining room."

It took the two policemen almost an hour to search Margaret Starling's private quarters. They compared notes on what they'd learned in their interviews as they went through her wardrobe, drawers, and the hatboxes neatly stacked on a shelf in the dressing room. Barnes even checked under Mrs. Starling's mattress, but it was all for naught. They found nothing except what was to be expected in a gentile lady's quarters. Witherspoon closed the drawer of her dressing table and straightened a perfume bottle he'd almost knocked over, and they went down to the study.

Barnes opened the double doors and they stepped inside. One wall was covered with bookshelves, a thick green-and-coral rug lay on the floor, and two coral upholstered balloon-backed chairs and a matching settee stood in front of the green marble fireplace. Tables, armoires, and cabinets, most of them cluttered with magazines, knickknacks, and table lamps, were artfully arranged around the room. A walnut desk with ornate carvings on the sides was in the corner, as was a leather chair.

"I'll start with her desk," Witherspoon said, crossing the room, going behind the desk, and opening the top center drawer.

"I'll take the armoires and the cabinets," the constable replied.

"Mrs. Starling was well organized." Witherspoon pulled the drawer farther out. "Stationery and envelopes neatly stacked on one side, writing implements in their own box . . . Oh, good, I've found her appointments diary."

Barnes left the door to the armoire open and joined the inspector. "Should we start at the beginning?"

"Eventually we'll examine the entire diary, but as it's getting late, let's just take a quick look at the last few months and see if anything odd jumps out at us."

He flipped through the pages until he came to October first. "This looks like a good spot to begin. Read along with me, Constable, and if I start to move ahead and you see something that strikes you as strange, let me know."

They read through the pages and found nothing but dressmaker's appointments, alms society meetings, luncheons, shopping expeditions, and dinner parties. When they got to November second, Witherspoon started to turn the page, when Barnes said, "Just a minute, sir. Look at that."

"Look at what? It's just a notation about meeting a friend while shopping on Oxford Street. We've had a dozen 'shopping' entries. Mrs. Starling apparently enjoyed that particular activity."

"But look there, sir, at the bottom of the page. She's added a name: Francine. Why would she do that?"

Witherspoon didn't think it significant, but he respected the constable's experience and instincts. "Perhaps she wrote the name to remind herself about something she needed to do. We'll ask Mrs. Wheaton who this 'Francine' might be. Let's see what else is in here." He resumed turning the pages. But it was more of the same: receptions, meetings, lunches, and dinner parties. Witherspoon closed the book. "According to the upstairs maid, Gretchen Terry, Mrs. Starling never missed appointments unless she was ill, and according to her diary there was an appointment listed for practically every day of her life. Yet twice in the last few weeks she's canceled her plans. Why?"

"Miss Terry said she'd gone to Tunbridge Wells first and then a few weeks later to Chelmsford, but there was nothing about either place in her diary," Barnes reminded him.

"Yes, and Miss Terry didn't know why she'd made those trips, but we'll ask Mrs. Wheaton. Perhaps she'll have some idea."

Barnes went back to the armoire while Witherspoon continued rummaging through the drawers.

"I've found letters," the constable announced. He pulled out a stack neatly tied with a pink ribbon, and untied the bundle. He put them down on the open armoire drawer and pulled out the top letter. "It's correspondence between her and Mr. Starling and it's dated September thirteenth, 1887." He read the first few lines then folded the pages and put them back in the envelope. He went through the next one and the next until he'd done all of them but they were all the same.

"Nothing here but letters between them when Mr. Starling was on the Continent on business. Mainly it's just household and health matters."

"I've not found anything of note, either," Witherspoon admitted. "Let me check this last drawer"—he yanked it open—"and then we'll have a word with Mrs. Wheaton. What's this, then?"

Barnes closed the armoire, crossed the room, and peered over Witherspoon's shoulder as he pulled out a wooden box and set it on the desk. "That looks interesting, sir. What is it?" The brown box was a good fifteen inches across and six inches high.

"It's a writing box, and quite an expensive one at that. It's mahogany with inlaid mother-of-pearl decorations on the corners and a silver filigree Celtic knot in the center. My late aunt Euphemia had one very similar to this."

"There's a keyhole but no key," Barnes observed. "Let's hope it's not locked."

"If it is and we can't find the key, we'll break it open," the inspector said as he lifted the lid. It opened easily and they peered inside.

There was nothing there but an envelope with Margaret Starling's name printed in big, bold letters.

CHAPTER 3

"It's been a very tiring day, Mrs. Jeffries." Witherspoon handed her his bowler and then unbuttoned his heavy black coat. "As soon as I walked into the station this morning, there was a message telling me and Constable Barnes to go to Putney."

"What on earth for, sir?" She hung up his hat and a moment later took his coat and hung that up as well. She knew why he'd been called to Putney, but she couldn't let on that, thanks to Wiggins, the household not only knew about Margaret Starling's murder but had learned a bit of information she'd need to relay to Constable Barnes the next morning.

"A murder, Mrs. Jeffries. A woman named Margaret Starling was killed in her own garden last night," he sighed. "Once again, we've a homicide to solve right here at Christmas."

"That always seems to happen, sir." She smiled sympathetically. "Perhaps this one will be a simple one, sir, and you'll catch the culprit immediately."

"I do hope so, but I'm not counting on it. Can dinner be delayed? I would love to have a glass of sherry."

"Of course, sir. Mrs. Goodge has made nice lamb stew, but it's not ready as yet." She led the way down the hall to his study and went to the liquor cabinet while he made himself comfortable in his favorite chair.

She took out a bottle of Harveys Bristol Cream sherry, poured the amber liquid into two small crystal glasses, and rejoined the Inspector. Handing him his drink, she took her own seat. "Now tell me everything, sir. You know how much I love hearing about your cases."

Witherspoon took a quick sip. "Well, as I said, I don't think this is going to be an easy case to solve. According to what we learned from her servants, the victim has recently been acting strangely, and she was suing her neighbor, a woman named Olivia Huxton. Additionally, I found out that she'd quarreled with the husband of her deceased niece."

"Oh, dear, that sounds complicated."

"And it gets worse, but I digress. Let me start at the beginning." He told her about his day, starting from the moment he arrived at the Starling home. "Of course, and though I'm not a medical man, even I could tell the poor woman must have been outside most of the night. Her flesh was nearly frozen."

"Didn't her servants notice she wasn't inside?" Mrs. Jeffries knew they'd all been gone, of course, but it was necessary to pretend ignorance.

"They were all given the evening out." He explained the series of events that led to the victim not being discovered until early that morning. "So, of course, that leads one to suspect that the killer knew about Mrs. Starling's habit of giving the servants a night out at Christmas."

"And planned the murder for when she was alone," Mrs. Jeffries murmured. "But why do you think she went outside? It was dreadfully cold last night."

"At first I thought she might have gone out because she'd heard something or someone had come to the back door, but her housekeeper assured us she was a sensible woman and she'd not have ventured out on her own with all her servants gone. Of course, to me the obvious reason was that she'd taken the lamp outside to look for her cat, but the servants said that the cat was safely inside when they arrived home from the theater. So she couldn't have gone out to find him and then been murdered, which would have meant the cat managed to get himself inside on his own. The back door was closed and locked from the inside."

"Could the killer have done that?"

"Possibly, but if you've murdered someone, why go to the trouble of putting their cat inside and leaving the gas lamp outside on the lawn? What's more, the back door key has been lost for several weeks now. That means either the murderer could have stolen it well before the last night, which may or may not prove to be the case, or he or she locked the door from the inside and then exited the home some other way."

"That doesn't seem to make much sense," she agreed. Still, she'd give this matter some thought precisely because it was so very strange. "You got much accomplished today."

"Yes, but we've so much more to do. It took ages just to interview Mrs. Starling's servants and search the pertinent areas of the house where she kept her business and personal correspondence. Luckily, we found her appointment diary and a very intriguing note."

"A note?"

"Indeed." He told her about finding the envelope in Margaret Starling's writing box. "The way her name was printed made one think it had been written by a ten-year-old practicing his letters, but when we opened it, the note inside was even more surprising."

"What did it say?"

"As well as I recall, it read something like this:

"'Dear Mrs. Starling,

"'You should know that your good character has become a slanderous topic of discussion amongst those who previously held you in high regard. Someone you trusted has shown an anonymous letter accusing you of senility, drunkenness, and a host of other character defects to the Board of Governors of the Angel Alms Society.

"'Sincerely,
"'A Friend
"'P.S. Be careful whom you trust.'"

The content of the note was surprising, but even more surprising was that it had been written on a typewriter.

"A typewriter?" she repeated. "Goodness, that's quite unusual."

"I thought so at first, but then I realized that typewriter machines are far more common than they were even five years ago."

"That's true," she murmured. "On your last really big case, Pierce and Son used typewriters for all their correspondence and invoices."

"As do most of the law firms here in London. We live in a modern world, Mrs. Jeffries, and from what I've seen, when a new, more efficient method of doing something comes along, it's adopted very quickly."

"I agree, sir, but I'm sure you've asked yourself this already: Why would someone bother to use a typewriter? They might be more common, but using one requires a certain level of skill, doesn't it?"

"Only if the operator wishes to type fast. Otherwise, anyone can use one." He grinned. "Truth to tell, I've played about with one a time or two, and all you need do is use your fingers to hit the keys." He stuck out his two index fingers and imitated striking the keys.

"Yes, I have as well; they had one on display at the Women's Institute. Where is the note now, sir?" She hoped it wasn't at the Upper Richmond Road Police Station. She'd not put it past Nivens to destroy any and all evidence Inspector Witherspoon found.

"Constable Barnes took it to Ladbroke Road." Witherspoon took a sip of his sherry. "He was going there anyway, and he said he'd noticed the evidence closet at Upper Richmond Road had a broken lock and that the note would be more secure at our station."

Mrs. Jeffries silently sighed in relief. No doubt Constable Barnes had come to the same conclusion and realized evidence would be safer somewhere Nivens wasn't in command. "I'm sure it will be, sir. How long did it take you to search the house?"

"We didn't have enough men to go over the whole house. The place is enormous, but according to the housekeeper Mrs. Starling kept all her important documents and correspondence in her study, so that's where we concentrated our efforts. However, to be on the safe side, Constable Barnes and I searched her room as well. There was nothing of interest there. Unfortunately, it was so late by the time we'd completed those tasks that we didn't have time to speak to Mrs. Huxton."

"That's the neighbor she was suing?" Mrs. Jeffries knew who she was, but again, it was important to feign ignorance.

"That's right." He tipped back his glass and drained it. "Let's have another one, shall we? I've not told you the worst of it yet."

"Of course, sir." She smiled serenely, poured him another one, and topped hers off. She was fairly sure she knew what he was going to tell her and was equally certain that was the reason for his second drink.

"Here you are, sir. Now, what's the worst of it?"

"As I said before, this case isn't in my district. But orders are orders, and Chief Superintendent Barrows sent me in to handle it. Unfortunately, the case should have been handled by the duty inspector at the Upper Richmond Road Police Station, and the duty inspector is Nigel Nivens. I'm afraid he's going to be very upset about it as well."

"But as you said, sir, it's not your fault that you were given the murder," she said softly. "Surely Inspector Nivens will understand you had no choice." She forced herself to say the words for the inspector's peace of mind, but she knew it was a lie. Nivens would do everything in his power to undermine the investigation.

"I was going to speak to him myself, but when we stopped in at the Upper Richmond Road Police Station, he'd gone for the day." Witherspoon frowned. "Mind you, his being gone was a bit annoying, as I wanted to make arrangements to get the local constables to question the neighbors."

"Of course, sir. You've found out really useful information on many of your previous cases because someone in the neighborhood saw or heard something important," she agreed.

Her mind was working furiously. She was sure that Nivens had deliberately absented himself from the station. He knew Witherspoon would need help from the local lads.

"Indeed I have, and that's why it's necessary to have the local constables help out and knock on a few doors," he took another sip. "But not to worry; perhaps I'm making too much of Nivens' absence this afternoon. I'm sure once I have a moment to speak to him we'll sort it out in no time."

The next morning Constable Barnes made sure he had a word with Mrs. Jeffries and Mrs. Goodge when he stopped in to get the inspector. When the constable had first realized that the inspector was obtaining information on his cases from an unknown informant, he'd been annoyed. But then he'd noticed the bits and pieces Witherspoon had picked up were very, very useful and, more important, that they were coming from a trusted informant—or, in this case, informants: the inspector's household and friends.

Being a smart old copper, he'd stepped back and watched how the cases unfolded. It didn't take long before he was convinced that their efforts were important. People who would spit on a policeman's shoe rather than talk to him would chatter like magpies to Wiggins or Betsy or any of the others. They ferreted out ancient history, buried facts, gossip, and hearsay and handed it to Mrs. Jeffries. She took the unrelated strands of information, turned them this way and that, and handed them the killer on a silver platter. The woman was the best detective he'd ever seen. Luckily, she and the rest of the household were so devoted to their inspector, none of them cared that they never got the credit. At that point, he'd boldly told the two senior ladies of the household what he knew, and ever since then they'd been sharing information.

"We heard that the vicar and the victim had some sort of argument recently," Barnes told them. "It's good that Wiggins found that out as well. Mind you, we've still a number of things to suss out; the Starling housekeeper had no idea who 'Francine' was nor why Mrs. Starling had gone to Tunbridge Wells or Chelmsford. But she did agree that such behavior was out of character for Mrs. Starling."

"Don't worry, Constable, it's still early days yet; you'll soon sort out all the bits and pieces," Mrs. Jeffries said. She and Mrs. Goodge had already given him a full report on what Wiggins had learned the previous day. The housekeeper had also repeated what Witherspoon had told her the night before so that he could fill in any missing information that might have slipped the inspector's mind.

"Let's hope so."

"Everyone is going to be out today, so hopefully we'll know more by tomorrow. Perhaps we'll even know who the mysterious 'Francine' is and why Mrs. Starling took those two trips."

"Ah, yes, that reminds me of something I wanted to tell you." The cook leaned closer to Barnes. "Everyone's a bit concerned about being seen by our inspector. If you could, please, if you spot one of them, try and distract our inspector. It's one thing if he sees one of the household in *this* neighborhood, but if he sees one of them across the river in Putney, he'll wonder what they're doin', and that's a question we'd rather he not ask."

"I'll do my best," Barnes assured them. "Now, what the inspector didn't tell you was that I overheard a rather interesting conversation in the kitchen." He told them about eavesdropping on the cook and scullery maid, then filled them in on a few small details that Witherspoon had overlooked. "I know it doesn't sound very important, but I thought I'd pass it along."

"Everything is important," Mrs. Jeffries said. "We want to get this case solved quickly. We have only five days until Christmas."

"I've a feeling we'll catch this killer by Christmas Eve," Mrs. Goodge declared.

"Fingers crossed that you're right." Barnes grinned at the cook, put his mug on the table, and got to his feet. "Right, then. I'll see you two ladies tomorrow."

As soon as he disappeared up the staircase, the two women went about getting the table set up for their morning meeting. Everyone already had a task assigned, but it was important to pass along what Mrs. Jeffries had heard from the inspector as well as the other details they'd gained from Constable Barnes.

Everyone arrived soon after the inspector and Constable Barnes left. Mrs. Jeffries and Mrs. Goodge took it in turn to tell the others the latest information, and less than a half hour after the meeting started, the kitchen was quiet.

Mrs. Jeffries picked up the empty teapot and took it to the sink. "Do you have any sources coming in today?"

"I'm sure someone will. I sent out those three notes yesterday and the laundry is due back today." Mrs. Goodge pulled her big green bread bowl out from beneath the worktable. "He's the only one I know for certain will be here today, and the trouble is the laundry lad probably won't know anything about anyone in Putney. It's much easier to find out useful bits when the inspector is in his own district."

"True, but don't get discouraged, Mrs. Goodge. We've had cases that were outside his district before and we've always solved them," Mrs. Jeffries replied.

"You're right. This one will be no different," Mrs. Goodge popped off the lid from the tin of flour she kept on the worktable. "I can feel it."

"Gracious, sir, this is a bit unexpected." Barnes stood in the center of the Huxton drawing room and slowly turned, his mouth slightly agape. The large room was elegantly appointed with pale gold painted walls, French-style upholstered furniture, and a polished diamond-patterned parquet floor. But it was the paintings and statues that held his gaze. A richly colored picture of a nude woman reclining on a couch hung above the black marble fireplace; between each of the three windows there was a statue of a woman, either nude or wearing only a few wisps of fabric; and along the wall opposite the hearth was a series of paintings depicting a horned man with absurdly hairy legs and pointy ears chasing a lovely young blonde girl. By the time his gaze focused on the last of the paintings, Barnes could feel himself blushing.

Witherspoon cleared his throat. "I believe the paintings depict the god Pan, and the statues appear to be Grecian in origin. One doesn't expect to see this sort of art in the homes of genteel ladies. Not that there is anything wrong with this sort of art."

"I'm glad you think so, Inspector." A tall woman of late middle age stepped into the room and closed the double oak doors behind her. She wore a high-necked white blouse and a blue skirt, and around her waist was a wide blue and silver braided belt. Her graying brown hair was pulled into a top-knot held up by a large silver filigreed comb. Her face was pale and her lips thin, and she stared at the two policemen out of a pair of deep-set dark eyes.

"I'm Inspector Gerald Witherspoon and this is my colleague, Constable Barnes," he said as she advanced into the room. "Forgive me, Mrs. Huxton. I wasn't disparaging your décor."

She waved him off impatiently. "I don't care whether you were or not, Inspector. Now, why don't the two of you sit down and we'll get this distasteful matter over with." She sat down on a sofa and gestured toward the two chairs opposite before clasping her hands together on her lap.

They sat where she had indicated and Barnes, after giving the god Pan one last glance, pulled out his notebook.

"I take it you know why we're here," the inspector said.

"Yes. Margaret managed to get herself murdered and you've no doubt been told by her servants that she and I were involved in a legal dispute."

"I hardly think she is at fault for being a victim," Witherspoon said.

She took a deep breath and closed her eyes briefly. "I'm

sorry. Please, forgive me. I shouldn't have spoken so flippantly. Margaret Starling and I were once very close friends, and even though we've been estranged recently, I'm very upset by the manner of her death. No one deserves to die as she did." She swallowed. "I've heard she lay outside all night. Is that true?"

"I'm afraid so, Mrs. Huxton." Witherspoon leaned back farther. "You've just said you and Mrs. Starling were once good friends. Can you tell us exactly what happened between you?"

"Is that really pertinent, Inspector?"

"We won't know that until you tell us what happened," he replied. "As policemen, it's been our experience that not all legal disputes are actually settled in court."

She stared at him defiantly. "I didn't kill her, Inspector, so I don't see how our personal difficulties have any bearing on her murder."

"That may well be true, ma'am," Constable Barnes interjected, "but we only have your word that you had nothing to do with her murder."

She gasped and looked at Barnes, her expression stunned. But before she could say anything, Witherspoon said, "The constable is correct, Mrs. Huxton, so if you don't mind, I'd like you to answer the question."

Her eyes narrowed angrily. "That's ridiculous. People such as myself don't commit murder. If we think we're going to lose in court, we simply hire better lawyers."

"I assure you, ma'am, people from the upper classes do commit terrible crimes, including murder." Barnes smiled cynically.

Mrs. Huxton said nothing for a long moment, her expression stony and hard. "If it's the only way to be rid of the two of you, I'll tell you everything. My relationship with Margaret turned sour last summer. Up until then we'd been both good friends and good neighbors. We often had dinner together and went to each other's social functions. I supposed that's what upset me the most." She looked away.

"What did?" Witherspoon pressed. There was much to do today, including getting some additional constables from the Upper Richmond Road Police Station. Inspector Nivens hadn't arrived that morning when he and Barnes stopped in to seek assistance.

"It's going to sound so petty, Inspector, but I suppose there's nothing for it but to tell you the truth. The final nail in the coffin of our friendship was when she had a garden party and didn't invite me," she explained. "But that's not what started our estrangement. It was the gooseberry bushes, you see."

"Gooseberry bushes?" Witherspoon repeated.

"I told you it was going to sound petty," Mrs. Huxton sighed. "For years those wretched bushes didn't produce anything except a few miserable berries. But last summer the berries suddenly burst forth into full splendor and they were delicious. There were plenty of them, so both households helped themselves until they were almost gone. One evening at the end of July, I was having a small dinner party with some of my friends from the art world. I'd not invited Margaret because she wasn't interested in art, but that's beside the point. I'd instructed the cook to take the last of the gooseberries and prepare a fool. Imagine my surprise when cook came and informed me that she couldn't do the fool because Margaret's scullery maid had just picked the last of the berries. Well, those bushes are mine, so I sent Liddy, my scullery maid over to ask for them back. I told her to explain to Margaret's cook that I was having an important dinner and that I needed them, as my guest had made a point of telling me how much he loved gooseberry fool." She paused and took a breath. "But Margaret's cook wouldn't give them back; she claimed the berries belonged to the Starling household and that Margaret was hosting a dinner party herself for her women's group. At first I was going to let it go, but then I realized that I couldn't." She jabbed her finger in the air as she spoke. "Those bushes are on my property, not Margaret's. So I went over and made my case. But Margaret wouldn't listen. She claimed the bushes were on her side of the property line. After that, we became more and more estranged. But things didn't come to a head until a week or so later."

"What happened then?" Witherspoon wondered why so often it was the most trivial, silly actions that led to the most dreadful consequences.

"We were still on somewhat civil terms until then, but early on Friday evening I went outside to see if the gardener had finished cleaning the lawn furniture, and when I looked across to her garden, there she was with the entire advisory board. I'm on the board as well but I'd not been invited."

"The Angel Alms Society advisory board?" Barnes interjected, seeking clarification.

"That's correct. Margaret saw me standing there and had the good grace to look embarrassed."

"Did you ask her why you'd not been invited?" Witherspoon asked.

"Of course, Inspector, and at first she tried to insist that it wasn't a garden party, merely a small gathering of the other advisers." Mrs. Huxton looked skeptical. "But when I mentioned that I could clearly see she was serving champagne and canapés, she then had the audacity to tell me that it was because she had something 'confidential' to tell the board. I pressed her, of course, reminding her that I was a member of the advisory board, but she told me it wasn't 'necessary' that I be included."

"Do you have any idea what the confidential matter might have been?" The inspector unbuttoned his overcoat.

"I do. I found out about it from Steven Marshall; he's on the board of governors. His wife is on the advisory board as well, and she was at the party—"

"Excuse me," Barnes interrupted, "but there's a difference between the advisory board and the governing body?"

Witherspoon winced inwardly as he realized he'd forgotten to tell the constable everything Mrs. Wheaton had told him about the matter.

"Certainly. Women make up the advisory board, while it's men who are on the board of governors. But one of the things we've been pressing for is to allow women to be governors, and we'd have won that battle if it hadn't been for that silly Reverend Pontefract. He's the vicar at St. Andrew's Church."

"We've been told he's on the board of governors," Witherspoon said.

"That's correct. The society is unofficially affiliated with St. Andrew's. The alms offices are located in the building next to the church—which, by the way, the church owns and lets to the society for far less than it's worth. But that's another issue we have with the vicar. But because of the affiliation, and because he's one of the governors and essentially our landlord, he's very influential. That was one of the few things Margaret and I agreed upon recently: that we were still going to push to get the society to accept women as governors." She sat back and folded her hands in her lap again.

"You've told us about one incident, Mrs. Huxton. Surely that can't be the only reason you and Mrs. Starling had become estranged," Witherspoon pressed.

"Of course it wasn't." Olivia Huxton smiled ruefully. "It was only the beginning. I felt wronged and very hurt, so I had a garden party of my own and I didn't invite her. After that, things got increasingly stupid and petty. I chased off her silly cat and she came around and accused me of hitting the animal. That's absurd, that fat Gladstone regularly attacks my BooBoo. He's a sweet spaniel and wouldn't hurt a fly. We stopped speaking, and right about then I heard a rumor that she was pressing the vicar to ask me to leave the advisory board."

Barnes stopped writing and looked at her. "Would he have done what she asked?"

"Probably. Margaret gave more money to St. Andrew's than I did, and there's nothing that Reginald Pontefract loves more than filling the church's coffers. What's more, he didn't approve of the art here in my home or of my political views. But that silly man's medieval ideas aren't important." She stopped. "Sorry, I still can't believe she's dead, and I never had a chance to apologize to her for what I did."

Witherspoon looked at her sympathetically. "What did you do?"

"I let pride dictate my actions and did something very, very stupid." Her eyes filled with tears. "God, I would give anything to take back that foolish letter." She sniffed, pulled a pristine white handkerchief out of her skirt pocket, wiped her eyes, and blew her nose. "I wrote an anonymous letter to the Reverend Pontefract."

"What did this letter say?"

"Stupid things, foolish things, exaggerations about Margaret's recent behavior." She sighed heavily and shook her head. "They weren't complete lies, but it wasn't the truth, either. I accused her of drinking too much, which, as I've already said, wasn't completely a lie. Sometimes she did drink to excess. I also said that she was making up stories about men on the board of governors and hinting that there was impropriety in financial affairs."

"Did you make that up?" Barnes asked bluntly.

"Not completely." She gave a harsh, ugly laugh. "That's why the letter was so believable. Margaret had told people she thought there was something going wrong with the finances and she had been acting erratic. But none of it was true enough for me to have written that stupid, stupid letter. I'm so ashamed of myself. It has caused no end of grief."

"But now that she's dead, she can't sue you for slander." Barnes watched her carefully as he spoke.

"I know, but she'd have lost the lawsuit anyway. The only proof she had that I wrote the letter was that she'd seen it when that idiot Pontefract showed it to her and she insisted it was my handwriting."

"Handwriting can be very distinctive," Witherspoon remarked, "and the courts have used it to prove the identity of the author."

She snorted delicately. "Oh, please, Inspector. If my writing looked like Graham McConnell's, I'd agree with you; his penmanship is so elaborate it's unreadable. But mine looks like the handwriting of any other woman who has been educated at St. Anne's School for Girls—a place where conformity in all things was not only encouraged but the only way to avoid getting one's hand smacked with a birch rod."

"Did you ever admit to her or anyone else that you were the author of the letter?" Witherspoon asked.

"I'm not a complete fool, Inspector. I never admitted it to anyone."

"But despite your assertion that your handwriting is similar to that of many other women of your class, if the letter is in your handwriting, simple comparisons to other things you've written should be easy enough to prove in a court of law," Barnes said. "All the judge and jury would need to see is a sample of your handwriting to compare to the letter."

"Which means that you could risk losing everything if Mrs. Starling had gone through with her court case," the inspector added.

"Not really," she replied. "The letter no longer exists. I made sure of that."

Betsy stopped on the corner and surveyed the busy High Street. Traffic was heavy in both directions and the pavement was crowded with pedestrians. Drat, that wasn't good. Shop clerks didn't waste their time chatting when they were busy. But she was here now and she'd agreed to see what she could learn about Olivia Huxton. She started down the street, moving quickly and peering into each shop window as she passed. At the baker's, there were half a dozen people waiting to be served and an even longer line of shoppers at the butcher's. She reached the greengrocer's and almost went in but then two women wielding shopping baskets shoved past her and got there first. The same situation prevailed at the fishmonger's, another butcher shop, and a chemist's. She'd reached the end of the street and didn't hold out much hope that it might be useful, because it was a grocer's shop, which meant it was generally filled with customers; but when she peered in the window, there was only one person inside. She opened the door and stepped inside.

"May I help you, miss?" the clerk asked as he handed a paper-wrapped bundle across the counter to a middle-aged matron.

Betsy walked slowly toward him, giving the matron time to leave. It was much easier getting young men to talk when they were on their own.

She smiled brightly as she neared the counter. He was a slender, dark-haired young lad with a narrow face and heavy eyebrows. "I do hope you can assist me. I'm so sorry to trouble you, but I'm afraid I'm lost."

"If I can, miss. Where are you going?"

"You'll think me an idiot, I'm afraid. But my neighbor asked me to do her a favor when she found out I was coming here to shop, and she gave me a note for a Mrs. Huxton who lives in the area. But I've lost the slip of paper that had her address on it. I'm hoping that her household shops here."

His thick brows drew together and he shook his head. "Sorry, miss, I've never heard of the lady. But if she lives in this neighborhood, you might try the dressmaker's around the corner. I understand it's quite a popular shop with the ladies."

Betsy smiled graciously, thanked him, and hurried off to find the dressmaker's. But her luck was just as bad there as it was at the grocer's shop. She tried the greengrocer's, the butcher's, and the fishmonger's but found out nothing. By the time she wandered back to the baker's, she was tired, hungry, and depressed. No one had heard of Olivia Huxton, and what's more, now that she'd bandied that name about, she couldn't use the same sad tale to find out about Margaret Starling. Maybe Wiggins had got it wrong or maybe the gossip he'd heard at the pub yesterday was nothing more than idle talk.

She stopped outside the baker's and peered into the shop window. This late in the day, they'd sold most of their goods, so there was only one other person in the shop. Pulling open the door, she stepped inside and walked to the counter. She didn't even bother to wait until the place was empty before she spoke, asking for what seemed the hundredth time if the clerk knew the address of one Olivia Huxton. But once again she was disappointed. He'd never heard the name.

Betsy stepped outside and shivered as a cold wind from the river blasted into her. She was back where she'd started, so she decided to take a look at the Huxton house and perhaps see if there was anything interesting at the Starling home next door. It should be fine—none of the constables here knew her by sight, and she'd take care to avoid anyone from the Ladbroke Road Police Station. Besides, she told herself, it was too late to go anywhere else this afternoon. Crossing the river to Putney was a lot more time-consuming than their investigations closer to home.

She turned onto Moran Place and surveyed the posh neighborhood, moving carefully and getting ready to flick the hood of her cloak up in case Inspector Witherspoon or Constable Griffiths suddenly appeared. But her luck seemed to have changed, and the only constables she spied were two that she didn't recognize. She passed the Starling house and was almost in front of the Huxton house when a woman wearing an oversized black mantle stepped out the side door and hurried down the short stone walkway to the street.

Slowing her steps, Betsy gave the woman time to stay a dozen feet in front of her. She saw that beneath the woman's garment was a black bombazine skirt. Maybe the lady was a housekeeper? Maybe she was Olivia Huxton's housekeeper? She studied her quarry more closely and saw that the mantle was frayed along the hemline. Suddenly the woman sped up as she came to the end of the street.

Betsy walked faster and she got to the corner just in time to see the woman disappearing through a doorway. She raced after her and skidded to a stop as she realized it was a pub.

"Oh, blast a Spaniard." She hesitated, unsure of what to do. Her husband wouldn't be happy that she went into a pub on her own; on the other hand, she was on the hunt and he went into pubs when necessary. What was good for the goose was good for the gander, she told herself. Yanking open the door, she stepped inside.

The pub wasn't crowded; only a couple of men in flat caps sat at one of the tables, and the woman she'd followed stood by herself at the bar. Holding her head high, Betsy strode across the small space.

The woman turned as she approached. Her face was lined, her nose a bright red, and beneath her cap her thin hair was more gray than brown. "Why have you been followin' me?"

Betsy saw that her quarry was drinking a shot of gin. She

cocked her head to one side and smiled. "I'm so sorry. I didn't mean to alarm you, but I'd like to speak with you."

The woman eyed her warily. "I've never seen you 'round here before. Do I know you?"

"What'll it be, miss?" The burly barman slapped a wet tea towel onto the counter and gave it a scrub.

"I'll have a gin and another for this lady here." Betsy jerked her chin toward the woman as she tugged off her gloves and put them on the counter.

"If you're buyin' me a drink, I guess I do know ya," the woman cackled.

"I'm a private inquiry agent," Betsy began.

"Stop lyin'. You're a bloomin' housemaid." She pointed toward the plain lavender dress peeking out from beneath Betsy's cloak.

Before she'd set off, she'd debated what to wear, and now she was glad she'd decided to wear her old housemaid's uniform and an old-fashioned brown cloak instead of one of her nicer outfits. "I'm dressed as a housemaid because I'm working—" She broke off as the barkeep brought their drinks.

Pulling some coins out of her cloak pocket, Betsy paid for the gin and then waited till the barman had moved away before turning back to the woman. "As I said, I'm dressed this way because I'm on an investigation. It's an important matter, and if you can answer a few of my questions, I'll be happy to buy you another gin." She'd learned this technique from Phyllis and hoped it would work, but as her gaze moved over the bloodshot eyes and red nose of her companion, she began to have doubts. The woman liked her drink; the question was: Did she like it well enough to talk freely. There was only one way to find out. "My name is Barbara Clark. What's yours?"

The woman said nothing for a few moments; she simply stared at Betsy out of watery blue eyes. But then she smiled slyly. "I'm Annabelle Waverly, and as long as you're buyin', I've time for a chat."

Betsy realized she'd blundered. Annabelle Waverly's smile, if that was really her name, gave the game away. The lady was one of those poor souls who couldn't stop drinking once they poured that first one down their throats. Drat, she'd known a lot of women like her from her childhood days in the East End. But as she was here, she might as well see if she could find out something. The worst that could happen was the woman would tell her a load of nonsense.

"Do you work at that house I saw you come out of?" She wasn't going to mention any names as yet. She took a sip from her glass.

"You mean the Huxton house? I work there, but I'm not one of their servants. I'm just helpin' out with the heavy cleanin'. Mrs. Huxton's havin' a fancy Christmas party. I work from half eight in the mornings till half past one. They give me a decent lunch there. The police were there this mornin'," she cackled. "You shoulda seen the housemaids, twitterin' like a tree full of birds, they were."

Betsy felt a bit better. At least she knew the right name. "Why were the police there?"

Annabelle looked at her, her expression cynical. "Why do you think? Her next-door neighbor that she's been feudin' with was murdered. Isn't that why you followed me here?"

"I'm not at liberty to discuss that," Betsy replied.

"Mind you, Mrs. Huxton is in a real state today; you should have seen her face after she saw all them police in Mrs. Starling's back garden." Her eyes narrowed shrewdly as she lifted her glass halfway to her mouth. "Come on, tell us the truth: That's why you're wantin' to ask me questions?"

"I've told you, I'm not at liberty to say, but I would like to ask you some questions about Mrs. Huxton." She paused and took another quick sip of her gin. It tasted awful.

"Ask 'em, then, unless you're wantin' to spend the rest of the afternoon here buyin' me gin." She laughed, drained her drink, and waved the empty glass at the barman.

Betsy wasn't sure this was a good idea, the woman was probably going to lie her head off just to keep the gin flowing. Still, this was the closest she'd come today to finding out anything. "Right, then: Why was she in such a state about Mrs. Starling's murder?"

"Because they used to be friends, and when she found out the woman had been murdered, her face turned white. We all saw it—the housekeeper and both the downstairs maids. We were in the big pantry off the dining room, polishing the silver and scrubbing the dust off the platters and the servin' bowls, when the scullery maid come in and announced that Mrs. Starling had been coshed in the head and was dead." She snorted. "That tossed her nibs off her high horse. She'd been bossing us, pickin' at every little thing, but when she heard the news, she looked like she'd been punched in the gut. Her face turned whiter than the table linens, and she had to steady herself against one of the chairs."

"So she looked surprised and shocked?"

"She tried to make it seem that way, but I was watchin' her eyes, and it wasn't shock I saw in them; it was fear." Annabelle snickered. "She's right to be scared."

"What do you mean?"

Annabelle drew back, her expression calculating. "This person who hired you—is he willin' to pay for information?"

Betsy had plenty of money; Smythe always made certain she had both coins and notes in her pocket or purse before she walked out the front door. She was quite willing to spend a bit to find out something useful, but she wasn't altogether certain Annabelle Waverly wasn't making it up as she went along. "That depends."

"On what?"

Betsy gave her a cool smile. "On whether what you've got to tell is worth anything,"

"It's worth plenty." Annabelle drained her glass and slammed it down. "Plenty, I tell you."

"You wantin' another?" the barman yelled from the far end of the bar.

"No, but bring one for her," Betsy answered, and nodded at Annabelle Waverly. "You do want another one, right?"

"Don't be daft. As long as you're payin', I'll drink."

"I thought you might," Betsy said. "Now, why don't you tell me what you know and then I'll decide if it's worth anything."

"That don't seem fair." She sucked her lower lip between her teeth and then released it as the barman brought another drink.

Betsy took her time paying him, because she wanted to give Annabelle a few seconds to consider her offer. True, she wasn't going to give her any money until she knew precisely what it was that the woman was selling. But she'd now bought her three gins, and she was fairly sure that alone would keep her talking. She hated the fact that she was taking advantage of this woman's weakness and had already decided against pouring any more gin down her throat.

"Ta, miss." The barman took the coins and went to the cash register.

Annabelle sipped her gin, her expression sullen. "You must think you're right special, don't ya?"

"No, I'm just like everyone else: I'm trying to make a decent living."

"Huh, you're not foolin' me. You might have put on a housemaid's dress and plain old cloak, but you made a bad mistake." She looked down at Betsy's feet. "Your shoes cost more than I earn in a month."

Betsy shrugged. "The reason I'm a private inquiry agent is because it pays decently and these shoes are an early Christmas present from my fella; he makes good money. Besides, what difference does it make? You either know something useful or you don't." She picked up her gloves as if she were getting ready to leave.

"Wait a minute, I'll tell ya," Annabelle said quickly.

"All right, tell me."

"I saw something Sunday night—something that her nibs would pay plenty for me to keep quiet about—but I'm not a blackmailer or anything like that."

"What did you see?"

"As I told ya already, I don't work for Mrs. Huxton or, for that matter, anyone else. I work for myself and the money isn't great, but it keeps a roof over my head and I generally get to eat at the houses. I do heavy cleanin', you see."

"But rich houses have plenty of servants," Betsy noted.

"They do, but sometimes, like at Mrs. Huxton's, they need extra help and they'll not hire a full-time live-in person for that; that costs way too much money, so they bring in someone like me." She waved her hand impatiently. "But my situation isn't important. Sunday evening I was workin' at the Larson house; it's directly across the road from the Huxton house, and Mrs. Larson needed an extra hand, because all of her relatives have come for Christmas. After I'd finished, I got my pay and put my coat on and I left. I came out the servant's door on the side of the house, and that side directly faces Mrs. Starling's home. I'd almost reached the street when I saw Mrs. Huxton coming down the front stairs of the Starling house. I moved back into the shadows; I don't know why, but there was something about the way she moved that bothered me. Now, I ask you: What was she doin' at the dead woman's house."

"You know for certain it was Mrs. Huxton?"

"It was; there's a streetlamp between their houses and I got a good look at her as she hurried past it. But that's not all—when she got to her own house, she didn't go in by the front door, she went to the side door and slipped in that way."

CHAPTER 4

Wiggins smiled at the young housemaid as he knelt and picked up the shopping basket she'd dropped. "Please let me carry this for you, miss. I feel such an idiot for bargin' into you." Of course, he'd deliberately "barged" into the young lady when he saw her leave the Huxton residence. She was a very young housemaid, with curly red hair, blue eyes, and more freckles on her nose than there were stars on a country night.

She smiled broadly and lowered her head, giggling before looking back up at him. "It was an accident, but if it'll make you feel better, you can carry the basket. I'm just going to the grocer's to get another cone of sugar. The mistress suddenly changed the menu for tonight's dinner."

"You work in the kitchen, then?" He took her elbow and they started off toward the High Street. Wiggins looked at both sides of the quiet street. He didn't want to run into

Inspector Witherspoon. For once, he wasn't all that worried about being spotted by the rank-and-file constables doing a house-to-house. None of them knew him by sight.

He relaxed and tried to think of a clever way to get the girl talking. Perhaps he should . . . drat, they were at the walkway of the house next door to the Huxton home, and there was Constable Griffiths coming down the porch stairs and heading toward them. What was he doing there? Blast a Spaniard! Wiggins pulled his scarf up far enough to cover his lower face. "It's really cold," he murmured.

"It's not so bad"—the housemaid smiled prettily—"though it's colder today than yesterday."

Wiggins hoped the scarf would muffle his words; he wasn't sure if Griffiths could recognize his voice. "You've been ever so nice about this, miss. Truly, though, I feel terrible. Are you sure you're all right?" He stuck his hand in his pocket and wiggled his fingers, trying to grab a coin. He caught a sixpence and pulled it out.

"I'm fine, really, but it's very kind of you to be concerned. My name is Cecilia Wilkins. What's yours?"

"Albert Jones." He dropped the coin and then stopped suddenly as Constable Griffiths came to the end of the walkway and turned onto the pavement. "There must be a hole in me pocket." He kept his head down as he pretended to look for the money. Griffiths moved past the two of them and crossed the road.

Still keeping his head turned away from the constable, Wiggins managed to find his money and get to his feet. "Sorry, I don't want to leave any of me wages in the road."

He took her elbow again. Now that the constable was too far away to identify him, Wiggins realized his appearance could be very useful. He wouldn't have to figure out how to get Cecilia talking about the murder. "Wonder what that policeman was doing here?"

"I know," she said quickly. "There was a murder next door."

"Actually, I do, too," he laughed. "That's why I'm here. But I'd no idea the murder was next door to you. That must be awful."

She slowed her steps and glanced at him. "You knew? Did you read about it in the papers?"

"You could say that." He could tell from the sudden change in her demeanor that he needed to be careful. He didn't want her to go quiet on him now. "I work for a newspaper, the *Sentinel*." It was a paper known for lurid headlines and stories.

"Cook reads it." She stared at him, her expression suspicious. "Is that why you're here? Because of Mrs. Starling's murder?"

"That's why my guv sent me down 'ere." He pulled his scarf down to his neck and gave her his best smile. "But I didn't bump into you on purpose, if that's what you're thinkin'."

She stopped and whirled around to face him directly. "That's exactly what I'm thinking. Give me my basket. I don't want to talk to a reporter. The way Mrs. Huxton's been lately, if she hears I've talked to a reporter, she'll sack me." She lunged for her shopping basket but he gingerly stepped back, out of her reach.

"Please, miss, hear me out. I promise you'll not lose your position, but if someone from these parts doesn't talk to me, I'm goin' to lose mine."

"Better you than me," she shot back, grabbing for the basket again. This time he relinquished his hold on it.

"All right, miss, I'll find someone else. There's bound to be someone from the Huxton household that wants an extra shilling."

She went still and stared at him in disbelief. "You're willin' to pay me a whole shilling just for talking to you? What if I don't know anything you can put in your newspaper? Do I still get the money?"

"You do," he promised. "As a matter of fact, I'll give you the money before you've said a word." It wasn't his custom to 'buy' information. Buying someone a pint or a cup of tea didn't count. But in this case he had a feeling she might know something. "There's a café at the end of the High Street; we can go there if you have time. I'd not like you to get in trouble for bein' gone too long."

"Don't worry about that. I can just tell 'em there was a long line at the grocers. Let's go to that café. It's cold, and a cup of tea sounds nice."

"What do you mean?" Witherspoon asked.

Olivia Huxton cocked her head to one side and stared at him. All vestiges of shame and grief had completely disappeared from her face. "Isn't it obvious, Inspector? When I found out Margaret had filed a lawsuit against me, I destroyed the letter."

"Reverend Pontefract returned it to you?" Barnes looked skeptical. "Why would he do that?"

"Of course he didn't return it." She shrugged. "But when I went to see him to discuss the matter, he got called away by the verger. The fool left it lying on his desk. I took it home with me and burnt it."

"You stole a letter from the vicar's desk!" Witherspoon exclaimed.

"There's no law against it," she replied. "I was merely reclaiming my property. It was my paper and ink, my words."

"You're admitting you destroyed evidence in a legal matter," the inspector insisted.

"It was only a civil matter," she shot back. "And, what's more, I destroyed the letter before Margaret was murdered, so I had no reason to kill her."

"When, exactly, did you write this letter about Mrs. Starling?" Witherspoon needed to establish a timeline here.

"Early October."

"When did you destroy the letter?"

"I don't recall the exact date; it was the sometime in the first week of December. I'd heard that Margaret and the vicar had a dreadful quarrel and I thought he'd be more amenable to my point of view. But I could tell from the moment I spoke with him that, instead of his being annoyed with Margaret, he was trying to come up with ways to soothe her ruffled feathers. So when the verger called him away, I knew I had to get that letter."

"Do you know why Mrs. Starling and the vicar quarreled?" Witherspoon asked.

"No, I don't, but Margaret had been quarreling with a number of people recently, so I wasn't surprised. Why don't you have a chat with Edgar Redstone; he's her late niece's husband. He hated her. He accused her of stealing his wife's inheritance and they had a dreadful row about it. He was shouting so loudly, the entire neighborhood could hear him."

"Who else hated her?" Barnes asked softly.

"Well, I wouldn't say he hated her, but Graham McConnell found her constant questions about the Angel Alms Society finances tiresome, and Merton Nesbitt—he despised her."

"Merton Nesbitt?"

"Yes. Mrs. Nesbitt was a close friend of Margaret's. Margaret testified against him in their divorce trial last summer."

"Where were you on the night that Mrs. Starling was murdered?" Barnes asked bluntly.

"Right here. I had dinner at half seven, my usual time, and then I read for a while before retiring."

"Your servants can vouch for that?" Witherspoon asked. There were dozens of other questions he now wanted to ask her, but the constable was correct in going right to the heart of her whereabouts at the time of the murder.

"Of course, Inspector. Feel free to speak to my housekeeper, Mrs. Cross, or any of the other servants."

"What time do your servants generally go to bed?" Barnes persisted.

"After their work is finished, Constable." She smiled slightly. "But they were all here that night. Would you like to speak to them?"

Barnes glanced at Witherspoon, who gave a quick nod.

"Yes, ma'am, I would." He got to his feet. "If it's all the same to you, I'll start with Mrs. Cross."

"She'll be downstairs doing the menus." She pointed to the door. "Ask whatever you like. I've nothing to hide."

As soon as the constable left, Witherspoon resumed his questions. "Does Merton Nesbitt live in London?"

"He does. He's a member of the Angel Alms Society

board of governors and he hated Margaret," she said. "He blames her for losing a very rich wife who not only left him but took all of her money with her and moved to Paris."

Downstairs, Barnes found the housekeeper in the butler's pantry. She looked up from an open ledger.

"Mrs. Cross, may I have a word, please?" Barnes asked.

Behind her spectacles, her eyes widened. "Does Mrs. Huxton know you're here?"

He studied her for a moment. She was a middle-aged woman with curly black hair devoid of gray and deeply etched worry lines around her mouth and eyes. "Mrs. Huxton knows I'm here and she's given permission for me to question the servants. I'm starting with you."

She closed the ledger and gestured to a rickety-looking chair. "Of course. Not that you need her consent to do your job, Constable. Forgive me, I didn't mean to be rude; I was just startled by your appearance. This has been a trying time for all of us. Mrs. Starling's murder is very upsetting."

Barnes sat down and pulled out his notebook. "I understand, Mrs. Cross. Was everyone in your household home this past Sunday night?"

"Yes, it was an ordinary evening. I served Mrs. Huxton's dinner at half seven and then we did the usual chores, tidied the kitchen, and at half nine everyone had gone to their quarters and I locked up the house and went to my room. I read for an hour and then retired for the night."

"Did you hear or see anything unusual?"

"No, nothing." She paused. "That's not true: At one point during the evening, BooBoo, Mrs. Huxton's spaniel, started barking."

"Do you recall what time this was?"

"It was half ten. I glanced at the clock on my mantel-piece."

"Half ten." Barnes made a note of it. It was possible the dog had heard something outside, perhaps even the killer. "Does the dog bark frequently?"

Mrs. Cross shook her head. "Not at all—he's very well-behaved—but he went on for a good few minutes, which surprised me. Generally, one word from Mrs. Huxton and he stops. But he went on that night. I almost went to Mrs. Huxton's room to make certain there was nothing wrong, but he finally stopped. He sleeps in her room."

"I see." Barnes wondered if the reason the dog kept barking was because his mistress wasn't there to tell him to stop. "You said you locked the house up. Are you the only one with the keys?'

"No, Mrs. Huxton has a set."

"Do you need a key to unlock the doors, or can they be unlocked from the inside?"

"You need to have a key to unlock the doors to the outside."

"I presume there's just the front and back door. Is that right?" he asked.

"There's an old side door as well"—she pushed her spectacles up her nose—"but it's not used."

"What do you think, sir?" Barnes asked as he and Wither-spoon left the Huxton house. "The servants confirmed that Mrs. Huxton was home when Mrs. Starling was murdered . . . well, all of them but one. There's a housemaid I couldn't interview; she'd been sent to the grocers, but I doubt she'll say anything different from the others. So it looks like Olivia Huxton has an alibi. Still, the dog barking is worrisome."

"Agreed, Constable." Witherspoon pulled on his leather gloves. "But a dog barking for a few minutes isn't evidence of anything except that perhaps Mrs. Huxton is a heavy sleeper, and Mrs. Cross did tell you that she'd had several glasses of wine with her dinner." He looked up and down the empty street. "Let's go to the Upper Richmond Road; we'll be able to find a hansom there."

"Where are we going now, sir?"

"St. Andrew's Church." He started walking at a brisk pace. "I want to have a word with Reverend Pontefract about that letter. It's close to the Upper Richmond Road Police Station, so after we interview the vicar we'll stop in and see if the postmortem report is there."

It took less than ten minutes to reach their destination. St. Andrew's, a huge redbrick building built in the early eighteenth century, stood on a street just off the Thames. Witherspoon and Barnes climbed the wide stairs, pulled open one of the double doors, and stepped into the narthex. The doors leading to the sanctuary were open. Halfway up the center aisle was a man with stringy salt-and-pepper hair and spectacles mopping the gray stone floor.

"Hello there," Barnes called. "We'd like to speak to Reverend Pontefract. Is he here?"

He stopped and stared at them for a few seconds before leaning his mop up against a pew. "He's in his study." He waved them forward. "It's this way."

They stepped into the sanctuary proper, moving past the stone baptismal font and the wooden pews. The stained-glass windows depicted scenes from the Bible and were done in brilliant hues of gold, red, green, and cobalt blue. The choir stalls and a pipe organ were on one side of the center aisle, while a tall, carved wooden pulpit stood on the opposite side.

"Are you the verger?" Witherspoon asked.

"I am, sir, I'm Tom Lancaster. Are you here to see the vicar about Mrs. Starling's murder? His office is just down there." He jerked his thumb to the left, where the aisle in front of the pews led to a hallway. "But you might want to hear what I've got to say before you go see his nibs."

"Do you have information about the murder?" Barnes pulled out his notebook and pencil. He found a clean page and then propped the notebook on the edge of a pew.

"The murder? Nah, can't say that I do. But I know that his nibs and Mrs. Starling had a nasty argument before she was killed."

"How nasty?" the constable asked.

He smiled. "I didn't hear everything, but I know she threatened him about something or other." He snickered. "Mind you, with this one"—he jerked his thumb toward the hall again—"there's no tellin' what she knew about him."

"Tell us what you heard," Witherspoon pressed.

"I heard her shouting that she'd go to the bishop, and then I heard him screamin' that if she did, he'd make her sorry."

"Lancaster!" a male voice shouted. "What is going on here?"

"Nothing, Reverend." Lancaster snickered softly and reached for the mop. "These policemen want to have a word with you. It's about that murdered lady, you know. Mrs. Starling. The one you was shoutin' at a couple of weeks back."

A man with short-cropped, graying brown hair and a

prominent nose hurried toward them. As a clerical collar was visible beneath the folds of his elegant black suit coat, the inspector suspected this might be the good reverend. But right now his appearance could equal that of any street tough. His eyes were narrowed, his cheeks flushed red, and his mouth set in a thin, flat line. "How dare you spread such malicious gossip about me!" he snapped. "I most certainly was not shouting at Margaret Starling."

"I'm just tellin' the truth, Father. Lying is a sin and you'd not want me to sin, would you?" Lancaster shrugged, turned his back, and resumed mopping. "Mind where you step, sir: The floor is wet, and it'd be a pity if you fell and hurt yourself."

The reverend glared at him for a moment and then turned his attention to Witherspoon. "Don't believe a word this man says. He's a liar. Come along, then; let's go to my study and get his distasteful business done with." Without waiting for a reply, he turned and stomped back the way he'd come, leading them down the hall and past two closed doors to the end of the corridor.

Witherspoon trailed after him and stepped inside the open door, then blinked in surprise. He hadn't expected a vicar's study to be this opulent.

A bookcase filled with volumes took up one wall, and on the opposite side were two windows, both draped with heavy gold brocade curtains tied back with gold tassels. A carved settee with two matching chairs, all upholstered in ivory and gold fabric, stood in front of the white marble fireplace. Two portraits, both of elderly gentlemen in full bishop's regalia, hung on the wall. Evergreens and holly decorated the mantel top, and a set of polished candelabra holding ivory candles stood on the two rosewood cabinets flanking the door.

Reverend Pontefract went behind a massive rosewood desk and plopped down. "I hope this won't take too long. I've an important meeting soon." He waved at the two straight-backed chairs in front of the desk. "Do sit down, please."

"Thank you." Witherspoon introduced himself and the constable as they took their seats. "Now, I'm sure you understand why we're here," he began, only to be cut off by the good Reverend.

"You're here because of Margaret Starling's murder, but despite what Lancaster may have said to you, I know nothing about that matter." He leaned forward putting his arms on the desk and clasping his hands together.

Witherspoon nodded as if he believed the fellow. "Nonetheless, we've some questions you may be able to help us with. Was Margaret Starling a member of this congregation?"

"She was"—he smiled smugly—"but she was hardly one of the genuine faithful. There were many a Sunday when she wasn't here."

"But she was a member?"

"Yes, she was, but as I said, I'd not consider her to be one of the most faithful members."

"How long has she been a member?"

Pontefract's heavy eyebrows rose. "How long? Well, I'm not sure. I've only been here myself for eighteen months. I was transferred here from St. Peter's in Highgate. Mrs. Starling was here when I arrived. Why? What does that have to do with her death?"

"Nothing as far as I know, but background information

is always useful," the inspector explained. "I understand that Mrs. Starling was on the advisory board for the Angel Alms Society. Is that true?"

"She was."

"I take it their mission was to raise money for the poor?" Witherspoon wanted to make sure there wasn't something else involved. It was easy to make assumptions based on nothing but what the name of an organization implied, but he'd learned from experience to take nothing for granted.

"That's correct." Pontefract relaxed a bit. "The society provides money and fuel—alms, as we call it—to some of the poor and deserving families in the parish twice a year, every Christmas and Easter."

"Where does the money come from?" Barnes asked bluntly.

"The community, the St. Andrew's congregation, various sources. But all fund-raising is handled by the society."

"And is it the society that determines who gets the money?" the constable persisted.

"Of course. However, I will admit that they do look to me for advice about what families in the parish are most deserving, but the board of governors makes the final decision."

"Mrs. Starling was on the advisory board. What do they do?" Witherspoon asked.

Pontefract lifted his shoulders in a dismissive shrug. "Not much, really. The advisory board was only formed a few years ago so the ladies could feel they had some say in the running of the society. Silly nonsense, if you ask me. That's what comes of all these women protesting in front of Parliament and agitating for the right to vote. But several women in the congregation essentially threatened that unless they were given some role to play within the society, they'd withhold funds not only from the society but from St. Andrew's."

"So someone made up a board that doesn't do anything so the church could hang on to their money?" Barnes stared at him directly.

"I would hardly put it in those terms," Pontefract sputtered. "The bishop was most upset when it happened. Everyone thinks the church is wealthy, but the truth is it takes an enormous amount of money to keep our doors open. So when some of our ladies threatened to withdraw their funds, the bishop very kindly came up with a plan to give them some say in the matter."

"Was Mrs. Starling one of the women?" Witherspoon interjected. He knew and approved of the constable's line of inquiry because it was effective. Barnes' blunt questions had rattled the man and loosened his tongue quite a bit.

"Yes."

"And exactly when did this incident happen?"

"Eighteen months ago. It was the first crisis I had to deal with when I was assigned here," he said. "Two days into my tenure, and Margaret Starling and two other women marched into my office with their demands. It was not a pleasant start to my relationship with her."

"That's understandable. Your verger said you had a disagreement recently with the deceased. Would you please explain the nature of the argument?"

"There was no argument," Pontefract said. "I've told you, Lancaster is a liar. You can't believe a word he says."

"Why do you keep him on, then?" Barnes asked softly.

"You're the vicar. If the man is a liar, why don't you show him the door and get someone else? Surely there's no shortage of men in the parish who'd want his position."

"Believe me, I've tried, but the bishop won't hear of it."

"The bishop doesn't believe he's a liar?" The constable struggled to keep the amusement out of his voice.

"Of course he does. The bishop knows good and well the man wouldn't know the truth if he found it written on the lectern Bible. But in this instance there's nothing we can do about the situation. Unfortunately, Lancaster is the distant cousin of a deceased church member who left St. Andrew's a huge legacy with the provision that Lancaster was to have a position for his lifetime."

"So you can't sack him," Witherspoon murmured. "Nonetheless, whether Mr. Lancaster is truthful or not, we've heard from other sources that you had a terrible disagreement with the victim."

"I don't know who told you such a thing," he began, only this time he was interrupted.

"Olivia Huxton told us." The inspector watched him carefully. Generally he didn't repeat what witnesses said when giving statements unless it was pertinent. In this case he decided it was most definitely apropos.

"That's impossible, she wasn't even here that day," he sputtered before he caught himself. "Oh, dear, this is dreadful. A man in my position oughtn't to be subjected to this kind of horrible abuse. I'm a man of the cloth, and I shall most certainly speak to your superiors about this."

The inspector smiled. "By all means, my direct supervisor is Chief Superintendent Barrows at Scotland Yard. In the meantime, please tell us what happened with Mrs. Starling."

Pontefract sat back, his shoulders slumped as he exhaled. "It's true, we did have words."

"Again, sir, I ask you what caused the argument between you and the victim?"

"Mrs. Starling accused me of ruining her reputation. She said my actions had compromised her position within the community and caused her great distress."

"What did she accuse you of doing?" Witherspoon was fairly sure he knew, but he wanted confirmation.

"I'd received an anonymous letter about her, the contents of which were most unflattering—scandalous, really. Naturally I showed her the letter, and she seemed to think that I'd agreed not to show it to anyone else. We had words when she claimed I'd gone back on my word and that I showed it to the board of governors. She insisted that I'd done it deliberately to hurt her."

Richard Wylie, the duty sergeant, nodded respectfully as Inspector Nivens and Constable Forman stepped through the front door of the Upper Richmond Road Police Station.

"Good day, sir. The postmortem report just came in." Wylie pointed to the brown envelope lying on the counter. "Should I put it in Inspector Witherspoon's office?"

"Witherspoon doesn't have an office," Inspector Nivens snapped. He stopped long enough to give Wylie a good glare. "He's merely using the duty inspector's office. But when I'm on the premises, that title is mine." He stuck out a gloved hand. "Give it here. I'll see that he gets it."

"Yes, sir." Wylie picked up the envelope and handed it across the counter. He waited until Nivens and his shadow, that little sneak Forman, had disappeared down the corridor into the duty inspector's office before he chuckled.

Constable Tony Sorrell, who'd just come out of the cloakroom behind the counter, leaned against the doorframe. He carried his helmet in one hand and his police whistle in another. "Is something amusing you, sir?"

"Indeed." Wylie chuckled again. "Let's just say that I'm doing my duty and making sure that justice is being properly served."

Sorrell shoved away from the doorframe and moved to the counter. "You're up to something, aren't you?"

Wylie's grin broadened even more. "I'm doin' what's right, Tony. Some of us around here don't care for the way some people"—he looked in the direction of Nivens' office—"are using this station to further their personal ambition."

Sorrell glanced toward Nivens' office as well and then looked back at his colleague. "Be careful, Sergeant. Inspector Nivens is a vindictive sort. Look what he did to poor old Hoskins last week."

"I remember. Nivens mucked up what should have been an easy arrest, but when he wrote the report, he made the poor lad take the blame for his own incompetence." Wylie looked disgusted. "Hoskins is young and he's a decent enough record that Nivens stink won't stick to him for long."

"That's not the point, sir. The point is"—again he glanced down the corridor to make sure Nivens was safely behind closed doors—"Nivens did it even though there were witnesses to what really happened, so be careful."

Wylie smiled. "Don't worry about me. I'm not some green

boy and I can take care of myself. Nivens isn't the only one with friends in high places."

"The gossip I've heard is that he hates Gerald Witherspoon." Sorrell put his helmet on and adjusted his chin strap.

"He's insanely jealous of him. But what he doesn't know is that some of us have a lot of admiration and respect for Gerald Witherspoon. You should hear the way his men speak about him, and they're not just sucking up to curry favor, either."

"I've heard they like him." Sorrell tucked his whistle in his trouser pocket.

"It's not just that; they respect him. Witherspoon has solved more murders in this town than anyone on the force. When he writes his reports, he makes certain all of his men get their fair share of credit."

"We know that Nivens doesn't do that. Constable Harlow helped bring in those Bascomb brothers that burgled those big estates along the river, but when the report was done, Harlow's name wasn't mentioned."

"Yeah." Wylie snorted. "I've been on the force a long time and I've seen more than one like Nigel Nivens. You mark my words, when Nivens leaves today, that postmortem report will be in his coat pocket, not on the duty inspector's desk."

"Come on, sir, Constable Forman is right there. Inspector Nivens won't do anything improper in front of him."

"You're a nice lad, and it's admirable that you hold your colleagues in such high regard"—Wylie gave Sorrell a skeptical glance—"but Forman's always been an ambitious toady. He'll do whatever Nivens wants him to do because he'll think that will put him another rung up the ladder. What's more, Nivens has already started doing his best to make sure

Inspector Witherspoon doesn't make any progress on this murder."

Sorrell stared at him, his expression curious. "What do you mean?"

"Exactly what I said. He knew that Inspector Witherspoon was goin' to ask for our lads to be used in questioning the neighbors about the Starling murder, but he made sure that didn't happen."

"Is that why there's two constables from the Ladbroke Road Police Station here?"

"Yes, and it's a good thing they've come. Both yesterday evening and this morning—the times when Inspector Witherspoon would be formally requesting assistance from Nivens—the nasty little sod made sure he wasn't here."

"Yeah, but wasn't Inspector Nivens out workin' that Lincoln robbery both times?"

"That's what he claimed, but I've my doubts."

"You're sayin' that Inspector Nivens is deliberately trying to sabotage the investigation?"

"Not the investigation." Wylie pulled out another envelope from beneath the counter. It was the twin of the one he'd handed Nivens. "Just Inspector Witherspoon. But not to worry: Dr. Littleham made sure to give me this." He held up the envelope. "A second copy of the postmortem report. Seems our police surgeon had his doubts about Nivens as well. He asked me to give this to Witherspoon directly, and that's exactly what I intend to do."

"Horatio, I appreciate you takin' the time out of your busy day to see me," Luty said as the tall, balding banker led her into his office.

She'd spent the morning chasing after information and hadn't learned anything they didn't already know: mainly, that both Margaret Starling and the neighbor she'd been feuding with were both rich. She'd almost given up and gone home, but she'd found herself close to one of her many solicitors' offices, and there she learned that Horatio Stillman had once served on the board of governors of the Angel Alms Society. As he was the only connection to Margaret Starling she'd been able to find so far, she'd not wasted a moment in coming to see him. Luty was determined to have something useful to report at their afternoon meeting.

"Nonsense, Luty, you're always welcome here. Let me take your cloak."

"Thank you, Horatio." Luty unbuttoned the peacock-blue garment and turned so he could slip it off her shoulders. He motioned at the closer of the two chairs in front of his desk. "Do sit down. Would you care for tea or perhaps coffee?" he asked as he took her cloak to the coat tree next to the door.

"No, I'm fine." She sat down, shifting to get comfortable on the hard wooden seat, and then looked around Stillman's office. It was a standard banker's lair: shelves filled with ledgers and black file boxes, an oak stationery cabinet sitting on a claw-foot table in one corner, and a portrait of the queen over the fireplace. But the one thing that wasn't typical was the beautifully drawn map of the world on the wall behind his desk.

She waited for him to take his chair before she spoke. "Now, you're probably wonderin' what I'm doin' here . . ." she began.

"I do hope you're not here because you're dissatisfied with

the way we've handled your mining business." He leaned forward, his long face creased with worry.

"You and your bank are doin' a fine job," she assured him. "I couldn't be happier. Actually, this is a bit awkward, and I hope you don't think I'm takin' advantage of our friendship, but my visit today is a bit more personal."

"Personal?" His bushy eyebrows rose in surprise. "In that case, please feel free to be entirely candid. Whatever you tell me will remain here in this office. You can count on my discretion."

"Thank you, Horatio, that's good to know. Truth is I need your help on a private matter, and you know how much I've always valued your opinion." Luty wasn't one to give out empty compliments, and in his case she wasn't just saying nice things to get him to cooperate. Horatio and his bank were performing their duties admirably; however, experience had taught her never to underestimate the value of flattery.

He settled back into his chair. "Why, thank you, Luty. That's a very nice thing to say. Now, tell me how I can help you."

"Well, this is kinda hard to admit and say out loud, but I'm not a spring chicken anymore. I've been thinking about what I'm goin' to do with all my money when I go."

He immediately started to object. "Now, now, Luty, don't say such things—"

She cut him off with a wave of her hand. "You're bein' kind, Horatio, but we all know that once you git past a certain age, the grim reaper can track you down anytime he wants"—she smiled as she spoke—"and you know as well as I do that people shouldn't leave these kinds of decisions to Her Majesty's government or to a bunch of lawyers. Don't get me wrong, Horatio: I know where I'm leavin' the bulk of the estate. But, as you know, it's pretty danged big, and I need your opinion about what to do with the remainder."

"Of course, Luty. Do you have any specific ideas or organizations in mind?"

Luty was ready for this question. "There's an organization across the river in Putney I had my eye on; as a matter of fact, that's one of the reasons I wanted to talk to ya. I've heard you know something about 'em. It's the Angel Alms Society. One of my lawyers told me you used to be on their board of governors."

"That's true, but I'm no longer associated with them." He shrugged and gave her a rueful smile.

"Why? Because one of their lady members got herself murdered? I heard that the poor woman that got her head bashed in and laid out on the ground all night was part of that organization. Her name was Margaret Starling. Is that the reason you quit?" Luty knew it wasn't, but she didn't want him going quiet on her now. Bringing up Margaret Starling was risky—she knew there had been gossip about her closeness to the Witherspoon household and his investigations—but dropping the dead woman's name would either keep the banker talking or shut him up altogether.

"Oh, no, I gave up my seat on the board several years ago," he protested. "Mrs. Starling's murder had nothing to do with it."

"Why'd ya quit then? Was they a bunch of crooks or flimflam artists?" She knew that she could get away with saying outrageous nonsense. People expected a certain level of bluntness from Americans and rich old ladies. Luckily, she was both.

"No, no, the people on the board are very honorable individuals. As for Margaret Starling, I was acquainted with her. She was a very gracious and nice person. If the manner of her death is one of your concerns about leaving them a legacy, then you can put that notion to rest. I hope the police catch her killer quickly."

"So do I," Luty agreed. "Uh, well, if it isn't too personal, Horatio, can you tell me why you left them?"

"It's not particularly personal," he admitted, "but it does involve someone else. Oh, dear, what am I saying? Of course you'll treat what I'm going to tell you with discretion . . ."

"I'd never betray your confidence." She crossed her fingers in her lap as she fully intended to share what he told her at the afternoon meeting. However, she'd do it in a way that didn't identify him.

"I left the board because it was simply too awkward for me to continue to serve," he sighed. "There was an incident, you see."

"What kind of incident?"

"It involved my nephew, a young man named Jasper Lewis. He's my youngest sister's only son. When I was on the board, they needed a clerk to work with the general manager, at that time a man named Ezra Travers. Ezra was and is a good friend of mine, and he knew that I was looking for a respectable position for my sister's son—" He broke off and smiled nervously. "Oh, dear, I'm not sure how to say this; one doesn't like to speak ill of one's own family. But the truth is poor Jasper is one of those people who doesn't quite understand that when one is working for someone else, that person has the right to make reasonable rules regarding how one does one's job."

"That's generally how most things in this world work," Luty said. "Them that's got the gold or the power get to make the rules. But go on, tell me the rest of it."

"Jasper did very well when Ezra Travers was the manager, but poor Ezra had a dreadful bout of pneumonia that impacted his health so badly, he had to give up his position. So the board of governors hired a new manager, a man named Graham McConnell. Mr. McConnell had far stricter requirements for his clerk than Ezra did, and Jasper simply wasn't able to keep up properly. He's a nice chap, but unfortunately he isn't the brightest of young men. I suppose every family has one like that. He was sacked, and after that it was awkward for me to be on the board, so I resigned."

Luty thought for a moment and then asked the question that popped into her head. "Can you be a bit more specific here? Exactly what rule did your nephew break?"

"I don't know all the details. Jasper was embarrassed, of course, so he merely said he was sacked because Mr. McConnell didn't like the way he worded the acknowledgments and thank-you correspondence to their donors. Apparently the new manager of the society felt that any mention of money was both gauche and ill-mannered. He only wanted the donors to be thanked for their generosity."

Luty nodded as if she understood, but she wondered why in the world anyone would be so fussy over a danged thank-you note!

CHAPTER 5

"Had you shown the letter to anyone?" Witherspoon asked.

Pontefract closed his eyes and let out a sigh. "Yes, I'd shown the letter to the board of governors. Margaret had asked me not to show it to them nor to anyone else, and I tried my best to do as she asked; but as the weeks passed, I realized the accusations in the letter were of such a nature that I felt the board had to see it."

"We understand it was an anonymous letter," Barnes said. "I'm surprised you took it seriously."

"Of course I took it seriously," he protested. "The complaints against her were very much like the behavior I'd observed. She'd become quarrelsome, intrusive, and demanding, insisting the board take action on matters that didn't concern her. I couldn't just ignore it, although in all fairness to me I did try to do as Margaret asked and keep the matter between the two of us. But after the alms society meeting on November twenty-fourth, I realized I had no choice."

"What happened at that meeting?" Witherspoon asked.

"She kept asking questions about all manner of nonsensical issues." He pursed his lips and shook his head. "She was only a member of the advisory board—she'd no right to keep interrupting the men—but she wouldn't stay quiet. That behavior was bad enough, but then I overheard her speaking to Ezra Travers—he used to be the society's general manager—and she was asking him the most ridiculous questions as well. That's when I realized I had to take action—that I had to make the board understand that she was becoming either unbalanced or senile."

Barnes stopped writing. "What kind of questions?"

"Silly ones—questions that didn't make any sense!" he exclaimed. "She asked him what percentage of the society's donations are made by notes and coin, rather than bank draft or checks. That is none of her concern, nor is it relevant to any of the advisory board's purposes. They're only supposed to advise the board about the specific needs in the community and to help with the day-to-day functioning of the society. They're responsible for the housekeeping functions: sorting the donated clothes and parceling out the food and coal to families in distress. None of them are supposed to be questioning the men on the board."

"What did Ezra Travers tell her?" The constable started taking notes again.

"I can't recall his exact words but he said he didn't know the exact amount, although it was a substantial portion of the annual giving." He shook his head in disbelief. "Then she asked him if there were people outside the parish who contributed regularly. Well, of course there are—she should have known that—but she kept pestering poor Ezra for details. You do understand why I had to show them the letter? It was Margaret's own actions that forced me to do so."

"Where's the letter now?" Witherspoon knew good and well it had been destroyed, but he was curious as to what the reverend would say about it. "Can we see it?"

"No, I'm afraid not." Pontefract leaned back in his chair. "It disappeared from the top of my desk when I got called away by the verger. I'd been having a discussion about it with Olivia Huxton. When I returned, both Mrs. Huxton and the letter were gone."

"You knew that Margaret Starling had filed a lawsuit against Mrs. Huxton?" Witherspoon said.

"It was no secret, Inspector," he sighed, and then shrugged. "I showed Mrs. Starling the letter because I thought she had a right to know what was being said about her, but I fear my concern was misplaced and a mistake. The moment she read it, she told me she was filing a lawsuit against Olivia Huxton. She insisted she knew the handwriting in the letter was Mrs. Huxton's. I tried to talk her out of it, of course, but she was adamant." He paused with a puzzled frown. "What I don't understand is who from the board would have told Margaret they'd seen the letter. I made it quite clear that she'd asked me not to show it to them or anyone else."

"Someone obviously told her," Witherspoon said.

"No, I don't believe that." Pontefract drummed his fingers on the desktop. "All of them promised to keep the fact that they'd seen the letter confidential. No one on the board wanted Margaret any more upset than she already was.

She'd been disrupting meetings for the past six weeks and everyone was tired of her antics. Someone else must have told her, but for the life of me I can't think who would have done it." He glanced in the direction of the sanctuary. "Lancaster is capable of it, but he didn't know I'd shown the letter to the board."

"These things have a way of getting out," the constable murmured. "When was the last time you saw Mrs. Starling?"

"At the morning service on Sunday. Why?"

"It's a standard question," Witherspoon interjected. "We're trying to ascertain the movements of both the victim and those individuals that had conflicts with her."

"That hardly includes me." Pontefract leapt to his feet. "We had a silly argument, not a conflict."

"But she was very upset about it, and according to what we've heard, you were upset enough that you threatened her," Barnes said pointedly.

"Surely you don't believe what that liar Lancaster said," he sputtered. "I most certainly didn't threaten Margaret. Lancaster hates me because, unlike my predecessor, I expect him to do his job properly. He'll say anything to put me in a bad light."

"Where were you on Sunday night?" Witherspoon asked quietly.

Pontefract's jaw dropped. "How dare you! I'm a priest in the Church of England and I will not be questioned or treated like a common criminal."

The constable fixed him with a cold stare. "So you're refusing to account for your whereabouts on the night Mrs. Starling was murdered?"

His hands clenched into fists. "Don't be absurd, I'm

offended you're asking such questions at all. But if you must know, after I finished with the Evensong service, I ate dinner in the rectory, then retired to my study to work on my sermon."

"Your servants can verify that?" Barnes asked.

He swallowed, his bulbous Adam's apple bobbing up and down. "Actually, I was home alone. None of the servants live in the rectory; it's too small. Not at all like what I was accustomed to at St. Peter's Highgate Hill. But one goes where one is sent."

"What time do the servants leave?" Witherspoon asked.

"At half past six. It's a ridiculously early time for me to eat my dinner, but the custom of the servants leaving at half past six was set by my predecessor, and apparently it wasn't subject to change."

"Did you have any visitors that evening?" the inspector asked.

"No, I was alone."

Witherspoon glanced at Barnes, who gave him a barely perceptible nod indicating he had no more questions, then both policemen got to their feet.

"Thank you for your time, Reverend," Witherspoon said politely.

Pontefract smiled cynically. "You're welcome, Inspector. I hope you catch whoever killed Margaret Starling, but I assure you, my petty argument with her had nothing to do with her death."

Barnes and Witherspoon walked back to the sanctuary. The constable looked around carefully as they reached the center aisle and turned toward the narthex. "Lancaster has made himself scarce."

"I suspect he accomplished his goal," Witherspoon said.

"He made certain we knew about the vicar's quarrel with the victim. He hates him."

"And the feeling is mutual." Barnes grinned.

"But if we've reason to speak to him again, we can come back. Let's see if Graham McConnell is in the Angel Alms Society office."

Mrs. Jeffries dropped her housekeeping ledger in the bottom drawer of the pine sideboard and closed it with her foot. "Mrs. Goodge, would you like me to make the tea?"

"It's made and everything else is ready as well. It's four o'clock; the others should be here any minute now," she replied just as they heard the back door open. Wiggins was the first to arrive, followed by Luty, who came in only a few moments before Hatchet and Ruth. Smythe and Betsy were the last to arrive.

"Where's my baby?" Mrs. Goodge demanded.

Betsy glanced at her husband. "I told you we should have brought her."

"And I say it's too cold out there for 'er," Smythe retorted. "I'm not one for coddlin' a child, but the wind off the river is fierce."

"We'll bring her tomorrow," Betsy said. "I promise." She knew that both Luty and Mrs. Goodge looked forward to playing with their godchild, especially at this time of the year.

"Well, all right . . . I don't want my Sweetness coming down with the sniffles." Mrs. Goodge picked up the teapot and poured the tea into the waiting cups.

Mrs. Jeffries took her seat at the head of the table. "Who would like to go first?"

"I might as well," Phyllis volunteered. "My report won't take long. I didn't find out anything." She looked at Betsy. "I hope you had better luck with the local shops than I did."

"Where did you go?"

"To those shops along the Upper Richmond Road," Phyllis said.

"I went to the ones on the High Street," Betsy said.

"Then I went and tried to find someone from either the Huxton or the Starling house, but I didn't see anyone and it was too cold to hang about very long." Phyllis shrugged.

Betsy smiled sympathetically. "My luck was a bit better than yours. But don't worry, there's always tomorrow."

"Don't fret, lass," Smythe said. "My day wasn't anything to write 'ome about, either." He glanced at Mrs. Jeffries, who indicated with a nod that he should go ahead with his report. "There's two cab stands within a quarter mile of the Starling 'ome, but none of the drivers I spoke to 'ad a ruddy thing to say. No one can remember pickin' up or droppin' off a specific fare that night."

"What do ya mean?" Luty asked.

"It was so miserable out, the few that I could find that 'ad actually been workin' Sunday night 'ad plenty of fares, but none that went to Moran Place. Mind you, I didn't 'ave a chance to speak to *all* the drivers that were doin' the night shift, so I'm goin' back to 'ave another go when this meeting's over."

"Do you really have to?" Mrs. Jeffries asked with a worried frown. "It's getting colder out there by the minute."

"I need to, Mrs. Jeffries. Otherwise we might miss somethin' important and we're runnin' out of time. But it shouldn't take too long."

"I'm out this evening as well," Hatchet announced. "My source isn't often available during the day. But at least I'll be inside."

Betsy looked at her husband. "What about the pubs? Any luck there?" She hoped he hadn't tried the one where she and Annabelle Waverly had been.

"I tried a couple along the Upper Richmond Road, but no one knew anythin', and it was gettin' so late, I didn't want to miss our meetin'."

"Let's hope you find out something useful, then." Betsy patted his arm and then looked at the housekeeper. "Is it all right if I go next?" As soon as Mrs. Jeffries nodded, she plunged straight in. "I got lucky today and met someone who was working at the Huxton house yesterday." She told them about her meeting with Annabelle Waverly, taking care to give them all the details about the encounter without mentioning that they'd been in a pub or that she'd ended up paying Annabelle a half crown. "But she didn't think anything of what she'd seen on the night of the murder until she saw Olivia Huxton's face the next day when the housemaid told them Mrs. Starling had been murdered."

"And she was sure it was Olivia Huxton she saw that night?" Mrs. Jeffries asked. "That could be important."

"I know." Betsy frowned, her expression thoughtful. "But there's something about it that's bothering me."

"What?" Ruth asked.

"Just because my source saw Olivia Huxton, I don't think we ought to jump to the conclusion that she committed the murder."

"Why do you say that?" Phyllis asked.

"Because I got a good look at both the Huxton and the

Starling house today. I had a look around, that's how I managed to find Annabelle; she was coming out of the Huxton
home and I followed her. The Huxton house and the Starling
house are separated by a row of gooseberry bushes, and this
time of year they're bare," she explained. "Annabelle said
she saw Mrs. Huxton coming down the front stairs of the
Starling house. It seems to me that if she had bashed her
neighbor in the head, she'd have gone back to her own home
by either slipping between those bushes or sneaking home
along the back of the property. Why would she risk going to
the front of the house, where someone could and did see
her?"

"Maybe she was panicked," Ruth suggested. "It does happen, you know. Unless one has a heart of stone, taking a human life could easily make someone behave without thinking."

"That's possible." Betsy picked up her mug and took a sip
of tea. "Anyway, that's all I found out."

"Who'd like to go next?" Mrs. Jeffries looked around the
table.

"I will," Wiggins offered. He grinned at Betsy. "You
aren't the only one who found a source from the Huxton
house. I met a housemaid and she told me a few bits and
pieces. It's mainly gossip but it might come in useful. The girl
is a friend with one of the maids from the Starling house,
and Mrs. Starling has been quarrelin' with more than just
her neigh—"

"We already know that," Mrs. Goodge interrupted.
"Sounds like she was squabbling with half of London.
There's that Edgar Redman—"

"Redstone," Mrs. Jeffries corrected.

"But he wasn't the only one," Wiggins insisted. "Cecilia

said the Starling tweeny told her that her mistress 'ad a spat with a fellow named Merton Nesbitt."

"When did this happen?" Ruth asked.

"Cecilia didn't know, but she thinks it must have been sometime recently." Wiggins shrugged. "She was just re-peatin' what the tweeny had told her. But that's not all she heard. All that quarrelin' was botherin' Mrs. Starling so much that in the two weeks before she was murdered, she'd gone to the church three or four times to pray on her own. Then, a couple of days before the murder, Mrs. Starling called the tweeny in to run an errand. She had a parcel all done up in brown paper and she'd wrapped it herself instead of getting one of her servants to do it. And instead of giving the tweeny the package, Mrs. Starling said something like 'No, this is too important. I'll take it myself.'"

"Did the girl know where the package was going or to whom it was addressed?" Mrs. Jeffries asked.

"She didn't. She said Mrs. Starling had been at church late that afternoon, then she'd gone into her study and ten minutes later called the tweeny to come take the package. Then she all of a sudden changed her mind. The tweeny told Cecilia Mrs. Starling hadn't even taken her coat off before she'd done up the parcel."

"I suppose it could have been a Christmas present," the housekeeper speculated.

"It doesn't sound like it, Mrs. Jeffries," Wiggins argued. "Cecilia said that her friend was wonderin' if she ought to tell the police about it."

"Of course she ought to tell the police!" Mrs. Goodge exclaimed. "And if she doesn't, we'll make sure to mention the incident to Constable Barnes."

Mrs. Jeffries glanced at the carriage clock on the pine sideboard. "It's getting late." she looked at Wiggins. "Anything else?" When he gave a negative shake of his head, she said, "Does anyone else have anything to report?"

"I doubt what I found out has anything to do with the murder," Luty offered, "but I'll tell ya anyway." She told them about her meeting with Horatio Stillman. "It's not much, nells bells: Horatio's nephew doesn't even work there anymore. Still, I thought I'd pass it along."

"Don't be so down in the mouth, madam." Hatchet grinned. "At least you found someone today who had some connection to the Angel Alms Society. That's better than I did."

"Yeah, but you're goin' out tonight and you'll probably find out all sorts of juicy gossip," Luty complained. "Right, then. Tomorrow I'll have a go at seein' what I can learn about Edgar Redstone or Merton Nesbitt's finances. That be okay?" She looked at Mrs. Jeffries.

"That's excellent, Luty."

"And I've some sources coming in," Mrs. Goodge added. "I'll see what I can learn."

"I'll take Graham McConnell," Hatchet offered as he rose to his feet. "If we're through here, I must go."

"Take the carriage," Luty ordered. "I'll take a hansom home."

He started to object, but she held up her hand. "Don't give me any sass, Hatchet. Smythe is going back to Putney; we can share a cab as far as Knightsbridge."

"Don't worry, 'atchet. We'll see that she gets 'ome safe," Smythe assured him.

* * *

"You're the one that was 'ere askin' questions this mornin', aren't you?" The driver stopped stroking his horse's nose long enough to turn and look at Smythe.

"I was. I'm lookin' to speak to someone who might 'ave been workin' two nights ago." Smythe shifted his feet in an effort to keep warm. He was at a cabman's shelter around the corner from the end of the Putney High Street, and although it was only five o'clock, the sky was darkening. Freezing wind blew in from the river as shoppers hurried toward the line of hansoms.

Two well-dressed matrons, both of them loaded down with parcels, rushed along the pavement to where Smythe and the cabman stood. One of them yanked open the cab door and climbed inside while the other called to the driver. "Number fifteen Burstock Road," she ordered as she, too, entered the vehicle. He shrugged at Smythe, gave his horse one last stroke, and then jerked his thumb toward the back of the line. "Go see Beckman. 'e was workin' that night," he said as he climbed up into the rig.

"Ta." Smythe nodded his thanks, hoping that the line of hansoms wouldn't move so quickly that Beckman would get away from him. Already the second and third cabs had been taken.

"You Beckman?" Smythe asked as he reached the fifth cab. "Can I talk to ya?"

"What about?" The driver, a young man with a huge black mustache, a slender face, and deep-set green eyes stared at him suspiciously.

"Something important." Smythe watched as the cab right

in front of Beckman's picked up a fare. "I know you're not wantin' to miss a fare, so if you'll take me to the bottom end of Moran Place, you'll not miss out. But before we go there, can you pull around the corner and stop so we can talk?"

Beckman stared at him curiously, then nodded. "If you're willing to pay the fare, that's fine with me. Get inside."

Smythe did as instructed and then grabbed the handhold as the cab pulled away. Two minutes later it slowed and came to a stop. Smythe got out and the driver got down from his seat.

"Right, then, what's this all about?"

"Night before last, did you pick up a fare and take them anywhere near Tavistock Road, Moran Place, Brindle Street, or Cedar Lane?"

The driver looked doubtful. "Course I did. This is where I work. I must 'ave taken half a dozen fares between them spots."

"Can you remember anythin' in particular about any of them fares? You know, what the fare looked like, what time you picked them up, and exactly where you dropped 'em off?"

"You're wantin' to know if I dropped anyone near Moran Place where that poor woman was killed?"

"That's right."

"Why is that your business?" Beckman eyed him warily. "You're not a policeman."

"I'm a private inquiry agent," Smythe replied. "And I've been hired by an interested party to look into her death."

"A private inquiry agent? You look like a street tough," Beckman challenged. "So why should I believe you?"

"What's it to you what I look like? I'm just out 'ere tryin' to earn a ruddy livin' and you're not 'elpin' much."

That was precisely the right tactic to use, because Beckman stared at him for a moment and then shrugged. "All right, I did pick someone up. I remember because it was gettin' late and the fellow was all bundled up in a long cloak and had a scarf wrapped around his chin. Mind you, it was really cold."

"Where did you take him?"

"To the corner of Moran Place and the Upper Richmond Road."

"What time did ya drop him there?"

"I don't know the exact time, but it was close to ten o'clock."

"Did ya get a look at his face?" Smythe asked.

"No, but as he was payin' me, his scarf shifted enough so that I could see what was underneath."

"And what was that?" Smythe asked.

"A clerical collar."

The Angel Alms Society was housed in a small building made of the same stone as St. Andrew's and located at the end of the churchyard wall. It was a single-story structure with a high peaked roof and a short, wide set of stairs leading to the front door.

"This was probably a carriage house," Witherspoon muttered as he and the constable stepped into the covered entryway.

Barnes tried the handle, which turned easily. "It's not locked, sir and it's getting late. Do you think anyone is here? Should we just go inside?"

"Yes. It's not a private home."

Barnes opened the door and they entered into a small,

poorly lighted foyer. Directly ahead of them was a coat tree hung with half a dozen garments, a battered brass umbrella stand, and a painting in a garish golden frame of an angel hovering over a sleeping, fair-haired little girl.

"May I help you?" The voice came from the left, where the foyer opened into an office.

"We'd like to speak to Mr. Graham McConnell." Witherspoon advanced into the room. Two paintings, both of them of golden-haired angels, hung on one side of the pale green walls, and a line of mismatched clothes cupboards and storage cabinets stood along the opposite side. Brown-and-white tiles, some of them cracked, covered the floor, and a set of striped brown-and-purple curtains hung at the one window.

A young man with thinning blond hair stood up from behind a desk. "You're the police." He hurried toward the short hallway. "Uh, let me see if Mr. McConnell's available."

"If he's here, please ask him to make himself available," Barnes called as the young man scurried toward a closed door. "It's rather important that we see him."

"Yes, sir." he reached the door just as it opened, and Graham McConnell stepped out. He stopped and stared at the two policemen. "Hello, Inspector. I didn't expect to see you."

"We'd like to speak to you, sir," Witherspoon said.

"I heard." He flicked a glance at the young man. "I'll take these gentlemen into my office. You may go back to work, Stuart."

"Yes, sir." Stuart scurried back to his desk.

Graham McConnell's office was far nicer than the outer trappings. A fire burned in the small fireplace; on the walls were portraits of well-dressed gentlemen in wing collars and old fashioned suits; and in front of the two windows was a large, ornately carved mahogany desk. McConnell went behind the desk and sat down. He pointed to a set of high-backed chairs with worn red velvet padding on the seats. "Sit down, please, and tell me what this is all about. I've already told you everything I know about Mrs. Starling's death."

"Not really, sir. The inspector said he only spoke with you for a few moments." Barnes pulled out his notebook and pencil as he took his seat. "There are always a few more details to go over."

McConnell flushed slightly. "I'm sorry, that was foolish of me. Of course you have more questions."

"Mr. McConnell, we understand you and the rest of the board of governors were somewhat upset with Mrs. Starling because she'd been disruptive at the alms society meetings. Is that correct?" Witherspoon took his seat.

McConnell looked surprised. "I wouldn't characterize it in quite that way, Inspector. Who gave you that information?"

"Reverend Pontefract told us," Barnes said. "He said that Margaret Starling had been asking a lot of what he termed silly questions for the last six weeks and that you and the rest of the board were very annoyed."

"Yes, I suppose that's true, but 'annoyed' is too strong a word to use. Mrs. Starling could be occasionally irritating, but I never lost my temper with her, nor did any other member of the board. She's worked very hard and diligently for the society, and her opinions, though at times controversial, were valued."

"How often does the society meet?" Witherspoon unbuttoned his heavy coat.

"Generally we meet once a month, except for the two months prior to Christmas and Easter. We meet every fortnight during those months. It takes quite a bit of time to decide who will be receiving alms and how much each family will get."

"What was the purpose of your last meeting? The one just prior to Mrs. Starling's death."

"That was the December fifteenth meeting and it was the annual disbursement meeting, the one where we go over the list of recipients. She was there that day, as she had been for every meeting since mid-November. Generally, members of the advisory board don't attend all the meetings, unless of course they've something to report, but there's no rule against it."

"Was she the only member of the advisory board who was at that meeting?" the inspector asked.

"She was the only one at that particular meeting or, for that matter, any of the meetings since mid-November."

"And you spoke to her at that time?"

"That's right." He smiled ruefully. "After the meeting ended and everyone else had gone, we had a brief discussion."

"What about?" Witherspoon asked.

He shifted uncomfortably and looked down at his desktop. "It was an awkward conversation, Inspector, and one that upset me a great deal. I've prayed about whether or not I should mention the conversation to you, and frankly I'm still not certain of the ethics of the situation. Mrs. Starling swore me to secrecy, and, what is even worse, I'm not certain she was in her right mind when we spoke."

Barnes looked up from his notebook. "Mr. McConnell, this is a murder investigation, so you need to tell us anything you know. That poor woman had her skull bashed in six ways to Sunday. I'd say that the only ethical thing you ought to be concerned about is doing everything you can to help us catch whoever killed her."

McConnell closed his eyes, his expression pained. "I know, Constable, and I've wrestled with my conscience about the matter. But what she told me sounded so ludicrous, I simply wasn't sure I ought to repeat it. I thought perhaps it would do more harm than good. But of course you're right: I ought to have told you." He took a deep breath. "Mrs. Starling said she had evidence that there was someone embezzling money from the society. When I pressed her for details, she refused to tell me who she suspected"—again he looked down at his desk—"but she said it was someone on the board."

Witherspoon leaned forward. "You didn't think that information was pertinent?"

"Of course it's pertinent!" he exclaimed. "But as I've just told you, I don't think she was in her right mind when she spoke to me. I don't like to speak ill of the dead, but Mrs. Starling had been acting peculiar for weeks before she was killed."

"In what way was she acting peculiar?" Witherspoon realized he was verifying what both Gretchen Terry and Pontefract had said.

"Well, as you've already heard, at board meetings she'd ask strange questions—questions that had nothing to do with the matter under discussion. She began acting as if she didn't trust anyone in the society or, for that matter, St. Andrew's Church. Don't just take my word for it—she was upset during our entire disbursement meeting; you can ask anyone on the board of governors. She kept interrupting the proceedings and asking questions, she was rude to everyone, and when Reverend Pontefract stated that the governors were under no obligation to answer her questions, she got very hostile and even asked him how he'd like it if she went to the bishop with what she knew."

"What did she mean by that?" Barnes asked.

McConnell shook his head. "I've no idea. Her behavior was shocking, to say the least. The governors were most upset, so we tabled everything on the agenda except for getting the Christmas alms. The meeting was adjourned as soon as the list of disbursement recipients was approved."

The inspector leaned forward. "May we have the names of the board of governors?"

"I'll have my clerk get a list ready for you." He went to the door, opened it, and called out, "Stuart, write down the names and addresses of the board members and have it ready when the officers leave." He returned and took his seat. "You can pick it up on your way out. Forgive me for not sharing this information sooner, but I wanted to preserve Mrs. Starling's reputation, now that she's not here to defend herself. But that was foolish of me, and I should have realized that I had to tell you what she'd told me. But honestly, Inspector, there's no evidence whatsoever that anyone on the board has done anything wrong. I think Mrs. Starling was going through a very difficult time in her life and she was starting to imagine things."

"How many board members have access to the society's funds?" Barnes asked.

"No one except myself and Reverend Pontefract. He's on the finance committee, but the majority of the donations come through here"—he hesitated—"though quite often people do hand him their donations directly. People like to impress the vicar. I saw you going into the church and I assumed you went there to speak to him."

"We did speak with him," the inspector replied. "As we're already here, perhaps we'll have another word with him."

But their hopes of asking the vicar any more questions were soon dashed. They stepped outside just in time to see the good reverend's hansom pull away from the front of the church.

Henry Devlin drew back in surprise. "Why on earth are you asking about the Angel Alms Society? Don't tell me you're interested in giving to them and you're no longer going to support us?"

"Don't worry, Henry, I'm not abandoning the Second Chance Temperance Charity. I'll continue with my usual contributions." Hatchet reached for his teacup and took a sip. He grinned at his old friend. Devlin was a ruddy-faced, blue-eyed Irishman with wispy gray hair.

They were sitting at a table in the large, cluttered Devlin drawing room that now served as headquarters for the charity in question. A desk stacked with papers, books, and ledgers stood next to the two windows. Several settees and couches, all of which had seen better days, were pushed against the far wall, and on the other side of the disused hearth were half a dozen storage cupboards and old wardrobes.

"Thank God for that," Henry sighed in relief. "You're one of our biggest supporters. If not for you, we'd be hard pressed to operate."

"You say that to everyone," Hatchet snorted. "But I have

it on good authority that you've plenty of donors. There's a lot of people like me in this world."

"True, but most of the ones who found themselves destitute and at the mercy of a habit that is well-nigh impossible to control without help don't end up doing as well as you did in life. But you're right: I am exaggerating. Charities are just like any other kind of business—we compete with one another for donor money—so when you mentioned the Angel Alms Society, I got worried." He picked up his own cup. "Tell me, why are you asking about them if you're not thinking of donating?"

Hatchet considered the question carefully. There were already a number of their acquaintances and friends that knew he and Luty as well as the others in the Witherspoon household helped with the inspector's cases. He didn't wish to add to that number. On the other hand, Henry was no fool. Furthermore, he was a decent man who'd given up a life of leisure and a fortune of his own to dedicate himself to this charity—a charity that was one of the few that tried to help men and women who'd climbed into a bottle so far, they couldn't see their own way out. "A friend of ours—mine and Luty's—is a man called Inspector Witherspoon."

"Ah, the one who solves all those murders." Henry nodded appreciatively and then brightened as he understood. "Good Lord, he's investigating the Starling murder."

"That's right, and being as the victim was closely associated with the Angel Alms Society, I thought I might have a go at finding out a bit about them . . . You know, the sort of information that the police might not find out on their own. Did you know Margaret Starling?"

Henry shook his head. "No, I've never met her, but I have heard of her, and of course I read about the murder in the newspapers. Poor woman, what a horrible way to die. All alone out in the cold."

"What can you tell me?" Hatchet put his cup down on the tabletop.

"Not very much. The Angel Alms Society is closely associated with but not part of St. Andrew's Church. Their charter requires them to have the current vicar on their board of governors."

"They must be an ancient society . . ." Hatchet began, only to be interrupted.

"You'd think so because of the name, no one gives out 'alms' anymore, but they've been in existence for only fifty years or so. The church is old but the society isn't. They picked the name deliberately to make it seem older than it actually is. I'm not sure how it's run, but I know they give out 'alms,' or money and fuel, twice a year, at Christmas and Easter."

"Who receives these alms?"

"Anyone can apply, but from what I've heard about them, it's generally someone 'deserving' from the local parish. I hate that word."

"'Deserving'? Why?"

"Because who is to say who is deserving and who isn't?" He pursed his lips and shook his head. "If people need help, they need help. Why should someone starve to death or freeze in the cold simply because society doesn't think them deserving? You either take Christ's instructions seriously, or you don't. God is the one who determines who is deserving, not humans." He waved his hand dismissively. "But you're not here to listen to me go on about my personal bugaboos. What else do you want to know?"

"Anything else that you might know."

Henry looked up, his expression thoughtful. "Well, I did hear a bit of unsavory gossip about them . . . Actually, it wasn't about the Angel Alms Society; it was about the new vicar at St. Andrew's. Apparently, he got into some trouble at his last parish and that's why he was sent down this way."

"Do you know what kind of trouble?"

"I've no idea what the details might be, but the gossip was he was a bit too free with his hands, and some of the ladies from his previous parish were not amused. Apparently the last young woman was from quite an influential family, she complained to her father, he went to the bishop, and Pontefract was moved to a smaller, less affluent parish."

"That's all they did to him? If the charges were true, why wasn't he run out of the church?"

"Don't be daft, Hatchet, they make certain those kind of charges are never properly investigated. The church hates scandals. It's much easier just to slap the priest on the wrist and move him along. Though I did hear that this wasn't Pontefract's first skirmish with the church authorities. He was warned that if there was one more complaint against him about *anything*, he'd be out the door."

"You've got a visitor, ma'am." Abigail, Lady Cannonberry's maid, met her at the front door, then glanced toward the drawing room as she took her mistress's cloak and hat. "It's that vicar—the one you didn't want to be alone with when he came to dinner that night. You remember, ma'am; it was about two years ago."

"Oh, my goodness, you don't mean Reginald Pontefract?"

"That's him." Abigail shook the cloak to get the damp off.

Ruth frowned. She'd neither seen nor heard from Pontefract since their last encounter. "Did he say what he wanted?"

"No, ma'am. I told him you were out and I didn't know when you'd return, but he insisted on waiting. I didn't know what to do. Everton is out shopping, so I asked Cook what to do, and she told me to put him in the drawing room." She hung up the cloak and hat. "But I've kept the door open a bit so I could keep an eye on him. He's not tried to steal anything."

Ruth couldn't help but smile. Abigail had no illusions about the world. She'd been raised in the East End and didn't think a vicar was any less likely to be a thief than the next person. "Thank you, Abigail. You've done an excellent job. I'll go see what the gentleman has to say for himself."

"Should I stay up here, ma'am? I remembered what you said the last time he was here: how, when he invited himself to dinner that night, you didn't want to be alone with him. So I put the sugar hammer in me pocket when I went down to ask Cook what to do with the fellow."

"That won't be necessary, Abigail. I can scream quite loudly if I need to, but I appreciate your concern." She went into the drawing room.

Pontefract tossed the magazine he'd been reading onto the settee and got to his feet as she entered. "Oh, thank goodness you're home. I was so worried you'd gone out for the evening, and your maid wouldn't tell me anything. Perhaps you ought to have a word with the girl about respecting one's betters. But do forgive me for barging in without sending a calling card or making an appointment. It was imperative that I see you."

She stared at him. His hair was disheveled, his coat was unbuttoned, and he was clenching his hands into fists. "Good evening, Reginald. It's nice to see you again. It's been quite a long time. Would you care for a sherry or perhaps a whisky?"

"Thank you." He swallowed and gave her a weak smile. "I could do with a glass of whisky."

"Sit down, please, and I'll pour us both one." She crossed the room to the liquor cabinet, where a cut-glass decanter filled with amber liquid sat behind a semicircle of matching glasses. She poured the liquor, giving her own glass just a tad more than she gave him. Ruth had a feeling she was going to need it.

"Here you are." She moved to the settee and handed him his glass. "You look upset. Is something wrong?"

He gave her a tight smile. "Wrong? I wouldn't say there was something wrong per se, but I do need your assistance." He took a drink, almost draining the glass.

"My assistance?" She sat down on the chair across from him. "Reginald, what are you talking about?"

"Are you still friends with that policeman? The one who solves all the murders?"

"Inspector Witherspoon? Yes, we're very good friends."

"Then you must help me—you must!" he cried. "I didn't do it. I didn't do anything, but they're going to blame me. It wasn't my fault that she died. I had nothing to do with it. I simply went there to have a talk with the woman, but she didn't even come to the door."

"What woman? Reginald, what are you talking about?"

"Your inspector thinks I killed her, and if you don't help me, he's going to arrest me. He thinks I murdered Margaret Starling."

CHAPTER 6

"I must have a glass of sherry," Witherspoon said as he handed his hat and coat to Mrs. Jeffries. "We've learned so much today, my head is spinning."

"It seems you've worked hard, sir. No wonder you came home so late. We were starting to worry." She hung up his garments.

"Dinner isn't ready, is it?"

"It won't be ready for another half an hour. Mrs. Goodge had made a lovely Lancashire hot pot and a nice crumble for dessert."

"Excellent. Then we can go into the study and have a drink." He headed down the hall with Mrs. Jeffries right on his heels.

She poured their drinks while he made himself comfortable. "Here you are, sir. Now do tell me about your day. As I said, sir, it got so late, we were concerned."

"It was simply one of those days, Mrs. Jeffries, we had so much to do that time got away from us." He took a sip of his sherry. "Our first interview was with Olivia Huxton, and I must say, she was both evasive and forthcoming simultaneously." He took his time, taking care to recall each and every word Mrs. Huxton had said. "So as you can see, on the one hand she told us everything, yet somehow I've a feeling she wasn't being completely truthful. Of course, that's the reason Constable Barnes interviewed her servants: We wanted to be certain they could vouch for Mrs. Huxton being home the night of the murder."

"Servants will sometimes lie to protect their mistress, especially if they feel their position is at stake." Mrs. Jeffries made a mental note to check with Constable Barnes for his impression of the Huxton household. He was a bit more adept at ferreting out lies than Inspector Witherspoon.

"True, but hopefully that's not the case here."

"And they confirmed that Mrs. Huxton was home all evening?"

"That's right." He took another drink.

"So now that Margaret Starling is dead, Olivia Huxton doesn't have to be concerned with the lawsuit."

"Correct, but I thought the most interesting thing about her statement was that she freely admitted to stealing and destroying the anonymous letter she'd sent to the vicar."

"She confessed to destroying evidence." Mrs. Jeffries took a sip of her drink as she tried to keep all the information straight.

"But she didn't know it was evidence at the time," he pointed out, "and as she rightly commented, she considered the letter her property. But I'm not certain about that. I should think that, once the letter is posted, it belongs to the recipient. Nonetheless, it is pointless to worry about it, as it's gone."

"She stole the letter so it couldn't be used against her in court, right?"

"I don't think that was the real reason she took it," Witherspoon said. "I think she was ashamed to have written it in the first place. She didn't seem that concerned about the lawsuit, even when Constable Barnes and I both told her that courts do use handwriting to verify evidence. She said something like 'If my writing looked like Graham McConnell's, I'd agree with you; his penmanship is so elaborate it's unreadable. But mine looks like any other woman's who'd been educated at St. Anne's School for Girls.'"

"You think she stole it simply because she was ashamed?" Mrs. Jeffries found that hard to believe. On the other hand, the inspector could be very perceptive about people.

"To be honest, that was my impression."

"Did she say what was in it?"

"Not word for word, but she did admit she'd written it out of spite and that it wasn't altogether true." He took a fast sip before repeating the accusations in the anonymous letter. "The information she gave us about everyone else in the case was useful."

"Let's see, Olivia Huxton told you that Mrs. Starling argued with the head of the alms society, the vicar of St. Andrew's, and even her late niece's husband—what did you say his name was?" She knew perfectly well what his name was, but she wanted him to repeat it so it wouldn't seem that she knew too much about the case.

"Edgar Redstone," Witherspoon said. "But we didn't have

time to interview him today. After we saw Mrs. Huxton, we went to have a word with the Reverend Pontefract at St. Andrew's Church. But before we could speak to him, we were waylaid by the verger, a man named Tom Lancaster."

"The verger had something to tell you?" Mrs. Jeffries asked.

"He told us quite a bit." The inspector repeated what Lancaster had said. "Unfortunately, the vicar arrived before we could learn more, and that was the end of that. By the time we'd finished with Reverend Pontefract, the verger had disappeared."

"You're going to speak with him again, I presume." She took another sip.

"Indeed we shall. Then, as it was right next door, we went to the Angel Alms Society and spoke with Graham McConnell."

"Isn't he the man who arrived at the Starling home the day her body was discovered?"

"That's right. He's been quite helpful, but like many people of his class he was reluctant to pass along some very pertinent information." He repeated everything McConnell had said.

"Goodness, sir, he should have reported this to you immediately!" Mrs. Jeffries declared. "Why do some people think they're doing the dead a service by remaining silent?"

"McConnell said he kept quiet because he was concerned that Mrs. Starling was imagining situations that weren't true, and as I've said before, her own housemaid and even Pontefract made the same claim against her." He drained his glass. "Still, he should have told us that only a short time before her death she'd accused Pontefract of embezzling from the society."

"I don't understand, sir. You said the society was separate from St. Andrew's Church, and if that's the case, how would the Reverend Pontefract have access to the finances?"

"I asked that question, and, according to Mr. McConnell, sometimes people give their donation directly to the vicar." The inspector shrugged. "McConnell says they like to do it to impress him."

"I see." Mrs. Jeffries frowned slightly, not entirely sure if what she'd just heard made sense. "Would you care for another one, sir?"

"That would be lovely," he replied.

She took his glass and refilled it. Information was coming fast, but what did it mean? What's more, it appeared that there was some truth to the notion that the victim was acting peculiar in the weeks before she died. But that didn't mean Margaret Starling was prey to an overactive imagination. Someone did murder her. She handed Witherspoon his sherry. "Did you interview anyone else this afternoon?"

He shook his head. "Not really. By the time we finished with McConnell, it was very late. We wasted so much time at the Upper Richmond Road Police Station waiting about for Inspector Nivens this morning that we felt as though we were behind schedule the entire day. But we did have a good look at the postmortem report."

"That was fast." Mrs. Jeffries took another sip and then put her glass on the side table.

"Yes. Dr. Littleham did a very efficient report and the results were what we expected: Margaret Starling was killed by multiple blows to the head."

"Did the report speculate on the time of death?"

"As near as the doctor could tell, it was between nine and eleven at night."

"Which means the killer probably knew the servants would be gone until after that time," Mrs. Jeffries murmured.

"The servants didn't get home until eleven," he said. "But then again, that tidbit of information isn't very useful. Mrs. Starling's habit of giving the staff an evening out at Christmastime was well-known."

"Which means the killer probably planned the murder well in advance."

"But I didn't. I'd never hurt anyone; I'm a man of the cloth, one of God's servants," Pontefract cried as he leapt up and stamped his feet.

"Reginald, sit down and calm yourself," Lady Cannonberry ordered. "Whatever is wrong, shouting and having a tantrum isn't going to help. I know Gerald Witherspoon; he's an excellent detective, and if you're innocent, you'll not be arrested."

"*If* I'm innocent!" he shouted. "How can you say such a thing? I know we've never been close, but I've always considered you as more than just a casual acquaintance. For God's sake, you're supposed to believe me."

Suddenly the drawing room doors burst open and Abigail, wielding the sugar hammer like a club, raced into the room. She skidded to a halt halfway across the room. "We heard screamin'. Is everything all right, ma'am? Cook's at the top of stairs with the butcher knife if we need more help."

Ruth was struck by an urge to giggle, because the situation was so absurd, but at the same time she hated seeing anyone, even Pontefract, so frightened and distressed. "Everything is fine, Abigail. You and Cook can go back downstairs."

Abigail's eyes narrowed as she glanced at Pontefract. "If you say so, ma'am. But if you need me, you just shout."

"Thank you Abigail."

Pontefract's mouth opened and closed for several seconds before he could get any words out. "Did that young woman think I was harming you? Oh, my gracious, what kind of street urchin have you let into your home? What a dreadful little guttersnipe. I've never been so insulted in my life."

Some of her sympathy for Pontefract vanished. "She's neither a guttersnipe nor a street urchin. Furthermore, if you continue to verbally abuse her in my presence, I'm afraid I'll have to ask you to leave."

"Ask me to leave," he moaned, and flopped onto the settee, his mouth gaping open in shock. "But . . . but . . . I need—"

Ruth interrupted. "She heard you shouting, Reginald, and as my butler is out for the evening, she did precisely what she should have done. Women are learning to stick together and to defend themselves when and if the need arises."

"But I would never harm you . . . Oh, goodness, I'm sorry." His eyes flooded with tears and he blinked to stop them from running down his cheeks. "I'm so sorry. You're right. I was making a spectacle of myself, and your maid is to be commended for coming to what she thought was your defense. I just lost my head for a few moments. Please forgive me."

"Of course, Reginald. Now, before you do anything else, finish that whisky and take some deep breaths to calm your nerves. Then you must tell me why you're so certain you're going to be arrested."

He did as he was told, drained his glass, put it on the side table, and inhaled heavily.

Ruth got his glass, crossed to the liquor cabinet, and poured him another. She topped her own off as well. "Now, tell me why you're so frightened." She handed him his drink and took her seat.

"Thank you." He took a quick sip. "I don't know if you're aware of this, but I'm no longer at St. Peter's in Highgate. I was sent to St. Andrew's in Putney eighteen months ago."

"Really," Ruth murmured, but now his showing up on her doorstep made sense.

"Yes, well, one goes where one is sent, but I digress. One of the women in my parish was murdered."

"I know that. Her name was Margaret Starling; it's been in all the papers." She didn't want to let on that she knew anything more than the general public.

"Inspector Witherspoon came to the church today to question me about her murder"—Pontefract took another deep breath—"but before he got to my study, the verger, Tom Lancaster, filled the inspector's head with lies."

"Why would he do that?" Ruth asked softly.

"He hates me and he told the police that I'd had a dreadful argument with Mrs. Starling—that we'd quarreled."

"Had you?" Ruth took a sip.

"Yes, but Margaret was quarreling with everyone. For goodness' sakes, she'd filed a lawsuit against her next-door neighbor. But none of this is important; what's important is that I had nothing to do with her death. But he's going to find out that I was there Sunday night."

"That's what you meant earlier when you said you'd gone there to talk with her?" Ruth asked.

He nodded. "That's right. I'd been upset all day over a number of things. She was also a member of the advisory board of the Angel Alms Society. We're loosely affiliated with the charity and I'm on the board of governors. Recently, Margaret had been asking a lot of questions about the charities' finances. Sir Gareth Cleary told me she'd convinced him that we needed to bring in an outside person to have a look at our books."

"Why would that upset you?"

"It didn't; we've nothing to hide. Margaret Starling has been at the center of a number of unpleasant incidents, and this was the final straw. So I decided to go and speak to her myself—to clear the air, so to speak. But when I got there, she didn't answer the door, and I gave up and left."

"Did you tell the police you'd been there that night?" Ruth was sure he hadn't informed them.

"I was too afraid." His shoulders slumped and he stared glumly at the floor. "Ruth . . . may I call you that?"

"Of course. Why were you so afraid? Your arguments with the victim sound petty—not the sort of motive one would have for committing murder."

He said nothing for a long moment, then finally he spoke. "Have you ever done something that you bitterly regretted? You know, given in to a stupid compulsion and done something you knew was wrong?"

"Of course. Everyone does that at one time or another."

"True, but when you're a vicar, you're supposed to be above such human impulses. People don't forgive you for not being perfect."

"None of us is perfect." She stared at him sympatheti-cally.

"I'm not, and that's why I was so scared. I did something . . . something that most definitely gives me a motive," he admit-ted. "I'm certain Margaret Starling had found out the reason I'd been sent away from St. Peter's. She kept dropping hints that she knew that my troubles at St. Peter's weren't the only reason I'd been given a smaller, poorer parish, and she told me that she knew if there was one more complaint about me to the bishop, I'd lose everything."

Ruth was surprised by his admission but struggled not to let it show on her face. It wasn't her place to pass judgment on him. "Whatever your troubles at St. Peter's might have been, if you've done nothing wrong at St. Andrew's, why are you worried? Even if she'd gone to the bishop, what could she have told him?"

He closed his eyes, hung his head, and exhaled. "That I was a thief. I kept three pounds for myself that should have gone to the Angel Alms Society. Margaret might have known about it."

Mrs. Jeffries and Mrs. Goodge gave Constable Barnes a concise report on what the household had learned. He, in turn, gave them additional details from the previous day's interviews.

"You've found out a lot in a very short period of time," Mrs. Jeffries said. "And, frankly, I don't mind saying that I can't make heads or tails of anything."

"You will, Hepzibah," Mrs. Goodge assured her. "I know it. I've a good feeling about this case."

"I hope you're right, Mrs. Goodge." Barnes put his mug

down on the table. "But as I see it, we've more problems with this one than we usually do. We've got that ruddy Inspector Nivens doing his best to muck up the investigation. Luckily for us, the duty sergeant at the Upper Richmond Road Police Station managed to get a copy of the postmortem to us. If we'd had to rely on Nivens, we'd be out of luck."

"Nivens deliberately withheld it?" Mrs. Jeffries was outraged. "That's awful. He's a policeman, sworn to uphold the law, and that's interfering in an ongoing investigation. Surely you can do something about him now?"

"We've no proof it was deliberate." Barnes shrugged. "But what Nivens didn't know was that the doctor made two copies of the report."

"Thank goodness," Mrs. Goodge said. "But it seems to have put the doctor to a lot of trouble. Fancy writing out two copies of a postmortem."

Barnes laughed. "Not at all, Mrs. Goodge. We're in the modern age, and reports aren't handwritten anymore. Dr. Littleham has a typewriter girl, and she's been trained to use something called carbon paper. It lets you make two copies at the same time."

"What will they think of next?" The cook shook her head. "But there must be some way to prove Nivens deliberately hid the original report."

Barnes drained his mug of tea. "I doubt it. Nivens is good at covering his tracks. And you know the inspector, he never likes to think the worst of fellow officers, even a useless one like Nivens." He got to his feet. "I'll see the two of you tomorrow, and hopefully by then we'll all have lots to talk about."

"Hopefully." Mrs. Jeffries smiled ruefully. "And hopefully we'll be able to understand exactly what it all might mean. Christmas is coming closer and closer."

"You'll do it, Mrs. Jeffries." Barnes headed for the back stairs. "You always do."

"I'm not so sure," the housekeeper mumbled as she got up. Thus far, nothing about this case made any sense at all. But she shoved that problem to the back of her mind and helped Mrs. Goodge arrange the table for their morning meeting.

As soon as everyone had arrived and taken their seats, Ruth said, "May I go first? I'm meeting a source for morning coffee and I've something important"—she paused—"well, it could be important . . . that I need to report."

"Of course. Go ahead. We're all ears," Mrs. Jeffries said.

Ruth told them about her surprise visitor. She took her time and told them everything he'd said. "Honestly, I was so stunned that he is involved in this case."

"What's more stunnin' is that he nicked three quid," Smythe said. "What's wrong with the man? Why risk your livelihood for a few pounds?"

"He said it was a momentary lapse in judgment," Ruth replied.

"Did he say how Margaret Starling might have known what he'd done?" Mrs. Jeffries asked.

"He said she'd been asking a lot of questions about how the donations were handled and he thinks she stumbled onto what he'd done accidentally. He grew alarmed when he found out that she'd convinced Sir Gareth Cleary and the board to have the books examined by an outsider. Someone named Nelson Biddlington."

"Nelson Biddlington!" Luty yelped. "Are you sure that's the name?"

Ruth nodded. "That's the name he heard. Why?"

"Nelson Biddlington is one of my solicitors." Luty looked puzzled. "But he ain't an accountant. So why would the society want him to look at the books?"

"I don't know. Reginald didn't say anything more about it," Ruth said.

"But 'is admittin' 'e was there that night takes the wind out of my sails." Smythe grinned. "Last night I found the 'ansom driver that took 'im to the Starling 'ouse."

"You're not alone." Hatchet looked at Smythe. "That's more or less what I learned last night as well, with one caveat: Apparently—and I suspect the good reverend was silent on this point—he was sent to St. Andrew's because he was too familiar with the ladies of St. Peter's, and that familiarity was not appreciated."

Ruth looked surprised and then she burst out laughing. "He didn't *mention* that specifically. He has a high opinion of himself, especially when it comes to women, but I don't think he's a killer."

"Why not?" Mrs. Jeffries asked.

"Because the murder sounds planned," Ruth explained. "The killer had to know that Mrs. Starling would be home alone and would have had to figure out a way to get her outside that night."

"And whoever did it would have to know where the shovel was kept and that it was available," Mrs. Goodge added.

"That's right"—Ruth nodded in agreement—"but Reginald Pontefract isn't very good at planning. He tends to react, not think or plan."

"Still, he was there, and we only have his word for it that he left without seeing Margaret Starling," Mrs. Jeffries said.

"Why don't I go have a chat with Nelson Biddlington?" Luty offered. "Maybe he knows something. There has to be some reason the board wanted him to look at the books."

"We've a lot to do today, sir." Barnes pulled open the door of the Upper Richmond Road Police Station and waited till Witherspoon had stepped inside. "Let's hope this doesn't take long."

"It shouldn't." Witherspoon smiled as he approached the desk. "Good morning. Is Inspector Nivens available? I'd like to speak with him."

"Of course, sir." Wylie pointed to the hall. "He's in the duty inspector's office."

"Thank you." Witherspoon headed in that direction.

"I'll wait here, sir," Barnes called after him.

Witherspoon knocked on the door and then stepped inside when he heard a muffled "Enter." "Good morning, Inspector Nivens."

Nivens was at the desk. He looked up from the open file he'd been reading. "Morning, Witherspoon. I suppose you're here for the PM report? Well, I was just thinking that before we go over that, I'd like to know how the case is progressing. It is, after all, in my district."

Taken aback, Witherspoon stared at him for a brief moment. "Actually, Inspector Nivens, I've already seen the postmortem report. I'm here to ask for some additional men. Two should do nicely. I was hoping I could have them this morning, and from what it looks like here, the station isn't terribly busy."

Nivens looked surprised. "What do you mean, you've seen the PM report?" He jabbed his index finger at the open file. "You couldn't have. It's right here."

"But I did see it and I'm wondering why you still have the report on your desk. It was done two days ago, and since that time I've been here several times. It should have been passed to me immediately."

"Are you implying that I deliberately withheld it?" Nivens voice was low, guttural, and meant to be intimidating.

"Yes."

"How dare you!" He shot to his feet.

"I dare because it's true. You deliberately withheld pertinent information in the investigation of a homicide. What's more, you've absented yourself from this station during those times when you knew I'd be here to request additional constables to assist in the house-to-house interviews and general police work."

An ugly red flush spread over Nivens' face as he balled his hands into fists. "That's absurd," he snapped, his voice rising. "I did no such thing, and what's more, if you dare to imply I behaved in such a manner, you'll be sorry." He banged his fist against the desk.

"Do you really think your threats frighten me?" Witherspoon smiled slightly. "You may do as you like. However, for now, I suggest you give me two of your constables, as I have a murder to solve. Furthermore, I've already sent a report about your behavior to Chief Superintendent Barrows—" He broke off as someone pounded on the door, and a second later it flew open to reveal Constable Barnes, Sergeant Wylie, and two other constables.

"We heard yelling." Barnes looked at Witherspoon. "All well, sir?"

"Get out, Witherspoon!" Nivens yelled before turning his fury to the crowd in his doorway. "All of you, close that damned door and get out of my sight!"

Witherspoon didn't move. "Not without my additional constables and"—he pointed at the file on the desk—"that copy of the PM report."

Nivens grabbed the open file, closed it, and shoved it across the desk. "Take the wretched thing, then. Sergeant Wylie, assign two constables to Witherspoon, and all of you, get the hell out of my office. Now!"

Ten minutes later Inspector Witherspoon and Constable Barnes, accompanied by two local constables, left the station.

"You lads, get on with it," Barnes ordered. "Split up and make sure you cover all the neighbors on both sides of Moran Place, and when you finish there, do the street directly behind the Starling home."

"Yes, sir," one of the constables replied. They nodded and hurried off. Barnes waited till they'd disappeared around the corner before he spoke. "It sounded like Inspector Nivens lost his temper, sir."

"He threatened me and I told him I'd already submitted a complaint to Chief Barrows about his withholding information and assistance on this case." Witherspoon waved at the hansom driver who had just pulled up.

"Really, sir?" Barnes couldn't keep the surprise out of his voice.

"Well, actually, I haven't done it as yet, but I'm going to do it. Let's grab that hansom before it disappears." He started toward the curb. "Frankly, I don't mind Nivens making it clear he doesn't like or respect me, but I must draw the line when he deliberately interferes in a homicide investigation, so Chief Superintendent Barrows will be getting a full report about his shocking behavior."

"Good for you, sir." Barnes wanted to burst into song as he trailed after him. "Where to now?"

"Let's see what Edgar Redstone has to tell us."

Edgar Redstone stared at them from the open door of his home. "Why do you want to speak to me? I've nothing to do with Margaret Starling—not anymore." He was a portly man in navy trousers and a white dress shirt with a frayed open collar. His thinning brown hair was disheveled and there was stubble on his chin.

"May we come in Mr. Redstone?" Barnes asked politely. "I'm sure you'll be much more comfortable speaking to us here rather than at the Upper Richmond Road Police Station."

Redstone stared at them with a cunning, speculative expression on his broad face. For a moment Witherspoon thought he might slam the door on them, but he finally stepped back and waved them inside.

He led them down a short hall and into a dimly lighted drawing room. The room was furnished with a dark green horsehair settee and matching armchairs, all of which had stacks of books, newspapers, and magazines on them. At the two windows, cream-and-gray-patterned curtains were tied back to let in the pale winter light, and on the floor was a faded oriental rug. A mahogany corner table, both the bookcases, and the end tables on each side of the settee were cluttered with objects: ceramic knicknacks, silver candlesticks, ornate picture frames, brilliantly colored enamel snuff boxes, and even a set of golden bowls.

There were faded spots where paintings had once hung on the green-and-gold wallpaper. Witherspoon suspected those pictures had been sold.

Redstone swept a stack of magazines off one armchair and an open copy of the *Times* off the other one. "You may sit." He flopped down in the center of the settee and stared at them.

"Thank you, sir." Witherspoon took a seat. "I'm assuming you understand why we're here."

"I'm not an imbecile, Inspector. You're here because someone murdered Margaret Starling, but as I've told you, my relationship with her is and has been at an end for quite some time now."

"You were married to her niece." Barnes propped his notebook on the arm of his chair and flipped it open to a new page. "Is that right?"

"I was."

Witherspoon shifted on the uncomfortable cushion. "When was the last time you saw Mrs. Starling?"

"I don't remember the exact date. It was around the time of my late wife's funeral."

"When did your wife pass away?"

"A little over a year ago, Inspector. She died of bronchitis two weeks before her mother died. It was a terrible tragedy."

Barnes looked at him. "You haven't seen Mrs. Starling since then?"

"No."

"Not even at the Angel Alms Society meetings?" the inspector asked quickly. "Aren't you on the board of governors?"

"I am on the board, so of course I've seen Margaret at the meetings." His thin mouth curved in a slight smile. "I thought you meant when had I seen her alone. Sorry, my mistake."

"Mr. Redstone, a witness has told us you saw Mrs. Starling recently and at that time you had a terrible row with her," Witherspoon charged. "Please stop wasting our time and tell us the truth. When was the last time you spoke to the victim?"

"Victim," he repeated, his eyes blazing with fury. "Margaret Starling was no more a victim than the man in the moon. That woman never had a bad day in her entire life."

"Until her life was ended by murder," Witherspoon reminded him. "You obviously had no love or respect for her. She was a very wealthy woman"—he gestured at the objects around the room—"and you're obviously in quite dire straits financially. Do you expect to benefit from Mrs. Starling's estate?"

His mouth dropped open in surprise. "Your implication is outrageous. I have no expectations and I've nothing to do with that woman's death."

"You accused her of stealing your wife's inheritance," the constable added.

"Because it's true," he snapped. "My wife should have inherited her mother's money, and when she passed away, it should have been mine. But because my wife died shortly before her own mother, Margaret got it all. It wasn't fair, and so I went around to speak to Margaret about it, to try and make her see reason. But she refused to so much as countenance sharing the inheritance."

"So you admit you were angry at her for not sharing money she'd inherited from her own sister, is that correct?" Witherspoon pressed.

"That's right, but as I said, the woman was so selfish, she adamantly refused to understand that her ridiculous behavior was bankrupting me. I wasn't the only one who was cheated out of what should have been rightfully mine; the Angel Alms Society expected to get half Marion's money. They were disappointed as well. Both Graham McConnell and Reverend Pontefract spoke to Margaret about it, but she kept insisting it was her money—only hers. She told them they'd get it when she died."

"Where were you on Sunday night?" Barnes asked.

"I was here." Redstone stared at them stonily.

"Can anyone confirm your whereabouts? A servant, perhaps?"

"There's my housekeeper, but she's here only in the afternoon and she leaves at six o'clock."

"You only have one servant?" Barnes waved his hand around. "This is a large house, sir."

"I know that, Constable, but when my wife passed away, I had to let most of the servants go."

"Why is that?" Barnes persisted.

"As the inspector guessed, my financial circumstances are quite dire," he said. "However, they are not the business of the Metropolitan Police."

"I'm afraid they are, sir," Witherspoon said. "Your dispute with Mrs. Starling was essentially one of finances, and she was murdered at a time when you don't have an alibi."

"Nonsense. Why would murdering Margaret now do me

any good whatsoever?" He laughed. "I've told you, I have no expectations and I know she didn't leave me anything in her will."

"How do you know that?" Witherspoon realized the man had made a valid point.

"The last time I saw her, when we had that dreadful argument, she made it clear that even though I'd been a good husband to her late niece, she owed me nothing and I wasn't to think I'd inherit from her."

"Once your wife had passed away, why would you have thought she might leave you something?" Barnes asked.

"Because when my wife was alive, we lived on the income from a trust set up by her mother, and because the money kept coming every quarter this past year, I foolishly assumed the capital from the trust was my late wife's property. But it wasn't. Margaret had merely allowed the disbursement to continue for a year so that I could make other financial arrangements. It would have been useful if Margaret had told me that, but she didn't. So when the money stopped, I went to see her and was stunned to learn that the trust now belonged to her. I asked Margaret if she could ensure that I received at least that part of the estate, but she claimed she'd done enough and that I had had ample time to find employment." He closed his eyes and shook his head. "She made it quite clear that when she was dead, she was abiding by my late mother-in-law's wishes and leaving every penny to charity. Specifically, to the Angel Alms Society."

"It's very kind of you to escort me," Phyllis told the young man. "I feel so silly; of course the London Rowing Club would be on the river. I don't know why I got so muddled in my directions."

"It's my pleasure, miss. This is a good neighborhood, but sometimes there are some rough sorts down by the river."

She gave him a grateful smile. He smiled shyly in return. He was dressed in a dark gray suit, white shirt, and blue tie. Beneath his bowler hat, his hair was blond, his eyes hazel, and his complexion pale.

After the morning meeting, she'd come to Putney hoping to find out a bit more about the Reverend Reginald Pontefract. Even though Ruth Cannonberry was more than capable of taking her own measure of the fellow, after Ruth had left the meeting, all the women had deemed it a good idea to find out as much as possible about the vicar.

Phyllis had volunteered, but when she'd arrived at St. Andrew's, she not found one single person to talk to, not even the verger. She hung around the church steps for a few minutes and then decided that it might be worth her time to go to the High Street and see if anyone there was in the mood for a bit of gossip. She was almost at the Angel Alms Society when this young man stepped out the front door. Phyllis instantly made up her mind not to let him get away from her.

"I'm Arabella Morgan," she lied. "I do hope I'm not keeping you from something important."

"My name is Stuart Deeds, and you're not keeping me from anything."

"Do you work at that building next to the church?" She gave him another dazzling smile.

He blushed. "I do, I'm a clerk at the Angel Alms Society. Usually I work until half past five, but today the manager had to go to the doctor. He told me I could go when I finished typing up the correspondence."

"You can use a typewriter machine," she gushed. "Goodness, you must be so very clever."

He blushed and ducked his head. "Not really, miss, but thank you."

"What does the Angel Alms Society do?" Phyllis tried to think of a way to bring up Pontefract's name. "Is it part of that church that's next to it?"

"Not really, no; what I should say is that it's not officially part of the church, but Reverend Pontefract, he's the vicar there; he's on the board of governors. He and Mr. McConnell—he's my guv—are always discussing something or other. Plus he comes into our office frequently. The society hands out overcoats and scarves to some of the beggars in the area. It's been such a miserably cold winter, and there's many on the streets that don't even have a decent coat."

"Are these coats and such donated?" She knew the question was idiotic, but she wanted to keep him talking.

"Oh, yes, there's some generous souls in this neighborhood." Stuart guided her around a cluster of young lads, giving them a good glare for not moving out of their way. "We've a good system. Even if I'm not there, the vicar can get in and help himself to whatever's in the donation cupboards." He chuckled. "But sometimes, we don't have what he needs."

Phyllis tried to think of what else to ask him, but her mind was suddenly blank, and she was afraid she'd made a mess of things. "Uh, you mean you don't have coats or scarves?"

"Not always. Yesterday morning Reverend Pontefract

came in looking for an overcoat. He'd promised some poor man that he'd get him one, but all we had were ladies' overcoats. He got a bit testy about the matter as well; he said he'd been in the coat closet last Saturday and had seen one that would have fit the man. I told him I'd not touched the closet in two weeks, so I've no idea where it went. I'm not sure he believed me."

"I hope Merton Nesbitt is cooperative," Witherspoon murmured as he and Barnes waited for someone to answer the front door. "I do wish we'd been able to talk to him yesterday."

"Yesterday was a busy day, sir, and we're here now," Barnes said as the door opened and a young, black-haired housemaid peered out at them.

"Yes?"

"We'd like to speak with Mr. Merton Nesbitt," the constable said.

She opened the door wide and ushered them inside. "His flat is upstairs on the top floor."

The foyer was wide and well furnished, with two brass umbrella stands, a coat tree, and a side table covered with a bright red table runner and topped with a tiny evergreen tree in a red-and-white ceramic urn. A staircase decorated with red-and-white Christmas bunting wound around the bannister was straight ahead.

"Do you work for Mr. Nesbitt, miss?" Barnes asked.

"No, sir, I work for Mrs. Retting; she owns the house." She pointed to the stairs. "There's only the two flats. Mr. Nesbitt's is on the left and Mr. Underwood has the one on the right."

"Do you live in, miss?" the constable persisted.

"Yes, sir, I do." Her pretty face grew wary. "Why are you asking me all these questions?"

"It's a police matter, miss. Don't worry, you're not in trouble"—Barnes gave her his kindest smile—"but can you tell me if Mr. Nesbitt went out this past Sunday night?"

She said nothing for a moment, her expression confused. "I wouldn't know, sir. Mrs. Retting's tenants come and go as they please. They all have their own keys. Sometimes the gentlemen go out in the evening, but I don't know about that night—" She broke off, then continued, "No, that's not true: Someone went out that night, because when I got up the next morning, whoever it was had tracked mud and leaves all over." She pointed to the gray-and-white tiled floor. "It took me ages to get it up."

"Thank you, miss" Barnes nodded. "The inspector and I will go on upstairs, then."

She nodded curtly and disappeared down the corridor.

"Well done, Constable," Witherspoon said as they started up the staircase. "We'll be sure to ask Mr. Nesbitt if he went out that night."

"And if he says he didn't, we'll see what the other tenant has to say; it had to have been one of those two who went out. The housemaid would have known if it was Mrs. Retting."

When they reached the top floor, they were both gasping for air. Barnes paused for a moment so he and the inspector could catch their breath before moving to Nesbitt's door and giving it a sharp rap.

"Who is it?" a man's voice asked.

"The police. We'd like to ask you some questions," Barnes said through the door.

The door opened and a middle-aged man with high cheekbones, brown eyes, and brown hair with just the right amount of gray at the temples to be attractive stared out at them. "What's this about?"

"Are you Merton Nesbitt?" Witherspoon asked.

"I am. Who are you?"

Witherspoon introduced himself and Constable Barnes and then said, "May we come in? We'd like to ask you some questions about the murder of Margaret Starling."

Nesbitt's eyes widened. "I don't see why you want to speak to me. I've nothing to do with this matter." He started to close the door, but Barnes stuck his foot in the opening.

"I think, sir, you have quite a bit you could tell us. We have it on good authority that you had threatened the deceased on more than one occasion," Barnes bluffed. "Now, you can either speak to us here or you can accompany us to the Upper Richmond Road Police Station."

"Oh, all right, then, have it your way, but you're wasting your time as well as mine." He flung the door wide, turned, and retreated into the flat.

The two policemen stepped over the threshold. The flat was decently but not lavishly furnished with two black upholstered chairs, a tweed settee, and a bookcase.

"Go on, then; let's get this over with." He flopped down on a chair and glared at the two police officers. He didn't invite them to sit down.

Barnes pulled out his notebook and opened it.

Witherspoon stared at Nesbitt. "What was your relationship with Margaret Starling?"

"I had no relationship to the woman; she was a friend of my wife's."

"You didn't like Mrs. Starling, did you?"

"I hated her. She ruined my life." He cocked his head to one side and smiled. "But that doesn't mean I killed her. From what I hear, Margaret had a number of enemies."

"How did she ruin your life?" The inspector shifted his weight a bit in an attempt to get more comfortable.

"She testified against me in our divorce proceeding. My wife left me and I was turfed out of my home."

"The grounds for divorce are very narrow, Mr. Nesbitt." Witherspoon was no expert on divorce law, but he knew legally ending a marriage was both costly and difficult. "Are you saying that Margaret Starling lied to the court when she testified against you?"

"No, she didn't lie. I was unfaithful to my wife—I'll admit it—but I'm hardly alone in that regard. What I objected to was the fact that Margaret instigated the divorce proceedings. Evangeline wouldn't have thought of such a thing if it hadn't been for Margaret's interference."

"Where does your former wife live?" Witherspoon thought it might be useful to speak to the lady.

"In Paris, Inspector." He smiled cynically. "She sold my home, packed up our belongings, and bought a house in Paris."

"She left the country?"

"Yes. She seemed to think the French are far more tolerant of divorced women than the English. That may or may not be true, but if she'd stayed here, she'd definitely be ostracized by our class of people."

"I take it your former wife was the one with the money," Barnes said.

"That's correct, so now I'm reduced to this miserable little flat and living off a tiny legacy left to me by a maiden aunt, and it's all thanks to that interfering old cow, Margaret Starling. I'm glad someone killed her."

Witherspoon glared at him. "Where were you on Sunday night?"

"I was here all evening."

"You cook for yourself?"

"Of course not, Inspector. I went out for an early dinner, but I was home by six o'clock. According to the newspaper reports, Mrs. Starling was killed late in the night, so it couldn't have been me."

"When was the last time you saw Mrs. Starling?" Barnes asked.

"A few days before she died, I went to see her."

"Was it a social call?" The constable didn't bother to keep the sarcasm out of his voice.

"Hardly, Constable. I went there to gloat."

"Gloat?" Witherspoon repeated.

"Oh, yes. You see, what Margaret didn't know was that I'd had a nice chat with the other members of the board of governors for the Angel Alms Society. She took something from me, so I decided to return the favor." His eyes narrowed and he broke into a smirk. "I wanted to let the cow know that I was getting back at her."

"How?" Barnes asked.

"Oh, it was easy, Constable. Margaret had been agitating for months to change the by-laws so women could be on the board. We were going to bring the matter up for a vote at the Christmas disbursement meeting, but I made certain it never even got on the agenda."

CHAPTER 7

Smythe stepped into the Dirty Duck Pub and stopped just inside the door so his eyes could adjust to the dim lighting. It was just past opening time, but the place was already busy. Sailors, dockworkers, tally clerks, businessmen, and bread sellers, their empty baskets propped on the hearth, lined the bar and sat at the benches along the walls. Every table was full to bursting as well.

Blimpey Groggins, the man he'd come to see, sat at the table closest to the fire with two others: a well-dressed man in a blue-and-gray-checked business suit, and a hard-looking man wearing scruffy clothes and a flat cap. He spotted Smythe, waved him over, then spoke to his companions. They got up, the businessman giving Smythe a curious glance as they left.

"You're a 'ard one to see." Smythe plopped into the stool opposite Blimpey. "Did ya get my message?"

"I did, and you'll be pleased to know that, despite the short notice, I've already found out a few juicy bits that your lot might find useful."

A portly man with a round red face, wispy ginger-colored hair, and sharp blue eyes, Blimpey owned the Dirty Duck as well as a number of other establishments in London. He was a buyer and seller of information. Blimpey's informants worked in the courts, all the prisons, the insurance companies, the shipping companies, all the newspapers, the hospitals, the docks, and Parliament, and there were even whispers he had a source or two at Buckingham Palace. He'd once been a burglar, but after a nasty fall from a second-story window and an even nastier encounter with an enraged mastiff, he'd changed occupations and put his phenomenally good memory to work. He was one of those people who never forgot a fact, and this ability had now made him very rich.

He catered to a diverse set of customers: businessmen needing market information, politicians looking to find a bit of dirt on their rivals, jealous wives suspicious of inattentive husbands, impoverished aristocrats searching for wealthy spouses, and anyone else who had the means to pay his exorbitant fees. But Blimpey had standards, and he drew the line at knowingly passing on facts that could cause physical harm to an innocent woman or child. Recently he'd made it clear to his customers that he'd rather not deal in information that was on the wrong side of the law. Most of his clients understood his decision, but there were a number of former customers who were still complaining about it. This new restriction was most probably due to the fact that he was now a husband and father. Respectability was important to him.

"You want something to drink?" Blimpey looked toward

the bar, where his man-of-all-work, Eldon, and a barmaid were busily dispensing pints.

"I'm fine," Smythe said. "Now, what 'ave you got for me?"

He had no concerns about paying for Blimpey's services. Smythe was a wealthy man. He'd gone to Australia after leaving the service of Euphemia Witherspoon, the inspector's aunt. He'd made a fortune there, come home, and stopped in to pay his respects to his former employer. He'd found Euphemia ill and being tended by Wiggins, a very young footman. The other household servants were robbing the woman blind. Smythe sent Wiggins for a doctor and tossed the rest of the staff out of the house. But it was too late to save the Euphemia's life. On her deathbed she made Smythe promise to stay on at Upper Edmonton Gardens to make certain her nephew, Gerald Witherspoon, would have a decent household that wouldn't take advantage of his innocent and unworldly character. Smythe agreed, but by the time he should have been ready to move on to his own life, he'd fallen in love with Betsy and become very fond of the others. The only fly in the ointment now was that he'd kept his wealth a secret from everyone but Betsy and Mrs. Jeffries. He hoped that when they found out they'd understand and forgive him for keeping them in the dark.

"That was quite a long list you gave me," Blimpey said. "But as I just told ya, I've found out a few bits and pieces. I've got people still workin', so what you don't find out today, we might learn tomorrow." He took a breath. "Let's start with Merton Nesbitt. He hated Margaret Starling because she testified against 'im in a divorce. Cost him dear, too; the wife was the one with the money, and she booted 'im of her 'ouse, sold it, and then moved to the Continent.

But from what we've 'eard, Nesbitt's never been violent. Mind you, 'e's broke and livin' off a small trust and what 'e can get by sellin' the few trinkets 'is wife didn't take when she left. Still, when 'e was in 'is cups, 'e wailed and moaned that it was all Margaret Starling's fault."

"But did 'e threaten 'er?" Smythe asked.

"Not that I know of, but wait, there's more to 'is story. Recently, Nesbitt told one of 'is mates that 'e'd got a letter from 'is former wife and that 'e 'ad 'opes of reconcilin' with the lady. Seems being a divorced woman is just as 'ard in France as it is 'ere. 'e claimed she'd told him she was lonely and 'inted that maybe the divorce was a mistake."

"Which could mean that now Merton Nesbitt 'ad a motive," Smythe murmured.

"Course it does. Someone like Nesbitt, a lazy upper-class sod that's never worked a real day in 'is life, wouldn't want Margaret Starling stickin' 'er oar in again and ruinin' it for 'im." He took a sip from his mug of coffee. "But time's a-wastin' and I've got to get 'ome early today. Nell and I are takin' the boy to see his great-aunt, and she'll 'ave my guts for garters if I'm late and we miss the ruddy train. So let's move on to the next one. We didn't find out much about Edgar Redstone—we're still workin' on that one—and we didn't find much about Graham McConnell. 'e's only been employed at the Angel Alms Society for two years, and before that he worked for a charity in Southampton. 'e goes down there once a quarter to visit 'is old mother."

Smythe nodded. "What did you find out about the Reverend Reginald Pontefract? 'e was involved in one of our other cases, but only as a witness, and our own sources 'ave found out a few ugly bits about 'im."

Blimpey chuckled. "Sounds like you already know what I'm goin' to tell ya. Turns out the good reverend 'ad a spot of bother at 'is last church, but it didn't 'ave a ruddy thing to do with that case of yours, either."

"Couldn't keep his 'ands to 'imself?"

He laughed outright. "Spot-on, Smythe. Accordin' to my source at Lambeth Palace, Reginald Pontefract was tossed out of 'is parish at Highgate—a very rich parish from what I understand—and sent south of the Thames because a number of young women claimed that 'e was overly familiar with their persons. That's the way the charge read."

"We found that out as well, but blast a Spaniard, that's disgustin'." Smythe frowned heavily. "Pontefract is a ruddy clergyman, someone a young woman would trust. Why didn't they just toss 'im out of the church altogether? Why send 'im somewhere else to do mischief?"

"Because 'e claimed it wasn't true—'e said the women were lying and as it was their word against 'is—the church fathers decided the easiest course would be just to get 'im out of the way." Blimpey nodded. "It's ugly, I'll grant you. This wasn't the only charge that's been laid at 'is doorstep, either."

"For God's sake, 'ow many complaints do they need before they take it seriously?" Smythe shook his head in disgust. "I've got a daughter, and men like 'im shouldn't be free to do as they like to innocent young girls, especially in a church."

"You'll not get an argument from me about that, but what I'm tellin' ya is the first complaint against Pontefract wasn't about 'im bein' too free with 'is 'ands. At 'is first parish, money went missin' from the Sunday collection, and there were those in the congregation that were sure Pontefract was 'elpin' 'imself to it. But nothin' was proved against him."

"Now, that makes sense." Smythe remembered what Ruth had told them. "No wonder he was so worried. Our source told us that Pontefract had admitted to her that he'd nicked three quid and he was afraid Margaret Starling knew about it."

"The church might look the other way a time or two when it's young girls accusin' Pontefract of actin' improperly"—Blimpey picked up his mug and took a quick sip—"but money is a whole different kettle of fish. If Mrs. Starling 'ad gone to them with proof 'e'd stolen money, they'd toss 'im out on 'is ear. That sounds to me like a motive to murder the woman."

Nivens leaned back in his chair and stared at Constable Forman, who was standing on the other side of the desk. "Why didn't you tell me that there was another copy of the postmortem report?"

He had his temper firmly under control now and had spent the last few hours giving his immediate problems a great deal of thought. The most pressing matter was finding out exactly what Gerald Witherspoon had written in his report to Chief Superintendent Barrows. But it wasn't going to be easy. He didn't have many sources of information at Scotland Yard, which was an unfortunate result of his actions and ambition. Forging friendships with colleagues and underlings never appealed to him; he'd always considered it a waste of time. That might have been a mistake, but right now he had to concentrate on his current difficulties.

Forman swallowed uneasily. "I didn't know about it, sir. No one said another one had been done. It's not standard procedure."

"Find out where and when it was delivered," Nivens ordered. "I want to make sure we don't have a traitor in our midst." That was a secondary matter, but it needed to be dealt with quickly. He had to find out who at the station was actively working to undermine him.

"A traitor, sir?" Forman edged toward the door. "I don't know what you mean."

"Don't be stupid, Forman," Nivens snapped. "If it was delivered here, then someone made certain it was given to Witherspoon. If it was delivered to the Ladbroke Road Station, then we'll need to keep an eye on Dr. Littleham. I know for a fact he was specifically told to send the report here. What's more, see if you can find out why he did two copies."

Forman's face fell. "To be perfectly honest, Inspector, I've noticed some of the lads have been avoiding me. I'm not sure anyone will tell me anything."

"For God's sake, Forman, you've bent my ear ever since I was sent here about how you want to be a detective, so use this incident to impress me. If the others won't tell you, get out and do some detecting work."

"All right, sir. Do you want me to ask Dr. Littleham directly why he did two copies?"

Nivens eyes narrowed. "Are you joking? Of course I don't want you to ask him directly. Use your head and figure out a way. For God's sake, Forman, you're no good to me if you can't find out a few simple facts."

"I'll find out, sir," Forman said quickly. "Really, but it might take a bit of time."

"We don't have time." Nivens drummed his fingers on the desktop. "Witherspoon might catch the killer, and I'll not have that. It simply can't happen—not when's he's barged onto my turf, stolen my case, and told a pack of lies about me to the chief superintendent."

Shocked, Forman gaped at him but said nothing.

Nivens was staring off into space with a calculating, speculative expression on his face. He looked at the constable. "Do you have any friends at Scotland Yard?"

Mrs. Jeffries picked up a clean rag, dabbed it in the open tin of silver polish, and pulled a dessert spoon from the box of silverware. She'd pulled the dining room curtains as far back as they'd go to take advantage of the pale winter sunshine. Downstairs, Mrs. Goodge was with one of her colleagues, and Mrs. Jeffries hoped the cook was learning something useful about this case. That would be very helpful. She'd decided to spend the morning polishing the silver because she was at her wit's end. She'd not been exaggerating when she'd complained to Constable Barnes and Mrs. Goodge that she had no idea who had killed Margaret Starling.

She smeared the spoon with a dab of polish and rubbed it vigorously. Polishing silver was the sort of mindless task that could help her see the connections between bits of seemingly unrelated facts.

First of all, she thought, who had the most to gain from this crime? She considered the question carefully. Margaret Starling's death meant Olivia Huxton wouldn't have to go to court and risk paying out damages in a slander lawsuit or having her social reputation ruined. Ruth's visit from Reverend Pontefract made it clear that he could lose his position as well as his reputation if she'd filed a complaint against him with the church hierarchy. But Pontefract had also told Ruth he only *thought* Mrs. Starling knew he'd stolen three pounds. He didn't know for certain that she'd found him out. He admitted he'd been to her house on the night of the murder, but that didn't necessarily make him the killer.

She tossed the cleaning rag onto an open copy of the previous day's newspaper, picked up a buffing rag, and polished the spoon. What about Merton Nesbitt or Edgar Redstone? Both had reasons to loathe the victim. They thought she'd ruined them financially, and she had. But her death would gain them nothing except some twisted emotional satisfaction. Was that enough? She wanted to think that couldn't possibly be the case, but the awful truth was that experience taught her that, for some people, destroying an enemy would be enough.

She finished with the spoon, put it to one side, and grabbed another piece of silverware. Mrs. Jeffries polished silver for two hours as she went over every detail they knew thus far. But it did her no good whatsoever.

"You're going around in circles," she muttered to herself. She closed the silverware box, picked it up, and put it away in the bottom drawer of the buffet. As she was gathering her supplies to go downstairs, she stopped. It suddenly occurred to her she might be looking at the case backward. Instead of asking who had the most to gain from Mrs. Starling's death, perhaps she should be asking who might have had the most to lose if the woman had stayed alive.

"Mr. Underwood said he was home all evening on Sunday night," Barnes murmured as he rejoined Witherspoon in the foyer. "He was sure it was Nesbitt who'd come in late and tracked up the foyer."

Witherspoon put on his bowler. "What time?"

"He didn't get out of bed to check the time, sir, but he heard Nesbitt's door slam." Barnes looked up the staircase. "Should we confront Nesbitt?"

"No. He'll just deny it, and a slammed door isn't particularly solid evidence." He put on his gloves. "I wonder if Constable Griffiths and Evans have had any luck verifying Nesbitt's and Redstone's whereabouts that night. That was a good suggestion; they're our constables and they know what they're doing. I'm not sure the local lads are up to the task."

"If either of them weren't home, someone in the neighborhood would have seen them going in or out of their homes." He opened the front door and stepped outside. "Where to now?"

"The Starling house," Witherspoon said. "I want to interview the servants again. Only one of them was forthcoming about how strange Mrs. Starling's behavior was in the weeks before she was killed. I think they can tell us more."

"You think they were lying?" Barnes started up the short stone walkway.

Witherspoon fell into step with him. "Not deliberately. But I suspect they didn't want to say anything that cast Mrs. Starling's character in a bad light. Murder is so shocking, and most people don't understand how important even insignificant details can be in catching the killer."

"I agree, sir," Barnes said. "They were holding back a bit. I sensed it as well. Plus I'd like to have a good look at the garden shed. Supposedly one of the first constables on the scene searched it, but I'd like to take a look for myself."

"Excellent. From what I've observed at the Upper Richmond Road Police Station, Inspector Nivens values loyalty from the rank-and-file lads rather than competence."

Octavia Wells reached for the blue-and-white coffeepot and poured the dark brew into the matching cups. "Margaret Starling was one of our best supporters." She handed Ruth her coffee. "I was so upset and angry when I learned she'd been murdered. I will do whatever I can to help your inspector catch whoever did this."

"She was a supporter of women's rights? I've never seen her at one of our meetings." Ruth stared at her friend.

Octavia was the treasurer of the London Women's Suffrage Society. Her hair was flaming red, her eyes brown, her complexion perfect, and her plump figure dressed by the finest seamstresses in London. She had long ago perfected the image of a silly matron obsessed with parties, gossip, and fashion, but in actuality she was smart and savvy and knew to the penny how much everyone in London's upper echelon was worth.

"She didn't come to meetings very often and she was a member of the Putney/Wandsworth group," Octavia explained. "She supported us with money rather than action. But she was highly respected and we'll miss her very much. Now, I know you're here because your Inspector Witherspoon caught the case."

"Yes"—Ruth nodded—"and we're not sure why it was given to him. Putney isn't his district."

"He got the case because I called the home secretary and told him to give it to him," Octavia explained. "Sorry, that probably doesn't make much sense to you. But my friend

Barbara Canton rang me early Monday morning and told me that Margaret had been murdered. Barbara's husband is a police superintendent. Well, I certainly didn't want that idiot Nivens on the case, so I did what had to be done and I called the home secretary. He owes me a favor, so I asked him very politely to send your inspector to take over. It's imperative whoever did this foul deed is brought to justice."

"You have a telephone?"

"Of course. You should get one as well. They're quite useful, and so many people have them nowadays. Lucky for us, the home secretary has one. Now, what do you need to know?"

"There are several people who had been quarreling with Mrs. Starling before she was killed. I was hoping you might know something about some of them." Ruth recited the names of the suspects.

Octavia thought for a moment. "The only thing I know about Merton Nesbitt is that his wife divorced him and she went to France. I've never heard of Edgar Redstone. As to this Reverend Pontefract, I've heard some ugly gossip about him. Apparently he's not to be trusted around young women."

"We've heard that as well, but what about Graham Mc-Connell?"

"That name doesn't sound familiar, either." Octavia took a sip of her coffee. "I'm sorry, Ruth, I'm not being terribly helpful. The only thing I know is that Ellen Ratchet—she's the correspondence secretary for the Putney/Wandsworth branch—said she saw Margaret Starling in Bayswater a few days before the murder. Ellen said she called out to Margaret, but she didn't hear her and simply continued walking and went into a private home." She smiled ruefully. "That's not particularly useful information."

"It could be," Ruth responded politely. "We never know what's going to be helpful. Did Ellen say where exactly she'd seen Margaret?"

"She didn't say, but it must have been Porchester Terrace. Ellen said she'd been visiting her sister, and that's where she lives."

"Did she say anything else?"

"Only that she wondered what Margaret was doing there and that she was carrying a parcel wrapped in brown paper."

"I don't understand, Inspector. You've already spoken to all the servants." Mrs. Wheaton looked confused. "Why do you need to speak to them again?"

"It's one of our methods, Mrs. Wheaton," Witherspoon explained. They were standing in the foyer of the Starling home. "Everyone was still in a state of shock when we did the first interview, and we've found that often, if you question people a second time, we learn some additional useful information."

"I've not had a chance to speak to Mr. Gormley," Barnes added.

"But he was interviewed by one of the constables."

"I know, but I'd like to speak to him myself."

"If you think it will help, then of course," she replied. "He is in the garden tidying up. And when you've finished with him, you can use the butler's pantry for your interviews."

"Thank you." The constable nodded and disappeared down the hallway to the back stairs.

She turned to the inspector. "You can use the dining room. I'll send the upstairs maid in."

"May I speak with you first?" he asked.

"Certainly, but I've told you everything I know." She caught herself. "All right, come along, then; let's get this done. Mrs. Starling's cousins are due here this afternoon. They'll be staying until after Christmas."

Witherspoon followed her. "Have you spoken with Mrs. Starling's solicitor?"

"The Biddlingtons? Yes. She has two of them; they're brothers. One of them is in Scotland until the twenty-third of the month, but Ronald Biddlington came on Tuesday." She shoved open the dining room doors and they went inside. "He was very kind and he told us that we could stay on until the will is read, and that won't be until after the New Year. We were all very relieved."

"I'm sure you were." Witherspoon pulled out a chair and sat down. Mrs. Wheaton remained standing. "Mrs. Wheaton, you'll be more comfortable if you sit."

She hesitated briefly before she took the chair next to him. "Sitting in here feels very odd, almost disrespectful."

"From what I've learned about your late mistress, I don't think she'd find it disrespectful in the least." He cleared his throat and tried to think of how to word the question he wanted to ask.

This morning Mrs. Jeffries reminded him that in all his previous cases he'd concentrated on the victims' actions in the days prior to their deaths. He'd realized that he'd asked her servants only the standard questions. He'd not delved deeply enough. "In the weeks before her murder, Mrs. Starling had a number of conflicts. But from what we've learned of her character, she wasn't by nature a quarrelsome woman. All of you, her servants, seem to have been devoted to her. She might have been opinionated and strong-minded, but she doesn't seem the type to have deliberately set out to make enemies. Have you any idea what was driving her behavior?"

"I've thought about that as well," Mrs. Wheaton sighed. "I think it started in October with that wretched letter. The vicar shouldn't have shown it to her. When she came home that day, she was dreadfully upset. She went into her study, wrote a note, and sent Fanny Herald to the Biddlingtons' office. He came for dinner that night."

"Mr. Ronald Biddlington?"

"No, his brother, Nelson. She demanded he file a slander suit against Mrs. Huxton. He tried to talk her out of it, but she was adamant—" She broke off with an embarrassed smile. "I wasn't eavesdropping, Inspector, I was helping serve that evening. But that's neither here nor there. What I do recall hearing is that Mrs. Starling seemed to feel that the vicar wasn't going to show the letter to the society's board of governors. Mr. Biddlington told her if no one but the vicar saw the letter and he kept silent on the matter, she had no basis for filing the suit. Apparently, it is only slander if your reputation is damaged. But she told Biddlington to file the suit anyway."

"Do you know why?"

"She was so hurt and angry. But it really wasn't like her, Inspector, and I think when she got over being so angry, she'd have withdrawn the lawsuit. But unfortunately she then found out the vicar hadn't kept silent. She'd not brought up the subject of the letter for ages, then all of a sudden—I think it was the first week in December—something happened and she discovered that he'd done precisely as she'd asked him not to do and shown the entire board the letter. When she went to see him, she was furious."

Witherspoon knew how the victim had found out, but now wasn't the time to share that information with her household. Not until they caught the killer.

Mrs. Wheaton's eyes filled with tears. "Between the letter, her worries about the finances at the society, and the arguments she'd had with Mr. Redstone and Mr. Nesbitt, I'm surprised she didn't have a stroke."

Arthur Gormley stared at Barnes out of watery gray eyes and then took an oversized handkerchief out of his trouser pocket and blew his nose. He was a tall man with a round red face weathered by hours spent outside. "You want to look inside the garden shed?"

"That's right," Barnes replied. "And I'd like to ask you a few questions as well."

"One of the constables has already asked me a lot of questions." He turned and picked up the pruning shears he'd put on one of the outstretched hands of the angel statue. "Come on, then. Have a look. But there's nothing but gardening equipment, rat poison, and paraffin." He started walking to the shed. "A constable already searched in there, so I don't know what you're expectin' to find."

Barnes trailed after him. "On the night that Mrs. Starling was killed, was the shed locked?"

Gormley gave a negative shake of his large head. "The shed's been here longer than the house. Them keys are long gone."

"Aren't you afraid someone will steal your tools?" Barnes asked.

"It's never happened before." They'd reached the shed, and Gormley turned the discolored brass knob. The door squeaked as it opened, and the gardener and Barnes stepped inside.

Two windows let in enough light so that Barnes could see properly. A worktable ran the length of the far wall. It held three rows of neatly stacked pots; half a dozen empty wooden seed trays, also stacked; a square clump of dirt under a damp burlap bag; hedge and pruning shears; and a tin of rat poison. Above the table was a set of shelves holding hand tools, seed catalogues, two tins of paraffin, and half a dozen open boxes containing nails and screws. Shovels, rakes, and hoes stood along the opposite wall. The concrete floor was chipped in spots but free from dirt or grease.

"Was the shovel used to murder Mrs. Starling stored in here?" It had been taken into evidence.

"It was right there." Gormley pointed to a spot on the wall within arm's reach of the door. "It's the heaviest one we've got. I use it in the winter to turn the earth over, but I'll never touch the wretched thing again. It should be burned."

Barnes stared at the empty space. Had the killer simply come inside and grabbed the first thing he or she could find, or had they been here before and knew the shovel was here for the taking?

"There's no lamp in here." Barnes looked around.

"No need of one. No one comes here at night."

Barnes stopped himself from pointing out that the killer had. Instead he said, "You keep a tidy shed."

"I do, I take pride in it," Gormley said. "Mind you, your lot could do better when tramping about someone else's patch."

"What do you mean?"

"One of your lads was smoking in here," He pointed to

the floor. "I found a spent match, and none of us smoke, especially not in here. This old wood could catch fire."

"When did you find it?" Barnes knew that none of the constables, even the ones from Upper Richmond Road, would dare smoke while on the job.

"Monday morning, I came in here as soon your lot searched it and made sure everything was as it should be."

"Excuse me, sir." One of the constables from Upper Richmond Road stuck his head into the shed. "If you've a moment, sir."

"I'll be right out," Barnes replied. He looked at the gardener. "Thank you for your help, Mr. Gormley." He stepped outside and motioned for the constable to follow him, He said nothing until they were at the edge of the terrace and out of anyone else's hearing. He gave the constable his full attention, noticing for the first time that the dark-haired young man had a baby face that didn't look old enough to shave, let alone be a police constable. "What's your name, Constable?"

"Brendon McNeil, sir, and I've found out something that might be important."

"Go on, then."

"One of the neighbors across the road, a Mrs. Larson, says that on Sunday night she saw the vicar from St. Andrew's at Mrs. Starling's house."

"She was sure it was him?"

"Yes. She said she'd seen a hansom cab pull up in front of Mrs. Starling's home and so she rushed outside to try and get it," he said eagerly. "She goes to St. Andrew's herself and she saw him quite clearly as he stepped out of the vehicle. She spoke to the driver and told him to wait a moment, and when she went to go back into her house, she said he was at Mrs. Starling's front door."

"She didn't greet the vicar, even though she's a member of his flock?"

"Mrs. Larson said she was in a hurry; she needed to get her aunt to the railway station before the last train left. She'd already sent a housemaid and a footman to the High Street to find a hansom, but they'd not come back, and she didn't want to risk losing this one by standing around in the cold, chatting with 'that idiot vicar'—her words, sir, not mine."

"Did you ask her what time she saw him?"

"Ten o'clock. She'd been checking the time because she didn't want her aunt to miss the last train."

"Good work, Constable. This could well be important," Barnes said. "Is the house-to-house done?"

"Yes, sir. Both Constable Peters and I finished, but the only thing we learned was what I've just told you."

Constable Griffiths smiled at Eliza Alston. But the portly white-haired woman didn't notice, as she was staring at the clock on the mantelpiece. "I don't want Mr. Redstone finding out what I've told you," she said. "I'm not expecting him back anytime soon, but with that one, you never know what he'll do."

The constable and the housekeeper were standing in Redstone's cluttered drawing room. Griffiths had come to Tavistock Road to interview the neighbors. Constable Barnes had made it clear that verifying the whereabouts of both Redstone and Nesbitt on the night Mrs. Starling was killed was important. Griffiths and Constable Evans had split up, with Evans heading to Cedar Lane to talk to Nesbitt's neighbors.

When Griffiths turned the corner onto Tavistock Road, he'd seen a man he assumed to be Redstone leaving the house and getting into a hansom. He saw the housekeeper through the window and decided to try his luck. If she knew nothing, he'd try the neighbors.

At first Mrs. Alston was evasive and told him she had left at six o'clock the night of Mrs. Starling's murder and had no idea if Redstone had been home or not. But then something, perhaps her conscience, had prodded her, and she'd told him plenty. He couldn't wait to pass it along to Constable Barnes and Inspector Witherspoon.

"Mrs. Alston, this is a murder investigation, but I will do my very best to be discreet about everything you've told me," Griffiths assured her. "But I do need to make absolutely sure of the facts. You're positive Mr. Redstone wasn't home on Sunday night?"

"Of course I am," she snapped. "You think I'd make something like this up? When he's in his cups, he does nothing but complain about Mrs. Starling, blaming her for ruining his life and turning him into a pauper. Mr. Redstone wasn't home the night Mrs. Starling was killed. I fixed his supper and left it on the sideboard, just as I always do, and then I left. But I'd just got to the pub when I realized I'd left my coin purse here. Well, I had to come back, didn't I? Mr. Alston won't eat his supper without his ale, and I always stop on my way home and get it for him. Mr. Alston visits his brother every Sunday afternoon, but the omnibus drops him off at the other end of our street from the pub, so I always buy the ale on Sundays." She picked up a cleaning cloth from the table. "When I got back here, Mr. Redstone was gone."

"If he wasn't here, how did you get inside?"

"I've a key; I let myself in, had a good look around to make certain he'd not had a fall or something awful like that, then I found my purse and left."

"What time did you arrive here?" Griffiths asked.

"About half past six."

"So he could have just stepped out for a walk," he pressed. "You don't know that he was gone for the evening."

"I most certainly do." She glared at him. "The next morning Mr. Selby from next door asked if Mr. Redstone was feeling better. Apparently, Mr. Redstone was in his cups again and Mr. Selby helped the hansom driver get him into the house. Mr. Selby told me it was after eleven when he came home."

"Have you any idea where Mr. Redstone went?"

"No, but it was obviously somewhere he could get drunk. Look, it's not my business, and he isn't one to appreciate questions. Now, if it's all the same to you, he might come back any moment. This isn't the best position I've ever had, but at my age it was all I could get, and I'd like to keep it."

"Of course." Griffiths knew when it was time to quit. "Thank you for your assistance, Mrs. Alston. I'll see myself out."

Everyone arrived for their afternoon meeting on time.

"Cor blimey, Mrs. Goodge, this is a real treat." Wiggins grinned from ear to ear as he settled into his chair. "Mince tarts, brown bread, and your raspberry jam."

"It's a cold day and I thought we could use a bit of cheer." The cook took her own seat. "Now, before we start, I've found out something, but I've no idea if it's useful or not and

I'd like to go first, because I've a pork roast in the oven. I've got to see to the potatoes and carrots as well."

"Do go ahead, Mrs. Goodge." Mrs. Jeffries finished pouring out the tea and began handing round the cups.

"On the night Margaret Starling was killed, Merton Nesbitt wasn't home. He was seen at the Three Swans; that's a pub on the Upper Richmond Road less than a quarter mile from the Starling home."

"Your source was certain of this?" Mrs. Jeffries asked.

The cook nodded as she got to her feet. "She was. She wasn't in the pub herself, but her friend was and she told my source. Nesbitt is well-known in the neighborhood."

"Why is that?" Phyllis asked.

"Because he's divorced, and during the trial or whatever it is they do nowadays, there was some scandalous gossip about him."

"You have to go to court to get a divorce," Betsy murmured. "Don't you?"

"You do now, but it used to be by a Private Act of Parliament," Mrs. Goodge said. "It cost the earth. When I was young, I had a position in a household where the husband was trying to divorce his wife. Mind you, he could never prove she'd been unfaithful, so despite spending hundreds of pounds, they were stuck with each other. It was a miserable place and they couldn't keep servants. I stayed only for three months myself."

"If Nesbitt was in a pub, why would he lie to the inspector? He must have been seen by dozens of people that night," Hatchet speculated. "Why tell a lie that is so easily disproved."

"He was probably scared to tell the truth." Mrs. Goodge went to the oven, opened the door, and pulled out the roast.

Grabbing a spoon from the counter, she began basting the juices over the meat.

"Nesbitt and the other suspects have been lucky so far," Betsy declared. "Nivens hasn't cooperated properly with our inspector. He's not given him any additional constables to help question the local people." She turned to her husband. "You ought to go to the Three Swans and see if you can find out when Nesbitt left that night. Or even better—find out if someone might have seen where he went."

"It'll take 'ours to get across the river this time of day. The Three Swans isn't goin' anywhere, so I can do it tomorrow. I've found out a few bits myself." He glanced at the cook. "I'm sorry, you done?"

"Yes. You go on." She put the basting spoon on the saucer next to the cooker and took the lid off the saucepan and frowned. "These need another twenty minutes before they can be drained. Sorry; go on, Smythe. I'm talkin' to myself."

"I 'ad a word with one of my sources, and it seems that Merton Nesbitt might 'ave 'ad a good reason for keepin' Margaret Starling quiet and out of 'is life." He told them what he'd learned from Blimpey Groggins.

"Nesbitt's wife was thinking of reconciling?" Mrs. Jeffries tapped her fingers against the handle of her mug. "He told this to his friends?"

"That's right." Smythe grinned. "Nesbitt isn't one to 'old 'is tongue or 'is liquor. 'e wouldn't want Margaret Starling stickin' 'er nose in 'is business and ruinin' it for 'im."

"How would she find out?" Phyllis asked. "Was Mrs. Nesbitt in contact with Mrs. Starling?"

"My source didn't know, but she could have been, and

Margaret Starling has a lot of influence over her. She wasn't just her friend; she was Mrs. Nesbitt's godmother."

"But is that a strong enough reason to kill someone?" Ruth asked.

"People 'ave been murdered for less than that," Smythe said. "'e's no money and his wife was 'intin' she might want 'im back. 'e'd not want anythin' or anyone muckin' that up for 'im."

"And now we know he wasn't home the night she was murdered." Mrs. Goodge took her seat again.

"But that's not all I found out," Smythe continued. "Turns out that Graham McConnell 'as only been at the Angel Alms Society for two years. Before that 'e worked for a charity in Southampton. 'is old mother lives there and 'e visits 'er once a quarter. That's it from me."

"Who'd like to go next?" Mrs. Jeffries glanced around the table.

"I will," Ruth offered. She told them about her meeting with Octavia Wells.

"Well, nells bells, she's the one that got us this murder!" Luty exclaimed.

Ruth smiled. "I'm afraid so. She has a telephone device and she called the home secretary and asked him to take Inspector Nivens off the case and put Gerald on it."

"So your source knew that Nivens is incompetent?" Hatchet asked.

"Oh, yes, she knows everything that goes on in London," Ruth explained. "Margaret Starling was a staunch supporter of women's rights, and Octavia didn't want her murder to go unpunished. But that's not the only thing she told me. A day or so before she was killed, one of our members saw Margaret in Bayswater. She was going into a house and she was carrying a paper-wrapped parcel."

"Bayswater," Luty said. "Where at in Bayswater? Do ya know?"

"She wasn't absolutely positive, but from the circumstances Octavia thought it must have been Porchester Terrace. Why?" She looked at Luty curiously.

"Because that's where I was today," Luty explained. "That's where Nelson Biddlington lives. I went to see him but he's not home. He won't be back to London until the evening of the twenty-third."

"He's the man that Margaret Starling wanted to have a look at the Angel Alms Society financial records," Mrs. Jeffries said. "So perhaps that's why Mrs. Starling was there."

"That's certainly possible," Ruth said. "Look, there's something I must ask. As you all know, Reginald Pontefract came to me because he's desperately frightened he's going to be arrested. But I've no idea how to broach the subject with Gerald. On the other hand, I don't think Reginald is a murderer, and I did tell him I'd try to help. Oh, dear, I don't know what is the proper or ethical course of action."

No one said anything for a moment. Finally, Wiggins broke the silence. "Does 'e think our inspector is goin' to arrest 'im just because he was at Mrs. Starling's house that night?"

"Yes, that's his main concern. He was there that night."

"But Nesbitt wasn't home, either. 'E was at a pub less than a quarter mile from the Starling house. 'e's got as much motive as Pontefract," Wiggins observed.

"True, but I'm still very much in a quandary. I told Reginald to tell Gerald the truth and to trust in both God and the legal system." Ruth shook her head, her expression sad. "But I don't think he believes very strongly in either. In any case, I'll not burden Gerald just yet. That simply isn't right."

"Stop worrying, Ruth, I'm sure it will work out fine," Mrs. Jeffries said. "Who'd like to go next?"

"Mine won't take long," Phyllis said. She told them about her encounter with Stuart Deeds. "He's a nice young man, but once he started talking, he did go on a bit. He said that for the last six weeks Margaret Starling was talking to the board members, asking them questions about the finances and how often the books were examined, who examined them, and what percentage of the donations was in coin and notes. It's quite a lot, actually. Stuart reckons about thirty percent, but he didn't know for certain, as Graham McConnell opens all the post and all Stuart does is the acknowledgment correspondence." She stopped and took a quick sip of tea. "Then he went on and on about odd things happening at the society: A man's coat went missing from the donation cupboard last week. Then he said there was a bit of paper jammed in the typewriter machine, and supposedly three bags of clothes have been donated to the society but he can't find them anywhere and he thinks someone stole them and he'll get blamed for it."

"Did he give you any details or dates as to when these things happened?" Mrs. Jeffries asked. A tiny idea nudged the back of her mind and then disappeared before she could get hold of it properly.

"I tried to get that out of him," Phyllis said. "But then the omnibus came and he got away from me. But if you think anything he said might be important, I'll make sure I talk to him again."

"Don't make a special effort to see him as yet. At this point I've no idea what is or isn't important." Mrs. Jeffries sighed. "Let's hope the inspector will be have learned something today that can help us catch Margaret Starling's killer."

Mrs. Goodge got up again and went to the oven. "Don't be so discouraged, Mrs. Jeffries. You'll figure this one out."

"Of course she will!" Betsy cried. "She always does."

But this time Mrs. Jeffries wasn't so sure.

CHAPTER 8

Constable Barnes waited outside the dining room while the inspector finished his second interview with Fanny Herald. He'd already told Mrs. Wheaton that they would be back the next day to complete the second round of interviews.

She'd not bothered to hide her relief. "That would be best, Constable. Mrs. Starling's cousins are arriving this afternoon, and frankly we're not certain what we should do. We've no idea if we ought to plan Christmas dinner for the guests or whether they'll be in mourning and not want any festivities. In any case, it's a dreadfully awkward situation. We've still to get the guest rooms properly aired, and Cook still hasn't received the meat order from the butcher—" She broke off with an embarrassed smile. "I'm sorry. By tomorrow things ought to be more settled." She then disappeared down the corridor without waiting for him to reply.

The dining room doors opened and Fanny stepped out.

She held a crumpled handkerchief to her mouth, her cheeks were tearstained, and her eyes were red. She took one look at the constable, choked back a sob, and ran to the back stairs.

Barnes stared after her for a moment and then stepped into the dining room. Witherspoon got up, his expression troubled. "Thank goodness you're here. Miss Herald is most upset and I've no idea why. One moment I was asking her questions about Mrs. Starling's last weeks, and the next she was crying." He waved his hands in a gesture of confusion. "Did you speak with the gardener?"

"Yes, sir, but the reason I'm here and not in the butler's pantry interviewing the kitchen servants is because the constables interviewing the neighbors on Moran Place had something interesting to report. It seems Reverend Pontefract was here on the night Mrs. Starling was murdered. Mrs. Larson across the road saw him. It's not that late, sir. We've time to go to St. Andrew's Church and have a chat with him." He broke off as the downstairs maid stepped out of the open door of the drawing room. She was carrying a tin of furniture polish and a cleaning rag.

"Do you want to speak to me next?" She directed her question to Witherspoon.

"No, no, we'll be back tomorrow, miss."

"Right, sir. I'll go back to my cleaning, then." She nodded politely and went back to the drawing room.

Neither of them spoke until they were outside. Witherspoon sighed. "I do feel bad about Miss Herald; she just started crying."

"We can talk about it on our way to the church, sir,"

Barnes suggested. "I've let Mrs. Wheaton know we're leaving and that we'll be back tomorrow to finish up the second round of interviews."

"Right. Then let's go."

They left the house and made their way to the Upper Richmond Road, where Barnes found a hansom. As soon as they were inside, Witherspoon said, "Honestly, Constable, I'll never understand women. One moment Miss Herald was fine, and the next she was weeping."

"What exactly did you ask her, sir?" Barnes grabbed the handhold as the vehicle lurched forward.

Witherspoon pushed his spectacles up his nose. "I asked her to tell me about Mrs. Starling's behavior since she'd found out about the anonymous letter sent to the vicar. At first she said she'd noticed nothing, but then she admitted there were two incidents she found troubling. The first one was in November, when Mrs. Starling had returned home from an alms society meeting. It was Miss Herald's afternoon out, but before she could leave, Mrs. Starling called her into her study and gave her a letter to post. She remembered it clearly because Mrs. Starling told her three times that the letter had to make the early afternoon post. She said it made her curious, so she took care to notice the name and address. It was to a Mrs. Minton in Chelmsford."

"Did she know the address?"

"Not the house number, but she remembered it was on Fordham Way," Witherspoon said. "The second incident took place over several days in the two weeks before Mrs. Starling's death. She said that Mrs. Starling kept going to St. Andrew's Church during the day and that she'd done it three different times. I said that perhaps Mrs. Starling had gone there for spiritual reasons. She said no, that wasn't it, because she'd seen her in the sanctuary and two out of the three times Mrs. Starling had simply stood in the back of the church as if she was waiting for something. The third time it happened was only a few days before Mrs. Starling was murdered, and that time she noticed that Mrs. Starling went into the small storage room at the front of the church. When she came out, she was carrying a book."

"Ye gods, was the girl spying on her mistress?"

"In a way, yes, and I think that's the reason for the tears," he explained. "The first time she saw Mrs. Starling, the housekeeper had sent her to get a set of curtain rings at the draper's shop. When she got there, she was told there were two kinds and which did the Starling household need? Well, she didn't know, so she was on her way back, when she saw Mrs. Starling going into St. Andrew's and she thought the mistress might know, so she dashed inside, but she said Mrs. Starling was walking up the center aisle, when she suddenly stopped, turned around, and left. Miss Herald said she was so taken aback—that there was something so odd about Mrs. Starling's expression—that she ducked behind a pillar until her employer had left the building."

"What about the second and third time?" Barnes asked. The hansom pulled up to the curb and he stepped out, holding the door for the inspector.

"The second time she admitted she had followed Mrs. Starling. It was her afternoon out and she'd been to see a cousin in East Barking and planned on going to the Evensong service at St. Andrew's. She was early, though, and saw Mrs. Starling going up the church steps. She followed her inside. She said the very same thing happened. Mrs. Starling was halfway up the center aisle, when she suddenly changed her mind and left."

"And Miss Herald leapt behind another pillar." Barnes paid the driver. "Did she happen to notice if other people had either come into the church from the churchyard or were already inside?"

"I was going to ask that very question," Witherspoon replied, "but then she started to cry. She did manage to tell me that the third time she'd seen Mrs. Starling go into the church, she followed her deliberately."

The two policemen climbed up the broad steps to the church.

"Did she say why she'd done it?" Barnes grabbed the door handle and pulled it open, and they stepped inside.

"She said by that time she was just plain curious. She thought perhaps Mrs. Starling was having some strange religious experience. I think we need to speak with her again," Witherspoon started up the aisle. "Now, let's go see what Reverend Pontefract has to say for himself."

"Of course, sir. Uh, do you need me to stay when you're speaking to the vicar? I'd like to question Tom Lancaster," Barnes said. His mind was racing. There was more to this story than a housemaid satisfying her curiosity. He wanted the real reason the tweeny had followed her mistress, and Fanny Herald would be more likely to tell Wiggins or Phyllis the real story rather than a middle-aged constable or inspector. He also thought the verger might be able to add a detail or two. Lancaster seemed like the kind of man who kept his eyes on everything.

They reached the vicar's study and Witherspoon knocked.

"Come in."

They stepped inside. The reverend rose to his feet, his expression sour. "What are you doing here?"

"We'd like to speak with you," Witherspoon replied. "It's very important."

"If you must." Pontefract sat back down. He didn't invite them to sit in the two chairs in front of his massive desk.

Constable Barnes spoke first. "Is the verger here? I'd like to have a word with him."

"Why do you need to see him? I've told you, the man is a liar."

"Please, sir, just answer the question. Is he here?"

"He's in the churchyard," Pontefract snapped. "At least, that's where he's supposed to be, but the fellow is so lazy, he's probably off sleeping in a pew somewhere. Good luck finding him."

"Thank you, sir." Barnes disappeared out the door.

From the expression on the vicar's face, Witherspoon suspected he'd be as uncooperative and obstructive as possible. "Reverend Pontefract, on the night of Mrs. Starling's murder, you said you were here all evening."

"That is correct," he replied. "After Evensong, I had dinner and then I worked on my sermon."

"Are you certain of that, sir?

"Of course I am." Pontefract looked annoyed. "There's nothing wrong with my memory, Inspector. I was here all evening."

"We have a witness who claims to have seen you getting out of a hansom cab in front of the Starling house and at her front door."

"That's absurd." Pontefract leapt to his feet. "Who said that? Was it that liar, Lancaster? I was here all evening."

"It wasn't your verger, sir. Not only do we have a witness that saw you, but we can easily find the hansom driver," Witherspoon warned.

Pontefract seemed to sink into himself for a moment, then he flopped into his chair. "My God, this is a nightmare. Yes, I'll admit it, I did go to see her, but I didn't kill her. I wanted to talk to her, to find out why she was asking all those questions about the finances of the charity."

"That was the only reason you went to see her?"

He nodded dully. "But she didn't even answer the door. No one did. I knocked and knocked and no one came. Then I remembered that she'd given her servants the night off, so I assumed she'd gone with them or perhaps gone to a friend's house. I left and came back here."

"Why didn't you tell us the truth to begin with?" The inspector watched him carefully. Reading people's expressions wasn't his strongest ability, but he had become much better at it than he used to be.

"I was afraid." Pontefract sighed heavily, closed his eyes for a moment, and lifted his chin toward the heavens. "Thanks to Lancaster's scurrilous comments, you already knew that she'd threatened to go to the bishop about me. Fear can make a fool out of any man."

"Even if Mrs. Starling had gone to the bishop, what could she have told him?" Witherspoon asked.

"I'm not sure." The vicar looked down at his desk. "She never actually said. When we were having our disagreement, all she said was 'How would you like it if I go to the bishop with what I know?' But she never told me specifically what it was that she knew."

Witherspoon sensed he was lying. "Then why were you so upset about the threat?"

"Because at my last parish there were some charges laid against me—charges that were never proven, I might add. Nonetheless, one's career could be badly damaged if more lies were told. I've done nothing wrong here, and truthfully I've no idea what she thought she knew about me. Perhaps she considered my sermons to be unorthodox, or perhaps she didn't like the way I conducted the service. Her behavior was so bizarre that there was no telling what she'd say. All I know is I didn't want someone of her stature and wealth making groundless charges to the bishop."

Witherspoon didn't care if Pontefract had violated church law or committed heresy. That wasn't his jurisdiction. "What time was it when you went there?"

"It was late, well after dinner. I'd had too much wine, and for some reason I convinced myself I could talk her into being reasonable."

"Reasonable about what? Going to the bishop? Or reasonable about her concerns over the alms society finances? You did claim that she'd been asking a lot of odd questions."

"Both, but mainly the bishop. Frankly, the finances of the Angel Alms Society aren't really my concern. My career is."

Barnes found Lancaster in the back of the sanctuary. He was carrying a bucket of water. "I'd like a word, please."

"Course. What is it?" He put the pail on the floor.

"In the days prior to Mrs. Starling's murder, I know she

was at the alms society for their meetings, but did she spend much time here in the church?" Barnes asked.

"On Sundays she was here, and a time or two during the week I saw her coming in during the afternoon or early evening."

"When did you see her?"

He thought for a moment. "I don't know the exact days, but it was in the last two weeks before she was murdered. Both times she went into the church, then a few minutes later she popped out again."

His statement confirmed what Fanny Herald had told the inspector. "When was the last time you saw her here?"

"Oh, that was just a day or two before she died. It was before Evensong service; I'd come in to light the lamps and make sure everything was at the ready." He cocked his head and scratched the stubble on his chin. "Come to think of it, she was actin' right funny that time. I saw her come out of the old chapel room."

"Chapel room?"

Lancaster pointed to the front of the church. "It's that first door in the corridor on the far side of the altar rail. It's a storage room now, but at one time it was a private chapel. A lot of churches had them, you know, so the lords and ladies wouldn't have to mingle with the rest of us."

"Right. Go on, then."

"It was one of them twilight days; it'd been raining and I'd not done the lamps, so it was gettin' dark. I didn't want to scare her, so I didn't say anything until she'd got to the pew where she'd put her carpetbag and cloak. Then I said hello and asked if she needed any help. Mind you, my eyesight isn't what it used to be, but it looked like she was carryin' a book. I thought she might be nickin' a hymnal, 'cause she saw me and then tucked it in her carpetbag right quick, grabbed her fancy cloak, and rushed out like the hounds of hell was at her heels."

"You thought she was hiding something?" Barnes asked.

"That's right. For a minute or two, I thought she might be stealin'. But then I realized someone as rich as her wouldn't be nickin' hymnals or tattered copies of the prayer book."

"Thank you, Mr. Lancaster," Barnes said.

The verger nodded, picked up his bucket, and went out the side door to the churchyard. Barnes pulled out his notebook and pencil and made notes of his conversation with the verger. He was almost finished when he heard the front door open. He looked toward the narthex and was surprised to see a constable from the Upper Richmond Road Police Station.

"I'm glad you're here, sir." Constable Sorrell hurried toward him. "I was afraid you and the inspector might have already left."

"How did you know where we were?"

"One of the servants at the Starling house overheard you say you were coming here," he explained. He pulled an envelope out of his inside coat pocket. "Sergeant Wylie sent me. This is for you and the inspector."

Barnes took the envelope, noting that it hadn't been sealed. "This is from Sergeant Wylie?"

"That's right. He had some information he needed to pass along as soon as possible."

Barnes read the note and then looked at Sorrell. "Did he say how he found out this tidbit?"

"He said to tell you a little bird told him." Sorrell tried not to smile but failed miserably. "Truth is, Constable Barnes, sometimes it's impossible not to *accidentally* overhear things. Sometimes, some people have very loud voices."

"I see." Barnes laughed and shoved the note in his pocket. "I'll make sure the inspector sees this right away. And please tell Sergeant Wylie he has our thanks."

"I will," Sorrell replied. "Uh, just so you'll know, Constable Forman is already on his way to Scotland Yard."

"Nivens wants him to find out what Inspector Witherspoon wrote in his report?" Barnes knew there hadn't been a report as yet, but Forman didn't need to know that. "Does he have connections to anyone at the Yard?"

Sorrell shook his head. "No, he's not been in the force long enough. Forman's a right bootlicker, and the boots he's lickin' now are on Inspector Nivens' feet. He thinks being the inspector's lapdog will help his career, but according to the sergeant, no one at the Yard will tell him anything."

"Good, but I'm more concerned about Dr. Littleham. I'd not like to see him damaged by having helped us."

"Don't worry about that, Constable." Sorrell grinned. "Sergeant Wylie wrote him a note as well."

Mrs. Jeffries was in the foyer waiting for the inspector when he arrived home. "I'm so glad you're home, sir. I was afraid that you'd be out late because of the Starling murder, and there's a storm brewing."

"It's going to be a bad one as well; it's already started to rain and the wind is howling." He handed her his bowler and then unbuttoned his heavy overcoat, slipped it off, and hung it on the peg. "Gracious, it's been quite a day. We learned a lot of information, and I, for one, need a bit of time to understand it all. Do we have time for a nice glass of sherry?"

"Of course, sir. Mrs. Goodge has made a lovely pork roast for tonight, and she's got it resting in the warming oven." She led the way to his study, went to the cupboard, and had both of them a glass poured by the time he'd settled in his chair.

She handed him his drink and took her own seat. "Now do tell me about your day, sir."

He took a sip from the delicate cut-crystal glass. "We started out at the Upper Richmond Road Police Station, and for once we managed to get some help from two of their lads. Unfortunately, I had to threaten Inspector Nivens."

Mrs. Jeffries, who was putting her glass on the side table, was so shocked her hand jerked, spilling a few drops of her drink. "You threatened Inspector Nivens? Goodness, sir, what happened?"

"I'm a bit ashamed of myself, Mrs. Jeffries—I do pride myself on controlling my temper—but this morning I was annoyed." He told her about his altercation with his fellow officer. "So not only did I threaten him, I also lied. I told him I'd already reported his behavior, which, of course, I haven't. But I fully intend to do so." He paused to take a sip of his sherry. "What's more, apparently some of the officers at Upper Richmond Road don't think highly of Inspector Nivens, and, well, they've done something I'm not sure I ought to approve of"—he paused—"but I do."

Mrs. Jeffries was still reeling, but she found her tongue enough to ask the right question. "What did they do, sir?"

Witherspoon chuckled. "Oh, dear, I shouldn't laugh, but

it is funny. Someone must have overheard both my exchange with Inspector Nivens and his conversation with a young constable after I'd left." He told her about receiving Sergeant Wylie's note and Constable Sorrell's conversation with Barnes. "There wasn't much in the note—only a warning that Nivens had sent a constable to the Yard to find out what was in my report about Nivens and that he was actively trying to hobble the investigation. That's the one thing I can't forgive, Mrs. Jeffries. But as they say, forewarned is forearmed."

"You're not worried about Nivens damaging you?"

"Not at all," he said, shrugging. "As a matter of fact, I'm both touched and humbled that so many officers are prepared to offer their assistance to someone outside their own district. But time is getting on, and we don't want to let Mrs. Goodge's nice roast dry out. After we left the station, we interviewed Edgar Redstone." He told her about their conversation. "I did find it interesting that he told us that Reverend Pontefract and Graham McConnell were even more disappointed than he was."

"You mean because they both assumed that the late Mrs. Redstone's mother was going to leave a large percentage of her estate to the Angel Alms Society?" Mrs. Jeffries asked.

He nodded. "He also made certain to mention that, with Margaret Starling dead, the society will get their legacy now."

"That should make Reverend Pontefract and the board of governors happy," she murmured. As he'd been speaking, an idea had flown into her head and refused to leave. She was always telling Witherspoon to listen to his "inner voice," so perhaps it was time for her to do the same. "Inspector, have you considered that you should speak to someone at the Angel Alms Society?"

"We've already interviewed Graham McConnell, and I've got the names and addresses of the board. They're on my list of people to see."

"What about the clerk, sir?" Mrs. Jeffries asked. "You made me think of him when you were telling me about the rank-and-file constables at Upper Richmond Road and how they'd found out Nivens was trying to interfere in your investigation. Perhaps that young clerk knows something."

Witherspoon looked at her over his spectacles, which had slipped down his nose. "That sounds like a very good idea. I'll put him on our interview list for tomorrow. Thank you for the suggestion, Mrs. Jeffries."

"Don't thank me sir," she chuckled. "You know good and well it was your own 'inner voice.' *Your* description of how the lads at Upper Richmond Road knew what Nivens was up to is what prompted me to think you should interview the clerk."

"Well, that's kind of you to say, Mrs. Jeffries," he said, and gave her a grateful smile. "After we left Redstone, we interviewed Merton Nesbitt. He claimed he was home when Mrs. Starling was murdered, but we're fairly sure he wasn't." He told her the details of their visit to Merton's flat and their conversation with the maid.

"She's sure it was Monday morning that the mud was tracked into the foyer?" Mrs. Jeffries said.

"Absolutely. And as neither she nor the owner of the house had gone out that night, it had to be one of the tenants. Mr. Underwood not only told us that he'd been home all evening, he also said he'd heard Nesbitt come in late that night."

"Interesting." She took a sip of sherry. "He admitted he

was the one to keep Mrs. Starling's request that women be allowed on the board off the agenda. He must have really hated her."

"He did. He felt her interference cost him everything."

Mrs. Jeffries silently thanked her lucky stars. This could be the perfect time to nudge the inspector to take a closer look at Nesbitt. Smythe's source said that Nesbitt told his friends that his wife might want to reconcile. "Perhaps he wanted to make certain she didn't interfere again."

"What do you mean?"

"Well, it's not unheard of for estranged couples to re-unite. Perhaps Nesbitt was going to write to his former wife to ask for a reconciliation. He'd not want Margaret Starling using her influence to ruin his chances of getting his wife and her money back."

"That's possible, I suppose. But there's very little we could do to find out if such a situation were true or not."

"You could ask Mr. Nesbitt's friends," she said. "Men do sometimes like to boast about such matters, especially if they've had a drink or two. But, of course, you know that. Where did you go after that?"

"We went to the Starling house. We wanted to conduct second interviews with the servants. Sometimes people will recall additional details after the shock has worn off a bit. Constable Barnes wanted to have a look at the garden shed as well." He took a sip of sherry. "I must say, Mrs. Jeffries, I'll never understand women."

"Goodness, sir, what happened?"

"Let me start from the beginning." He repeated what he'd heard from Mrs. Wheaton and told her about Constable Barnes learning that a match had been found in the garden shed. "The gardener was sure the match hadn't been dropped by a member of the household, and Constable Barnes is equally certain it wasn't a police constable who tossed it onto the floor."

"You think the murderer dropped it?"

"I do. There's no lamp or light in the shed, and we know that she was killed after dark. It's very possible the killer used it to get the shovel out of the shed." He finished his sherry and set the glass on the side table.

"Would you like another, sir?"

"No. I'm very tired, and another sherry might put me to sleep." He put his hand over his mouth to hide a yawn. "After I spoke to Mrs. Wheaton, I spoke with the tweeny, Fanny Herald, and it was dreadfully uncomfortable. She started to cry." He repeated everything he'd told Constable Barnes about the awkward interview. "Honestly, I quite understand why Miss Herald behaved the way she did. I'd be curious as well. What I don't understand is Mrs. Starling's behavior."

"Are you sure Fanny Herald was telling the truth?" Mrs. Jeffries wasn't sure what to make of it, but once again a thought flitted into her head and then flitted out before she could grab it.

"Yes. Constable Barnes spoke with the verger at St. Andrew's and he recalled seeing Mrs. Starling there in the late afternoon on several occasions in the two weeks before her death. The third time he saw her, Mrs. Starling was coming out of the private chapel. It's now a storage room, but I must say, hearing someone use that term reminded me of 'priest's holes' and hiding places. You know, when King Henry dissolved the Roman churches and monasteries. Many Catholics refused to convert, and they had hiding places for their priests and their rosaries."

"I didn't realize St. Andrew's was that ancient," Mrs. Jeffries remarked. Dozens of thoughts were swirling in her head, but she didn't have time to think about them now. She needed to listen.

"Neither did I, but apparently at least some part of the building is quite old," he said.

"Did the verger say anything else?" She didn't want to rush him, but the roast was going to be dry if he took too much longer.

"That's all Constable Barnes told me. Oh goodness, I didn't tell you that one of the constables interviewing the neighbors on Moran Place reported that Pontefract was seen at the Starling home Sunday night. That's why we broke off the interviews and went to the church." He recounted what the vicar had told him.

"So he admitted to being at the Starling home that night but insisted he had nothing to do with her murder," she said. "That's interesting. Do you believe him?"

"At this point I'm not sure what to believe. Information is coming so quickly that it's difficult to make sense of what really happened that night."

"Are you sure you wouldn't like another sherry, sir?" Mrs. Jeffries asked, more to buy a bit of time to think than anything else.

"You've talked me into it, Mrs. Jeffries. But if we ruin Mrs. Goodge's roast, I'm blaming you." He laughed as he handed her his glass. "Thank you, yes. Honestly, Mrs. Jeffries, it's a very complicated case and I've not told you all of it. After we left St. Andrew's, Constable Griffiths tracked us down and told us he'd found out that Edgar Redstone wasn't home that night."

She kept her back to him and listened as she filled their glasses.

"So, in addition to speaking to the rest of the Starling servants, the board, and the clerk at the Angel Alms Society, we've got to reinterview Edgar Redstone as well as Merton Nesbitt. We've so much to do tomorrow."

"Don't get discouraged sir. At least now you've more help," she reminded him. She took their drinks and went back to her seat. "Despite Inspector Nivens' nasty attempts to thwart the investigation, you've two more constables as well as the two from Ladbroke Road. Can't they do some of the interviewing for you?"

"Well, I'd trust Griffiths or Evans to do a proper job." He hesitated. "I'm sure the constables from the Upper Richmond Road Police Station are competent as well. But in a murder investigation, sometimes it is the tiny details that points one in the right direction. I don't mean to boast, Mrs. Jeffries, but my lads know my methods. They know to include everything in the report, not just what they *think* might be important."

"I understand what you mean, sir," she replied. "You're worried they'll leave something that appears inconsequential out of their reports. But you could pair a constable from Upper Richmond Road with both Griffiths and Evans. That might be useful and it would save you a great deal of time."

He sipped his sherry, his expression thoughtful. "That's a good idea. I'll speak to Constable Barnes tomorrow and we'll see what we can do. Otherwise, I'm worried we'll not get this one solved before Christmas, and I was so looking forward to spending time with my dear Ruth and my godchild."

"Nonsense, sir, you've made great progress," she spoke more enthusiastically than she felt. "You now have several more avenues of inquiry, and you know that most of your suspects lied about where they were on the night of the murder."

"True, but that doesn't make it easier. The difficult part will be finding out which one of them killed her."

Mrs. Jeffries checked to see that the back door was locked and then took her old-fashioned oil lamp up the back staircase to her room. She blew out the flame and pulled a straight-backed chair up to the window.

Across the street she could see the bare branches of the trees twisting and turning in the wind. Rain pounded against the glass panes and a lightning bolt slashed across the sky, followed by a clap of thunder.

She had no idea what to do about this case, and the reality was that they were running out of time. Closing her eyes, she leaned her head back against the headrest of the chair and took a deep breath. Another burst of thunder jerked her to attention just in time to see a streak of lightning cut through the sky. She stared at the raging storm, letting her mind wander and not trying to make sense of where it went.

The key to the back door was missing: Was it possible the killer had stolen it in order to force the servants to use the front door on the night of the murder? Had he or she planned it that way to prevent anyone from coming to the victim's aid? No, that didn't make sense. Why go to the trouble of committing a terrible crime and then walk away, leaving the victim still alive? Furthermore, the key had been missing for weeks, but perhaps that was simply a coincidence.

A gust of wind slammed against the window, but she barely blinked. When the body was discovered, the murder weapon—the shovel—was leaning against the angel statue. Why didn't the killer leave it lying by the victim? Why walk five or more feet and stand it against a stone figure? Had the murderer done that deliberately to confuse the investigation, or had he or she simply been unable to leave it lying on the ground? She'd once had a neighbor in Yorkshire who was like that. Poor Helga Ridgeway was so obsessed with order that she'd go out in the middle of a snowstorm to reset flowerpots that had been upended. Was the murderer like Helga? No, she thought to herself, don't overthink it. Maybe it was simply a routine gesture. The killer had a shovel in his or her hand and out of habit propped it up on the nearest object.

Across the road, the wind split a branch off and sent it hurling through the air and out of her line of sight. Her eyes narrowed as another idea took hold. The cat wasn't home by the time the servants left for the theater. But it was safely inside when they returned, which meant that only Mrs. Starling could have let it inside. No, that's not true, she told herself; the killer could have let the cat into the house. But would that only work if the murderer had the missing key because the door was locked? The Starling housekeeper said that the door could be locked with a key only from the outside. She hunched her shoulders, moving them in a circle to relieve the stiffness.

She stared into the storm, mesmerized by the wildness of the wind and the bolts of lightning splitting the sky in two. Who had the most to lose if Margaret Starling stayed alive?

She couldn't get that thought out of her head. Edgar Redstone and Merton Nesbitt gained nothing from her death, unless it was really true that Nesbitt's former wife might be thinking of reconciling—in which case, he might have a reason for wanting the victim dead. But as motives went, it was a bit on the flimsy side. Nesbitt could easily take himself to France, and if his former wife was serious about reconciling, he could make certain they married in Paris.

As for the vicar, Pontefract had the most to lose if the victim had gone to his superiors in the church, but he didn't know for certain that Mrs. Starling knew about the money he'd pinched. She shivered. The room was getting colder. Getting up, she closed her curtains and got ready for bed.

But sleep eluded her. She stared at the ceiling, trying her best not to think but to let her mind wander. Who had killed Margaret Starling? Who had the most to lose if she were alive now? The Angel Alms Society was going to benefit from her death—that was true—but surely a charitable organization didn't commit murder just to keep its coffers full.

She rolled onto her side and closed her eyes, breathing slowly and evenly, and soon she was drifting off to sleep. But just as she was about to go under, she realized that there was one aspect of the case they'd not examined thoroughly. She sat bolt upright, staring into the darkness. Ye gods, they'd been so distracted by all the anger and rage directed at the victim, they'd not seen what was right in front of their noses!

"Should we take her with us this morning?" Betsy wiped a piece of boiled egg off Amanda's chin. "It's not that cold outside, and the storm's passed. Seeing her would mean so much to Mrs. Goodge and Luty."

Smythe put his coffee mug on the table and looked at his daughter, who was sitting on her mother's lap, grinning like a drunken sailor.

"Me wan go, me wan go," she chanted, her little fists bouncing gleefully up and down.

They were in the spacious kitchen of their downstairs flat, having breakfast. "Do ya think that's a good idea, love? We've a lot to do today."

"How do you know?" Betsy put the toddler on the floor and began clearing the dishes. "Mrs. Jeffries claims she doesn't have a clue about this case. What's more, all of us seem to be finding out the same information."

"Leave the dishes for Mrs. Packard," he said. "And stop frettin' over this case. Mrs. J. will solve it; she always does."

"Me wan go, me wan go." Amanda was at her daddy's knee, her tiny finger jabbing his thigh. "Me wan go . . . me wan go."

There was a knock on the back door and Amanda shrieked in delight, "Mrs. Packwa here!" Moving as quickly as her chubby little legs could go, she headed for the door.

"It's too early for Mrs. Packard." Betsy raced after her daughter, scooped her up, and then opened the door.

A blond-haired, blue-eyed young lad who looked to be about ten stood there. He was rail thin and wearing brown trousers with patches on the knees, a navy-blue coat with most of the buttons missing, and a greasy gray flat cap. "Hello, ma'am," he said, then whipped the cap off and nodded politely at Betsy. "Blimpey sent me." He grinned at the little one and she giggled.

"Come in, then." Betsy opened the door wider and the boy stepped inside.

He gazed around the spacious kitchen. "Cor blimey, this is nice. It's so warm in 'ere, and you've got one of them nice cookers and a sink. Me mam would give 'er right arm for a cooker and a sink like that."

"What's your name?" Betsy asked.

"Me name's Roy and Blimpey sent me 'ere with this note." He pulled an envelope out of his trouser pocket and started to hand it to Betsy, but she pointed to her husband. "Give it him."

"Oi." Amanda tried saying his name. "Oi, you wan play? Oi, Oi," she chattered, trying to get his attention.

"This is Amanda," Betsy said, introducing her daughter. "Don't mind her. She loves older children."

Roy gave the child another grin before hurrying to the table and handing Smythe the envelope.

He opened it, pulled out the note, read it, and put it on the table. "Thanks for bringing this." He looked at Roy. "'Ave you 'ad any breakfast?"

"Just a cuppa tea and slice of bread," he replied.

Betsy plopped Amanda on the floor again and went to the large oak pantry sideboard opposite the dining table. Opening the top cupboard, she got down a plate of jam tarts and a hunk of cheddar cheese.

She put the items on the shelf, opened the top drawer, and took out a crisp, white linen serviette that she put next to the tarts. Then she got a knife and carved off a generous six-inch hunk of cheese. Within moments she had the tarts and the cheese wrapped in the cloth.

Roy's eyes widened as she handed him the bundle. "Here, this is for you. A growing lad needs lots of good food."

"Thank you, ma'am." He cradled it against his thin chest.

"This'll make me mum so 'appy. Now we'll 'ave us a decent supper tonight."

Smythe dug a coin out of his pocket and handed it to him. "Seein' as it's Christmas, take this as well."

His mouth opened in surprise, his eyes widening ever more as he reached for the money. "Cor blimey, it's a shilling. Thanks ever so much. This'll buy plenty of food. I 'ope Blimpey sends me 'round 'ere again."

"Merry Christmas, lad," Smythe laughed. Both he and Betsy knew what it was like to be poor, and neither of them ever let anyone leave their home hungry.

"Oi, oi, wan play?" Amanda grabbed the sleeve of his jacket.

"Amanda, behave," Betsy warned. "He's got to go. Here, come along, then. Let's walk him to the door."

"Oi go? Wanna play," Amanda declared, but she dutifully took his free hand and escorted her new friend to the back door.

"Good-bye, little Amanda," he said, causing her to giggle uncontrollably. "And thanks again for the food." He stepped outside.

As soon as the door was closed, Betsy turned to her husband.

"What did the note say?"

"Not much; only that Blimpey was called out of town. Apparently, Nell's auntie is ill and they're stayin' with 'er till after Christmas. But 'e wanted me to know that 'e's found out more about Graham McConnell. The man's mother is dead."

"Dead? But I thought he went there once a quarter to see her," Betsy said. "That's what Blimpey told you originally."

"Yeah, but 'is note said that's not true." He picked up the paper and began to read, "Upon further investigation, my source found out McConnell's mother 'as been dead for two years. I don't know if this fact is important, but I thought I'd send it along just in case."

"If his mother's dead, then why does he go to Southampton every quarter?" Betsy asked.

Smythe shrugged. "Who knows? Maybe 'e's got a lady friend down there—someone 'e doesn't want the board of governors to know about."

CHAPTER 9

"Constable Barnes, how much do you know about embezzlement and fraud?" Mrs. Jeffries asked after the constable had added some additional details about the previous day's investigation.

"I've arrested my fair share of those types. Why?" He stared at her curiously. "What are you thinking?"

"I'm not sure," she said. "I could be completely wrong, but last night I realized something that might be important."

"What?" Mrs. Goodge demanded.

"I can't say yet. All I know is that we might be looking in the wrong direction." Mrs. Jeffries looked at the constable. "In your experience, do embezzlers keep a set of books with the details of the money they've stolen? Oh, dear, I'm not sure I'm asking the question properly."

"I know what you're wantin' to know," he said. "Most small embezzlers don't bother, especially if they've just pinched off a bit here and there. But the ones that have worked out a system to steal on a regular basis generally keep a record of sorts. Most of them want to know how much they've stolen. Add to that, embezzlers, at least the clever ones, usually have more than one way to steal. They're not just putting their fingers in the till a time or two. Some of them are very sophisticated—they set up fake payable accounts and false bank accounts, and every month or quarter they pay themselves for goods or services that don't exist."

"I see," Mrs. Jeffries said. "Constable, can you and the inspector speak to Sir Gareth Cleary today?"

"He's the chairman of the board of governors, right?" Barnes asked.

"That's right, and I think it's important to find out when, exactly, Mrs. Starling began voicing her concerns about the alms society finances."

"You want me to find out specific dates?" Barnes looked skeptical. "What if he doesn't remember?"

"If you can't get a specific date, try and see if he can recall about when she first spoke to him. Also, find out if he has heard the name 'Francine' in connection with Mrs. Starling and if he can tell us who she might be."

"I'll do my best, Mrs. Jeffries, but the inspector might have other plans. We've a lot on our plates. The inspector wants to finish the second interviews with the Starling servants, and I know he'll want to speak to Edgar Redstone again."

"I know, but I think this might be important." She glanced at the clock on the pine sideboard. "I've a couple of other requests, Constable, and they might be even more difficult for you."

*   *   *

"Here's my baby." Mrs. Goodge grabbed Amanda and sat down with her on her lap. "Hello, my darling. Are you all ready for Christmas? We're going to have a lovely time this year!"

Amanda giggled and clapped her hands together.

"Luty and Hatchet are right behind us," Betsy said as she took her seat.

"Then it's good that I can get my cuddles in before Luty gets here."

"I am here," Luty announced as she and Hatchet came into the kitchen. "Oh, good, everyone's here."

They spent the next few moments hanging up their outer garments, then Luty took her seat and Mrs. Goodge graciously handed their mutual godchild over to her friend. "Here, you can have her now. I've got to check if those Christmas buns have started to rise. But go ahead with the meeting; I can hear well enough from my worktable."

"We've much to get through this morning, and I've tasks for each of you," Mrs. Jeffries announced. "So, everyone, listen carefully." She told them what she'd learned from the inspector and then added a few details they'd heard from Constable Barnes. "But as I told the constable, I've a feeling we might be looking at this murder from the wrong side."

"What does that mean?" Phyllis asked.

"We focused too much on those who hated Margaret Starling and not enough on what she was actively doing when she was killed," Mrs. Jeffries explained. "I don't want to say too much, because there is a very good chance I could be wrong." She sighed heavily. "Oh, dear, this might be a wild-goose chase as well, but I feel we must do it."

"What do you want us to do?" Hatchet asked.

"Give me a moment." She took a sip of tea to get her thoughts in proper order. She looked at Luty. "First of all, I'd like you to find out which bank the Angel Alms Society uses, and after that I'd like you to go to Nelson Biddlington's home on Porchester Terrace and see if you can find out if Margaret Starling went there a few days before she died."

"That sounds simple enough." Luty rubbed her finger along Amanda's cheek, causing the little one to giggle. "But you should know there was no one home when I went to Nelson's house yesterday. He ain't due back until tomorrow, so there might not be anyone there today, either."

"Try anyway." Mrs. Goodge put the cloth back over her huge bread bowl and took it to the counter by the cooker. "If the master is coming home tomorrow, there should be one or two servants there today getting things ready for him."

"Unless you've something else for me to do." Hatchet looked at Mrs. Jeffries. "Why don't you let me find out what bank the alms society uses for their deposits? Luty isn't the only one with sources in the financial world."

Mrs. Jeffries nodded. "All right. Wiggins, your task is going to be difficult, but I think you can do it. Today is probably Fanny Herald's afternoon out, and I want you to make contact with her."

"Isn't she the tweeny from the Starling 'ouse?" he asked.

"That's right. And I'd like you find out some very specific information." She told him what she needed.

When she'd finished, Wiggins stared at her as if she'd lost her mind. "Cor blimey, Mrs. Jeffries, that's a lot. Isn't she the one that started cryin' when the inspector was interviewin' 'er?"

"Yes, and that's precisely why I want you to talk to her. I know it is asking a great deal."

"And you can do it," Phyllis interjected. "Use your charm, Wiggins. From what the constable overheard in the kitchen about her, she sounds like the type to get her head turned easily."

"I'll do my best," he shrugged. "But don't expect too much. I'm not that charmin'"

"You'll do fine," Mrs. Jeffries assured him. "Phyllis, I'd like you to take one of Mrs. Goodge's apple tarts to Stuart Deeds. Tell him it's a thank-you gift for the way he helped you find that rowing club. Now, I suggest you do it around noon, and we'll hope that he comes out of the society offices for lunch."

"What do you want me to find out?"

Mrs. Jeffries told her.

Wiggins laughed. "Cor blimey, Phyllis, you're goin' to 'ave to be even more charmin' than I am to find all that out."

"She can do it," Betsy said confidently. "I've faith in both of you. But before we go any further down this road, Smythe needs to tell you about our visitor this morning."

"Oi came," Amanda cried. "Oi came but he not play."

"Who's this Oi," Luty demanded.

Smythe told them about their visit from Roy and then looked at Mrs. Jeffries. "Does this 'elp or 'urt your idea?"

"It helps," Mrs. Jeffries replied. "As a matter of fact, it helps a great deal. Do you think your source can find out precisely why McConnell goes to Southampton every quarter? Is that possible?"

"That source isn't goin' to be doin' anything until after Christmas," he said.

"Oh, dear, that's unfortunate." Mrs. Jeffries looked at Betsy. "But perhaps there is another way. Do you have someone to take care of Amanda today?"

"Of course. We brought her this morning only so Mrs. Goodge and Luty could see her. What do you want me to do?"

Mrs. Jeffries told her. "If you make contact with McConnell's housekeeper and she's friendly, find out if she knows why he went to Southampton."

"What should I do?" Ruth asked. It was the first time she'd spoken except to say hello when she arrived.

"You've been right quiet," Wiggins said. "You all right?"

"Not really," she admitted. "Despite praying for guidance, I still don't know if I should mention Reginald Pontefract to Gerald. I don't want to burden him while he's trying to solve this murder, but I did promise the vicar I'd help him."

"The best way to help him is for the real murderer to be caught," Phyllis noted.

"And to do that, I've got a chore for you," Mrs. Jeffries added. "I want you to go to Chelmsford." She told her specifically what she wanted her to do. "That won't be too onerous a task, will it?"

Ruth smiled. "Doing something is better than sitting around my drawing room, fretting."

Mrs. Goodge came back to the table and took her seat. "Good, it sounds like we're well on our way to getting this murder solved."

"Do you have any sources coming today?" Phyllis asked.

"Not a one," the cook said. "Today the greengrocer is delivering the evergreens and holly so I can decorate the dining room for our Christmas dinner."

"What about the tree?" Betsy asked. "When is it coming?"

"Today, and we'll all decorate it at the party on Christmas Eve. So everyone had better get crackin' if we want this case solved before the big day."

Sir Gareth Cleary rose from behind his desk as the two policemen were shown into his study. "Come in, Inspector, Constable. I've been expecting you."

"Good day, sir. I'm Inspector Witherspoon and this is my colleague, Constable Barnes. "Thank you for seeing us so promptly."

The man behind the desk reminded him of a portrait he'd seen of Benjamin Franklin. He had a round, kindly-looking face, a receding hairline, and long, wavy hair that brushed the edge of his collar. A pair of oval wire-rimmed spectacles were perched on his nose. He went well with the old-fashioned room. Wooden wainscotting, so dark it looked black, covered the lower half of the forest-green walls. Gray velvet curtains tied back with green tassels hung at the two windows. There was a portrait of the queen as a young woman hanging over the black marble fireplace, and a bulldog lay in a huge basket on the hearth. He lifted his head to stare at them and then went back to sleep.

"Of course, sir, as I said, I've been expecting you." He motioned to the chairs in front of the desk as he took his seat. "Please sit down. I assume you're here because of Margaret Starling."

"I'm afraid so."

"Dreadful business, absolutely dreadful. I still can't believe that she's gone. She was such a big part of the Angel Alms Society. We shall miss her very much. Now, what can I do to help you?"

Witherspoon, who wasn't really sure why the constable had been so insistent that they interview Sir Gareth this morning, glanced at Barnes.

"We've been told that Mrs. Starling attended all the alms society meetings since the beginning of November," Barnes said. "Is that correct?"

"That's right." Sir Gareth took his spectacles off and laid them on the desk. "She's always been one of our most stalwart members."

"So it wasn't unusual for her to be in attendance?"

Sir Gareth sat back and folded his hand across his ample middle. "It was. She's always been very committed, but her attending so many meetings, especially at this time of the year, was odd."

"But isn't this the time of year that your society selects the recipients of the alms?" Witherspoon asked.

"That's true, but that had nothing to do with Margaret. The advisory board took care of housekeeping matters. You understand, they repaired and sorted the donated clothing, made sure there were provisions in the emergency food cupboard—that sort of thing. They had nothing to do with the selection of the alms recipients. The vicar of St. Andrew's and the board made those decisions."

There was a loud snort and a series of short staccato ones, followed by the loudest snore Witherspoon had ever heard. Both policemen looked at the bulldog. He was still sound asleep.

"Sorry, Alfred is very old and he snores horribly. But he gets very distressed if he isn't with me," Sir Gareth explained.

"That's quite all right, sir." Witherspoon smiled at the sleeping animal. "I'm a dog lover myself."

"Did Mrs. Starling tell you why she was attending so many of the meetings?" Barnes asked.

"Not at first, but I've known Margaret for many ye—" He caught himself. "Sorry, I'm still thinking of her in the present, not the past."

"That's easy to do when you've lost a friend." The inspector smiled sympathetically. "Do go on."

"The meetings are long and rather boring, so I confronted her and asked why she was suddenly coming to all of them. She told me she had some grave concerns about the finances of the society."

"What kind of concerns?" Witherspoon asked.

"At first she refused to say; all she would tell me was that she'd heard some very disturbing information. But she wouldn't be specific. It was only later that I learned exactly what those concerns entailed."

"Did you take her seriously?" Barnes put his pencil in his left hand and flexed the fingers of his right one.

"I did. Margaret wasn't one to exaggerate. I pressed her, but she said that she'd get back to me when she had additional information, and a few weeks later she did."

Barnes flipped to a clean page in his notebook. "When was the first time she spoke to you about this?"

"November seventeenth. I remember because it was getting late and I was in a hurry to leave, as I had a luncheon engagement. She started asking me questions about how the actual finances were handled, who got the money, how often the books were examined, and who examined the records. I must say, I was quite surprised, and had it been anyone but Margaret asking those questions, I wouldn't have taken it seriously."

"But you did take her seriously. Why?" Witherspoon asked.

"First of all, because I knew her character. Margaret didn't make idle chitchat to make herself look important. Secondly, at the previous meeting, the one on November third, I overheard her speaking to Graham McConnell. At that meeting Mr. McConnell announced that donations for the quarter were much lower than usual. After the meeting, she asked him about an individual contribution, one from a former member who'd left the area, and McConnell said the woman gave the same amount she always gave: ten pounds. Margaret argued with him, saying she was certain he was mistaken, that she'd spoken to this person and learned she was giving more each quarter, not the same."

"Do you recall the name of this individual?" Witherspoon asked quickly.

"It's Mrs. Ordway—Francine Ordway," he replied. "She moved to Tunbridge Wells at the beginning of last year. McConnell brushed her aside, saying that donors often exaggerated the amount they gave and that Mrs. Ordway was elderly and forgetful."

"And it was the next meeting that she approached you with questions," Barnes clarified. "Is that correct?"

"That's right, but it was what she told me at the following meeting, the one on December first that was so surprising. She told me she'd gone to Tunbridge Wells. Mrs. Ordway insisted she sent fifteen pounds a quarter to the society, not ten. I'll admit, I was in a quandary. I said that perhaps Mr. McConnell had been mistaken; that happens, especially at this time of year when everyone is so very busy. Margaret said she had another avenue of inquiry and that she'd speak to me later. Then she left."

"Did she bring the subject up again?" Barnes was fairly sure she had.

"Yes, at the next meeting, the one on December fifteenth. She told me she'd spoken to another person who donated to the society, Mrs. Harriet Minton. She lives in Chelmsford and Margaret had gone to see her. She said Mrs. Minton claimed she sent three pounds a month to the society. It was at this point that I agreed we should bring in an outsider to examine the records."

"I don't understand," Witherspoon said. "What was wrong with Mrs. Minton's donation?"

"Everything, Inspector. The last recorded entry for the donation was in September."

"Did you ask Mr. McConnell about it?"

"I did, and he said that they'd not received any money since the September entry. But he did point out that Mrs. Minton sometimes sent the money to the alms office and sometimes she sent it to the church."

"What do you mean, you've found out nothing?" Nivens demanded. "You've had plenty of time, I sent you to the Yard yesterday and you've learned nothing. What kind of detective are you?"

"I did my best, sir," Forman said, "but no matter who I asked, no one would tell me anything." He knew he'd made a mistake. Falling in with Nivens wasn't going to do his career any good. Now he had to think of a way to salvage the situation without making Nivens too angry. The man wasn't completely powerless.

"What about the other matter?" Nivens snapped. "Did

you at least find out about that? Surely someone here saw who received those two postmortem reports."

Forman swallowed nervously. "I asked Sergeant Wylie, sir, but all he said was that when he returned from the lavatory, one of them was on the counter. He had no idea how the second got into Inspector Witherspoon's hands."

"Blast," Nivens muttered. "That won't do. There must be some way to stop him. I'll not let him solve this case. Not this time. If he mucks it up, Chief Superintendent Barrows will have to give it back to me. Have you been keeping an eye out for his servants?"

"I'm trying to, sir, but I don't know what they look like." Forman felt sweat break out on his forehead. "But I did what you told me, and this morning I've watched to see if there was anyone looking suspicious and hanging about the Starling neighborhood."

Nivens slumped in the chair. "This isn't working, I'm going to have to take more direct action."

Forman panicked. He was only willing to go so far and no farther. "What do you mean, sir? If we get caught mucking about with the evidence—"

"We'll not get caught," Nivens interrupted, "and I certainly don't need you questioning my authority. Now, get out there and find Witherspoon and that blasted Constable Barnes. Keep an eye on them and then report back to me before you go off shift today. That's an order."

Wiggins stared at the young woman he hoped was Fanny Herald. He was at bottom of St. John's Road, in the spot where it ended at the edge of a field. He'd gone to the Starling home, and as Mrs. Jeffries had predicted, at one o'clock a housemaid dressed in a navy-blue overcoat came out the servants' entrance and went toward the High Street. He'd followed her, thinking he'd use his old standby, bumping into the girl, when she suddenly darted into the post office. He'd waited and she came out and carried on walking. He'd been sure she was going to the railway station, but instead she went on to the Upper Richmond Road. He had kept his distance, watching her as she made her way past the Angel Alms Society and then St. Andrew's Church to the edge of a field. She'd stopped and now stood there.

He walked closer and heard her crying, faint sobs she was trying to muffle with a wadded-up handkerchief over her mouth. Throwing caution to the winds, he went over to her. Her back was to him and her sobs were loud enough that she didn't hear him. Not wanting to startle her, he cleared his throat before he said, "Excuse me, miss, but are you all right?"

She whirled around, her face a mask of fury. "None of your blooming business!" she yelled. "Now leave me alone."

"I'm ever so sorry, miss. I didn't mean to intrude, but you looked so upset, I just 'ad to make sure you were all right."

She glared at him for a few seconds and then her face crumbled. "Am I all right," she repeated, her voice cracked. "Of course I'm not all right. I've made a right fool of myself." Tears flowed down her cheeks and her nose was wet. "Now the mistress is dead and we're all going to get turfed into the street. I've nowhere to go. My gran can't take me in again and I don't know what to do."

He wondered if the tears were because she was terrified of being on the streets or if it was something else. But whatever was upsetting the poor lass, he wasn't just going to leave her standing here scared and blubbering in the wind. "Miss, we've all made fools of ourselves one time or other. Now, look, I know I'm a stranger and you don't know me from Adam. I mean you no 'arm and me mum raised me to be a gentleman. She'd be ashamed of me if left a lady in distress 'ere on the edge of cow field. There's a nice café on Disraeli Road; please let me buy you a cup of tea. You'll feel ever so much better."

She swiped at her face. "You'll buy me a cup of tea? Well, that's better than nothing. All right. My name is Fanny Herald. What's yours?"

"Albert Jones." He took her elbow. "It's just up 'ere, miss."

Five minutes later he seated her at one of the tables in the workingman's café before going to the counter to get their tea.

"'ere you are, Miss 'erald." He put the tea down in front of her.

"Thank you, Mr. Jones." She gave him a tremulous smile. "I'm so sorry to have made such a spectacle of myself, but the past few days have been hard."

"I understand, miss. Would it 'elp to talk about it? Sometimes a chat can make you feel better." He wasn't certain whether he wanted her to say yes or no. He didn't want her to start crying again. He knew he was here to find out what she knew, but he hated seeing anyone look as scared and miserable as she did.

"I'm not sure even where to start." She took a sip of tea. "My mistress was murdered last Sunday night. You've probably heard about it because it's been in all the papers. Her name was Margaret Starling."

"I'm sorry. That must be awful for you."

"Not just me, but for the rest of the household as well."

She brushed a strand of hair off her cheek. "The police have been asking everyone questions. We've no idea what we're going to do once the solicitors read her will; we'll probably all be tossed into the streets. It's fine for people like Mrs. Adkins—she's the cook, and she'll not have any trouble getting another position—but for girls like me, it's goin' to be hard and I've got no place to go." Her eyes filled with tears again.

"What kind of work do you do?" he asked quickly.

"I'm a tweeny." She took a breath and brought herself under control. "I'm not even a properly trained lady's maid. I'm going to have a devil of a time finding another position."

"You could go to one of them domestic employment agencies," he suggested. "Lots of people get work like that."

Her expression changed. "I've not thought about that. Do they have positions with room and board? That's what I'd need—a roof over my head."

"I think so. If you've good work and character references, you should be able to find something that will suit you."

"How can I get a reference? My mistress is dead," she muttered.

"Don't be daft. You can get one from the 'ousekeeper and you can get a character reference from a churchman or a doctor or someone like that," he pointed out.

She brightened again. "That's true. I go to Evensong services on Thursdays, so perhaps the vicar will give me one. Or maybe Mr. McConnell . . ." Her voice trailed off and she looked down at her lap. "But I'll not ask him. It's 'is fault I've been in such a state."

This was the opening Wiggins wanted. "Is this Mr. McConnell a friend?"

"Friend? No. I thought he was kind—I thought he liked me—but now I think he was just using me so I'd say nice things about him to the mistress." She snorted. "He didn't even look at me when he come to the house on Monday. It's not like I was sweet on him or anything like that. For God's sake, he's old enough to be my father, and he's got a head like a turtle."

"He sounds a right scoundrel," Wiggins agreed.

"He is. He uses people. That's what Mrs. Starling said about him, and he tried to use me to sweeten her up. Then he had the nerve to treat me like I was some jezebel who'd set her cap for him. He's the one that come after me—he's the one that sat next to me every Thursday at Evensong and then insisted on walkin' me home—and now I know it weren't because he liked me; he just wanted me to put in a good word for him so Mrs. Starling wouldn't set her solicitor on him."

"Perhaps we ought to stop in at the Starling house and have a word with Constable Griffiths. He and the constable from Upper Richmond Road should have had time to speak to the rest of the servants." Witherspoon said as he and Barnes headed for the Lower Richmond Road in search of a hansom cab.

A hard blast of wind hit them as they turned the corner, and Barnes reached up and tightened the chin strap on his helmet. "Right, sir. It'll be interesting to hear what Constable Griffiths has to say about the other lad. Mind you, they seem a good sort, and we can thank them for keeping us informed about Inspector Nivens' silly antics. There's a cab dropping a fare, sir. If we hurry, we can get it before anyone else does."

They raced up the street, with Barnes taking the lead and hurrying ahead. He had the door open by the time the inspector reached it.

"I'm wondering if we should interview the other members of the board," Witherspoon said to Barnes as they climbed into a hansom. "Your suggestion that we speak with Sir Gareth Cleary was most informative, Constable. Perhaps some of the other board members will add to what we know."

"We did learn a lot, sir." Barnes braced himself as the vehicle lurched forward.

"On the other hand"—Witherspoon reached up and grabbed the handhold—"I think we should speak to Mr. McConnell again. He omitted mentioning a number of pertinent details about what happened during those meetings."

Barnes nodded in agreement. "And I still need to ask him where he was on the night of the murder."

Witherspoon looked surprised, started to say something, and then shrugged. "Well, sometimes we miss a step or two, Constable, but not to worry, we'll ask him now."

"I'll tell the driver we've changed destinations." Barnes banged on the roof of the vehicle and then stuck his head out the tiny window as the cab slowed. "Take us to St. Andrew's Church."

Phyllis cradled the small basket against her middle as she stood across the road from the Angel Alms Society. Mrs. Goodge had wrapped not one but the last two of her delicious apple tarts in a fancy pink serviette and tucked them into a basket she'd dug out of the back of the pine sideboard.

She watched as a man who she assumed was Graham McConnell rammed a black top hat onto his head and hurried down the broad steps. Moving quickly, he turned in the direction of the Upper Richmond Road and disappeared.

Phyllis started to step off the curb but hesitated. Did she dare simply walk inside? What if McConnell returned? Well, if he did, she had a shilling in her pocket; she could always say she'd stopped in to make a donation as well as thank his clerk for helping her when she was "lost." It had to be done and she was determined to do it properly. She had to speak to Stuart Deeds. There was no guarantee he'd come out to lunch, and this might be her only chance. Taking a deep breath, she hurried across the road, climbed the steps, and went inside.

"Hello," she called softly. "Is anyone here?"

"Can I help you?" Stuart Deeds stepped into her field of vision. He looked surprised and then a pleased smile curved his thin face. "Well, hello. How nice to see you again, Miss Morgan. Do come in."

"I hope I'm not disturbing you, Mr. Deeds, but I had to come." She gave him what she hoped was merely a polite smile.

"Come sit down, Miss Morgan." He led her into the outer office, pointing at a chair in front of a narrow desk. "My guv is gone, so we've time for a nice chat."

She sat down and he went behind the desk and took his own seat.

"You were so very kind to me when I was lost that I felt I had to thank you for going to all that trouble." She put the basket in front of him. "Here, this is for you: a small token of my appreciation."

Delighted, he smiled at her as he opened the serviette. She winced inside. She could see he thought she liked him, and nothing could be further from the truth. Guilt speared through her, but she ruthlessly shoved it aside. She was working for justice, and sometimes that was hard and put one in a difficult situation.

"Apple tarts," he laughed. "How wonderful. Did you make them?"

"No, no," she replied. "My grandmother made them. She's a wonderful cook."

"They look delicious, but as it's close to lunchtime; I'll save them for dessert." He tucked the serviette over the tarts and set the basket to one side.

"Speaking of lunch—" he looked at her expectantly—"I don't suppose you're free, Miss Morgan?"

She smiled apologetically. "I'm so sorry, but I've another engagement."

Another shaft of guilt hit her as his face fell. "Perhaps another time, Mr. Deeds."

"Oh, do call me Stuart. And may I be so bold as to call you Arabella?"

"Of course, Stuart. Please do." She was glad he'd remembered the name she'd used at their previous meeting; she'd thought it was Isabelle. "I was hoping you could tell me a bit more about this society. I'm thinking of making a contribution, but as you know, money doesn't grow on trees. I want to ensure that my donation would be put to good use." She'd decided on this line of inquiry after hearing specifically what Mrs. Jeffries wanted her to learn.

"I assure you, it would. The Angel Alms Society is a highly regarded charity. It is overseen by a board of gover—"

"How often do they meet?" she interrupted.

"Usually once a month, but at certain times during the

year, during the months leading up the actual alms distribution, they meet every fortnight," he explained. He went on to give her additional details on how the charity was set up and managed.

She forced herself to be patient. Stuart certainly loved the sound of his own voice. When he paused to take a breath, she pounced. "Are you at any of these board meetings?"

"I attend all of them," he announced proudly.

"Excellent. You have such a wonderful way of explaining things, Stuart. Can you give me a description of say—oh, I don't know—one of the meetings from the past month?"

He drew back, his expression puzzled, and she was afraid she'd gone too far, too fast. But then he brightened. "You want to hear what a meeting is like?"

"Naturally, from what you've just told me, that seems to be where the most important decisions might be made. Now, do tell me and don't be afraid to tell the truth. I want to know everything, warts and all."

"In that case, let me tell you about our last meeting." He rolled his eyes. "There was ever so much going on."

She listened carefully. Stuart enjoyed talking and he was a natural gossip. She had to interrupt him only a few times to find out exactly what she'd come here to learn.

As if he'd read her mind, he gave her an embarrassed smile. "I hope you don't think I'm being a gossip, but Mr. McConnell did seem to expect me to tell him everything after the meetings."

"I'd never think you a gossip, and I've already told you that I came to see you because I wanted to understand everything about the charity. Do go on," she encouraged.

"It's very well run, if I do say so myself." He smiled

proudly. Finally, after several more minutes of talking about the charity and the office, he said, "I do hope I've not discouraged you. Perhaps telling you about my stationery drawer being untidy and mucked about wasn't helpful."

"Oh, no, that's the kind of detail I wanted to know," she replied. "Do you have any idea who might have gone through your desk?"

"Just between you and me, I think it was either the verger at St. Andrew's or possibly even the vicar. Both of them have keys. Mind you, I don't think the vicar was stealing anything; I imagine he simply needed something and didn't think I'd notice the drawer was so untidy. But I've my suspicions about the verger: I think he stole those three bags of clothing I overheard Mr. McConnell mention to Mrs. Starling."

Without thinking, Phyllis blurted, "Exactly when did he mention the clothing to her? Was it at one of the meetings?"

Again he drew back, but this time his eyes narrowed. "That's an odd thing to ask."

For a moment she almost told him the truth, but at the last second she decided against that course of action. "I'm sorry if my question seemed strange to you." She gave him another smile. "It's just that you tell things so well, it's almost like one of those mystery stories. You know, the sort that Mr. Doyle writes for *The Strand Magazine*." He was still staring at her, so she threw caution out the window. "I just finished reading Mr. Doyle's 'The Story of the Brazilian Cat' in this month's issue and it was wonderful. You should think about writing for them, I'm sure you'd be fantastic."

His expression lightened. "Really? You think so? I've always wanted to be a writer."

"You tell everything so well; that's why I asked that

question. But it was silly of me to ask; of course you wouldn't recall a minor detail like that."

"Thank you." He beamed. "But actually I do. It was the morning of December sixth. We were coming in to open the office, and Mrs. Starling walked past on her way to the church. Mr. McConnell tried to stop her; he said we had received these three bags of clothing and when could she and her committee come to sort them? But she didn't even stop; she yelled she was in a hurry."

"You do have a good memory." She meant it, too. "How did you recall the date?"

"I wrote it in my diary." He pointed to a red-leather-bound book on the corner of his desk. "I've found that when one works for Mr. McConnell, one must remember everything. He doesn't like answering questions. But back to my suspicions. I think the verger must have pinched those clothes and while he was here he mucked about with my stationery drawer and played with the typewriter. There was a tiny piece of paper jammed inside it."

She was saved from having to comment by the door opening. Stuart got up and raced to the foyer. "Hello, Inspector, Constable. I'm afraid Mr. McConnell isn't here just now. But I expect him back after lunch."

Phyllis was already on her feet and moving toward the back of the small building. She silently prayed that she'd find a back door.

"Actually, we'd like to have a word with you," she heard Constable Barnes say.

But there was no back door. Moving as quietly as possible, she rushed across the expanse of the outer office and down the short hallway to a closed door.

"I'm with someone now, but do come in. The young lady and I are almost finished with our business."

Phyllis opened the door and stepped into Graham McConnell's office.

Betsy knew she'd made a mistake. She should have waited till Graham McConnell's housekeeper came out to do the shopping and accidentally bumped into the woman. But instead she'd boldly walked up to the three-story white stucco building and knocked on the front door leading to McConnell's ground-floor flat. McConnell's middle-aged housekeeper, Mrs. Ellen Pillington, wasn't impressed when Betsy announced she was a private inquiry agent. Truth be told, the housekeeper looked her over from head to toe, her expression one of disbelief.

"Why are you asking about him?" Ellen Pillington folded her arms over her chest and eyed Betsy with a disapproving frown. "Why is his comings and goings any of your business?"

"They're not," Betsy replied. "I told you, I'm a private inquiry agent, and Mr. McConnell's name has come up in the course of an investigation we're conducting. May I come in and speak to you?" She was tired of standing on the doorstep, and if the woman wasn't going to cooperate, she wanted to know now so she could get back to Upper Edmonton Gardens and tell Mrs. Jeffries.

"It's not my house and I've no intention of letting you inside nor answering your questions. A woman private inquiry agent . . . That's ridiculous."

"Excuse me, Mrs. Pillington, I need to get out, please." The voice came from behind the housekeeper.

Giving Betsy one final glare, the housekeeper moved aside. "Sorry, Mrs. Walcott."

Mrs. Walcott, an attractive black-haired matron in her mid-thirties, stepped outside, smiled at Betsy, and went down the walkway.

Mrs. Pillington slammed the door shut.

Betsy made a face at the closed door and turned. She was surprised to see Mrs. Walcott standing on the pavement, waiting for her. "Don't mind Mrs. Pillington. She's like that with everyone."

"Really? She must not have many friends." Betsy nodded politely and started to move past the woman.

"She doesn't have anyone, that's why she is so desperately devoted to Graham McConnell. Are you really a private inquiry agent?"

"I am," she replied. It wasn't really a lie: She was making inquiries and she was a private citizen. "These days there are a number of women in the profession. My employers discovered that most women are more comfortable speaking with other women rather than male agents." She was gilding the lily a bit, but if you were going to pretend to be something you weren't, pertinent details made the lie more believable.

"Forgive me, I wasn't eavesdropping, but I couldn't help but overhear your conversation with Mrs. Pillington." She glanced at the front window and grinned. "The curtain twitched; she must be watching us. I'm going to the High Street to shop. Would you care to walk with me?"

"I'm going that way myself," Betsy replied. She'd long ago learned to trust her instincts, and now she was certain this woman had something to tell her. She hoped it would help catch Margaret Starling's killer. Christmas was getting close.

CHAPTER 10

Stuart led the way into the outer office, stopping short when he saw the empty chair where Arabella Morgan had been sitting. "Oh, dear, where's she gone? There was a young lady here. She was thinking about become one of our donors."

"Perhaps she's gone out the back door," Witherspoon suggested.

"It's been boarded up for years." He looked confused. "Could you wait here, please, I'll just check Mr. McConnell's office. Perhaps she felt faint or needed to . . . I don't know. I'll be right back."

"Take your time, Mr. Deeds," Barnes called after him.

Inside the office, Phyllis raced to the window, silently praying she could get it open. She heard Constable Barnes and knew from his warning that she had only seconds.

Pushing the heavy curtains to one side, she put her hands underneath the top of the frame and pushed up with all her might. It opened. "Thank God," she murmured. Her heart pounded and her mouth was suddenly dry. There were footsteps outside the door, so she swung her legs over the sill, held on to her hat, and jumped out. The window was a good four feet from the ground and she landed hard, wincing as pain shot up her legs.

From inside, she heard the office door open. "Arabella—Miss Morgan—are you in here?" He must have spotted the open window, because a second later she heard him say, "Goodness me, have you gone out the window?"

Gripping her purse and holding her hat fast on her head, she ran for it, not caring where she went as long as it was away from the open window. She dodged to one side, keeping low and praying Stuart wouldn't stick his head out and see her. She reached the corner of the building, when she realized she was in the oldest part of the churchyard. Directly ahead, ancient headstones covered in lichen marked the burial spots of the faithful, and beyond them was a terrace leading to the side door of the church. She sprinted to the wall separating the churchyard from the road and, keeping low, raced toward the door.

Behind her, she heard what she hoped was the window slamming shut. She hugged the wall until she reached the edge of the terrace, and just as she stepped onto the cobblestones, the door opened and a man carrying a burlap sack and a broom stepped out. "Hello." He grinned. "Havin' a nice look around, are ya?"

"Thank you, I am," she smiled politely, and walked past him. "It's a lovely churchyard." She reached the door but he didn't budge. "May I get past, please? I'd like to go into the church."

"Of course, miss." He stepped out of her way. "But I'm wondering how you got in here. This door's been locked all morning."

"I'm afraid you're mistaken." Phyllis was quite pleased with herself for remaining calm. "I used it only five minutes ago."

He said nothing. He simply stared at her with an expression that said he didn't believe a word she said. Phyllis didn't care, even if both Stuart Deeds and this fellow told the inspector about her, all they'd be able to report was that a woman named Arabella Morgan had behaved oddly.

"Do you think that young man is a reliable witness?" Witherspoon whispered to Barnes. "He seems quite imaginative. If the back door's been boarded up, uh, where could this young woman have disappeared?"

Barnes knew the "young woman" was either Phyllis or Betsy, so he tried to come up with an answer that sounded reasonable. He hoped whichever one it was had gotten clean away. But he didn't want the inspector dismissing Deeds's interview out of hand. "Perhaps the young lady was here earlier and he forgot she'd left."

"I'm so sorry," Stuart said when he returned. As he crossed the room, he stopped long enough to grab a rickety-looking chair from the ones placed against the wall. He put the chair next to the one in front of his desk. "You must think me mad, but I assure you there was a young lady here. I've no idea where she went."

He gestured at the chairs as he went around the desk and sat down. "Please make yourselves comfortable."

"So Mr. McConnell is at lunch?" Witherspoon asked.

"No, Inspector, he's gone to the doctor."

"I do hope it's nothing serious." The inspector sat down.

"It's his arm, Inspector. I think it might be some sort of nasty rash, or perhaps he got it badly scratched. I saw him putting an alcohol tincture on it yesterday and it appeared very inflamed. Now, how can I help you?"

Barnes took the rickety chair and winced as it squeaked. Witherspoon gave him a fast, sympathetic glance before turning his attention to the clerk. "You know why we're here, Mr. Deeds. We're investigating Margaret Starling's murder."

"She was a nice lady. Quite opinionated sometimes but nevertheless, she always treated me decently."

"How long have you been employed here, Mr. Deeds?" Barnes could hear the chair groaning under his weight so he braced his feet against the floor.

"Eighteen months."

"You're the clerk. Are you the one who keeps the financial records?" Barnes carefully pulled his notebook out of his trouser pocket but even that small movement made the chair creak.

"No, no, Mr. McConnell takes care of all the financial records. The ledger is in his office."

"What are your responsibilities?" Witherspoon asked.

"I make sure the office is always staffed during our business hours. Mr. McConnell frequently has to be away. He does an enormous amount of fund-raising within the parish and of course the community. It's not easy getting people to give their hard-earned money to the poor. I also handle all the correspondence, sending out the thank-you and acknowledgment letters for gifts we've received. I keep an inventory

of everything that is donated, the clothes and fuel, sometimes food—"

Barnes interrupted: "Isn't that what the advisory board
does?"

"We work together," he explained. "Especially with the
clothing, when the items arrive, I make a general entry in my
ledger; it's just a basic description, something like 'Two hatboxes donated today.' Then the ladies go through the individual items to see what needs to be repaired, and then I
make a more specific notation in the ledger."

Barnes stopped writing. "I don't understand. Why two
notations?"

"It's easier to keep track of everything that way." He
leaned to one side and opened a drawer. Taking out a thick
ledger, he pulled it open and slid it across so that both policemen could see. He pointed to an entry. "Here, on December
twelfth, I've written, 'One carpetbag.' Then beneath it I've
written, 'Six white handkerchiefs, three ladies' blouses, one
navy-blue boy's overcoat.' Those items are what we found in
the carpet bag, but as you can see, there's no notation that
any of them needed to be repaired."

"Mr. McConnell informed us you've recently had three
bags of clothing donated," Barnes said, "and he wanted
Mrs. Starling's committee to come and sort through them.
Is that correct?"

Stuart shifted in his seat, looked down at the ledger for a
few seconds, and sighed heavily. "Honestly, Constable, I've
no idea what Mr. McConnell is talking about. As you can
see from the ledger, there's nothing recorded after December
twelfth. If those bags were here in this office, I'd have written
it in the ledger."

"Then why did Mr. McConnell tell us he'd stopped in to see Mrs. Starling on Monday because he wanted to fix a time for her committee to sort through them?" the inspector asked. He'd finally realized what Barnes was doing.

"I don't know," Deeds admitted glumly. "To be honest, I'm worried that they were here and someone stole them. It's not like Mr. McConnell to make mistakes."

"Why don't you just ask him about it?" The constable inched his feet farther apart as a distinct creaking noise came from one of the chair legs.

"Mr. McConnell doesn't like people questioning what he says; he's one of those people that think their word is law." Stuart shrugged. "That's one of the reasons he got so annoyed when Mrs. Starling began making inquiries about the society's finances. He got so angry about it, he insisted that after every meeting I hang back and pretend to be tidying up so I could report back to him who she'd talked to and exactly what she'd said to them."

"He directed you to spy on Mrs. Starling?" Witherspoon clarified.

Panic flashed across the clerk's face, as if he knew he'd said too much. "Well, I'd not characterize it like that. He is the general manager. He had a right to know what she was up to."

"You can give me the message." Constable Griffiths stared at Forman. They were standing outside the Starling home and he and Constable Quinn had just finished the second round of interviews with the Starling servants. He'd noticed that when Forman approached them, claiming he had an important message for the inspector, Constable Quinn snorted and looked at him with undisguised disgust. "We'll be meeting Inspector Witherspoon soon and I'll pass it along to him."

"Right, then." Forman cleared his throat. "Tell Inspector Witherspoon that if he needs more men, Inspector Nivens will be glad to accommodate him."

"That's it?" Griffiths stared at him in disbelief. "We should have already had what we need to work this murder. So you're telling me that Inspector Nivens is just now doing his duty?"

Beside him, Constable Quinn, a brown-haired, fair-skinned lad with a face full of freckles, snickered.

Forman gave him an ugly glare. "Inspector Nivens has done his duty. There's more than just the Starling murder to investigate. He can't let all our officers go to Inspector Witherspoon."

"That's news to me!" Constable Quinn exclaimed. "Other than the Lincoln robbery, a couple of knockabouts, and two petty thefts, it's been quiet the past week."

"That's not true," Forman retorted, but then his shoulders sagged. "Look, I'm just the messenger. I don't know what's goin' on; I just do what Inspector Nivens tells me."

"And it doesn't matter to you if what he's doin' is wrong," Quinn charged. "You're a policeman—you know what's right, and from what I hear, he's got you doin' lots that's wrong."

"I just wanted to get a leg up," Forman muttered. "I didn't know Inspector Nivens was going to actually try to hobble Inspector Witherspoon's investigation. I thought he was just bein' a bit stroppy because he was annoyed at losing the case himself. But now I'm in it up to my ears and I don't know what to do. If I don't do as Inspector Nivens tells me, he'll come after me."

"What exactly did he ask you to do?" Griffiths asked. He wanted to hear it from Forman. He knew what had been going on at the Upper Richmond Road Police Station, because Quinn as well as half a dozen other constables had been dropping hints for days now. As much as Griffiths and the rest of the rank and file might dislike Nivens, he felt a surge of sympathy for the pale-faced, frightened-looking Forman.

"He, uh, he asked me to go to Scotland Yard to try and find out exactly what Inspector Witherspoon had said in his complaint. He also asked me to find out who had passed the postmortem report to the inspector and now he wants me to find out where Inspector Witherspoon and the constable are right now and keep an eye on them. I'm to tell him what they're doing and if it looks like the inspector is getting ready to make an arrest."

"So Inspector Nivens has deliberately interfered in this investigation. Forman, you need to go to Scotland Yard and see Chief Superintendent Barrows. Tell him everything you know."

Forman's eyes widened and he drew back. "Are you mad? If I do that, Nivens will have my guts for garters. His family and friends will see to it that nothing happens to his career, but mine will be over right quick."

"If you don't do it," Griffiths said calmly, "you'll be in even worse trouble, I can assure you of that."

"Lady Cannonberry, I'm so delighted to meet you." Janet Madrigal's round, pudgy face was flushed with pleasure. She was an older woman with salt-and-pepper hair styled in old-fashioned sausage curls and wearing a crimson-and-gold-striped dress with puffed sleeves.

"Forgive me for barging in like this without so much as a calling card or a note, but I'm on a rather important errand and I'm hoping you can help me." Ruth had spent the train journey there coming up with a plan to find out what Mrs. Jeffries had asked her to do. But in the end she'd realized that sticking closely to the truth might be the best way. Not that she was going to be completely honest. She'd decided Gerald's name wasn't going to be mentioned.

"Not at all, Lady Cannonberry. Please come in and make yourself comfortable." She led the way into the drawing room.

The walls were papered with bright coral cabbage roses on a pale green background; a huge mirror in an elaborate gold frame was over the fireplace; and a wooden ivory-colored fire screen painted with intertwined coral and pink cabbage roses stood in front of the hearth. Overhead, a chandelier with bell-shaped ivory lamps blazed with light.

Mrs. Madrigal gestured at the couch. "Please sit down and make yourself comfortable. Would you care for tea or perhaps coffee?"

"No, thank you. Please don't go to any trouble; as I said, I feel very badly for interrupting your day." Ruth sat down.

"Lady Cannonberry, please stop apologizing. I had nothing important planned for today. Now, my housekeeper said you wished to speak to me about Margaret Starling?" She sat down on a chair opposite Ruth.

"That's correct."

"Dreadful tragedy . . . absolutely dreadful." She shook her head. "I don't know what the world is coming to: Nowadays a woman isn't even safe in her own back garden. Were you a friend of Mrs. Starling's?"

"No, I never met her, but she was a highly regarded and

respected member of a group I'm also involved with. Several of our members have asked me to come and speak to you about a very delicate matter."

"What's the name of this group?"

"It's the London Women's Suffrage Society; we're part of the National Union of Women's Suffrage Societies. Margaret was a member of the Putney/Wandsworth branch."

Mrs. Madrigal regarded her steadily, and Ruth was afraid she'd made a mistake. Not all females believed in women's rights.

"She was also a member of the Angel Alms Society," Mrs. Madrigal said softly. "As was I when I lived in London. But I've nothing to do with her other interests. Don't misunderstand: I believe in women's rights as much as the next person; I'm simply confused as to why you've come here."

Ruth drew a deep breath. This was the difficult part. "I'll admit it must seem odd, but our group wants to make certain that the person who murdered Mrs. Starling is caught and punished."

"As do I"—Mrs. Madrigal nodded in agreement—"but isn't that up to the police?"

"Absolutely. We're certainly not trying to do any investigating on our own, but I did learn something that might be pertinent. Unfortunately, when I told a policeman at the Upper Richmond Road Police Station what I'd heard, he was very dismissive and essentially told me to mind my own business. I'm not going to do that. Mrs. Starling deserves better."

"Everyone deserves better than being murdered," Mrs. Madrigal concurred, nodding. "But even if I can answer your questions, what makes you think the police will listen to you then?"

"Because I've found out they've put another policeman in charge and I've heard that, unlike the man I spoke with, this policeman listens to members of the public who come forward. If you can answer my questions, the information I have to give could be very helpful in catching the killer."

"All right. Then go ahead and ask."

As arranged, Constable Griffiths and Constable Evans, along with the Upper Richmond Road lads, met up with Witherspoon and Barnes in a café on the Upper Richmond Road.

The inspector waited till everyone had a cup of tea and a bun before he spoke. "How did it go this morning?" Witherspoon directed his question at Constable Evans. He'd sent him and Constable Firth to the hansom cab shelters to question the drivers as well as to all the pubs along the Upper Richmond Road.

"One of the hansom cab drivers told us that he'd taken a cleric to the Starling home on the night of the murder, but you already knew that. None of the other drivers reported taking anyone else near the house. We did a bit better with the pubs. Merton Nesbitt was at the Three Swans on Sunday night. He was there from half past eight to closing at eleven o'clock."

"So that probably eliminates him," Witherspoon said. "The PM report estimated the time of death as between nine and eleven."

"I'd not let him off just yet, sir," Barnes said. "Even the doctors admit that it's impossible to be accurate in determining when someone was killed. Nesbitt could have done it before he went to the pub."

"That's true." Witherspoon turned his attention to Constable Griffiths. "Did you learn any additional information from the servants?"

"Not really, sir. No one said anything more than was written in your initial report. But Constable Quinn and I haven't compared notes."

"Constable Quinn, what did you find out and, more important, what was your impression of the household?"

Quinn's mouth gaped open in shock. "Find out, sir? I was going to include it in my report, sir. I was going to write it up for you; that's what Inspector Nivens has us do."

Griffiths chuckled. "Inspector Witherspoon thinks all policemen, regardless of their rank, have eyes, ears, and brains. He expects us to use them. Now, stop looking like a surprised squirrel and answer the question."

Quinn licked his lips. "Well, sir, the young lady I spoke with, a maid named Louise Rector, told me that she knew when the back door key went missing. She said it was November twenty-fourth; she remembered because it was her birthday and Mrs. Starling had given her permission to go out that evening with her family. She said when she went to grab the key so she could get back inside, it was gone."

"Why didn't she tell anyone?" Barnes demanded.

"She didn't want to get another maid into trouble—a girl named Fanny Herald. She's the tweeny, and apparently Mr. McConnell from the alms society had escorted her home from Evensong service that night. He walked Fanny all the way to the back door and lingered for a good ten minutes, chattin' with Miss Herald. Mrs. Starling was a good mistress, but like most mistresses she felt responsible for the morals of her female servants. She wouldn't have approved of Fanny staying outside and talking with McConnell. She would have expected the girl to come straight inside when she got home."

"It would have been useful if she'd told me this when I spoke with her," Witherspoon muttered.

"She told me she hadn't thought much of it until recently. She said this Miss Herald's acting strange, really upset, and crying at the drop of a hat. She thinks the girl might know more than she lets on."

"You were going to put all this in a *written* report?" Barnes cried. "You should have told us this right away!"

"Now, now, Constable Barnes," Witherspoon soothed. "We mustn't blame the constable for following his station's procedures."

"I don't, sir. I blame someone else," Barnes said softly. "And we both know who it is."

"Yes, well, we'll deal with that at a later time. Does anyone else have anything to report?" No one did, so Witherspoon gave the constables their assignments for the afternoon, sending Griffiths and Quinn out to interview more locals, while Constable Evans and Constable Firth were told to have a chat with Edgar Redstone. "Make sure Mr. Redstone understands we know he lied to us when he claimed to be home on the night of the murder."

Then they finished their tea and left.

"I'd like a quick word with you, Constable," Griffiths said to Barnes as they stepped outside. "It's just a small matter about the paperwork going to Ladbroke Road."

"I'll meet you at the corner," Witherspoon told his constable. "We'll take a hansom to the alms society. I think it's going to rain. I do hope Mr. McConnell is available. I've a lot of questions for him."

As soon as the inspector was out of earshot, Quinn made himself scarce while Griffiths told Barnes about their encounter with Forman. "So I sent him to see the chief superintendent. I hope that was all right."

"It was," Barnes assured him. "And I'll make sure our inspector follows through on his threat to write a full report about Nivens' conduct. That man has no right to call himself a police officer."

Mrs. Jeffries paced as she waited for the others to arrive for their afternoon meeting.

"You're going to wear a hole in floor if you don't sit down." The cook put a plate of brown bread on the table next to the big teapot. "Don't worry, they'll be here any minute."

"I know, I know. I'm just a bit apprehensive. I gave them all such difficult tasks, and I'm worried that I'm wrong."

"You're always worried that you're wrong"—Mrs. Goodge took her seat—"but you're not. I've had one of my feelings, so stop your fretting."

"I wish they'd all get here."

"They'll be here within the next five minutes, you mark my words."

The cook was almost right: Everyone except Phyllis was at the table within the interval Mrs. Goodge had predicted.

Phyllis came rushing in two minutes later, her cheeks were flushed; a long strand of hair had slipped out of her topknot and she was out of breath. "I'm sorry I'm so late, but I had to leap out a window."

"A window?" Wiggins got up. "Are you all right? Did you get hurt?"

"I'm fine; it's just it was quite an odd experience." Phyllis started to giggle. "I'm sorry, I can't believe I did it. But I managed to get there, find out what we needed, and then get away without being caught by the inspector."

"Your day sounds more exciting than mine, though, all in all, mine was interesting as well. Mind you, I didn't need to leap out a window." Betsy poured a cup of tea and set it in front of Phyllis's chair. "Come have some tea and catch your breath."

Phyllis sat down. Wiggins took his seat as well. "Cor blimey, my day was strange, too. There must be somethin' in the Christmas air."

"I'll go first, then," Hatchet offered. "My report won't take very long. It took most of the day, but I found that the Angel Alms Society uses the London and Southwestern Bank; it's on the Putney High Street. But what took so long was that I also discovered another little tidbit." He paused and took a sip of his tea.

Luty gave him a disgruntled look. "Stop bein' so melodramatic and tell us what you found out."

Hatchet chuckled. "I found out that Graham McConnell has a bank account in Southampton."

"The bank here in London told you *that*?" Luty retorted.

"Don't be absurd, madam. You know how bankers are. They keep their mouths shut as tightly as their vaults. However, bank clerks who make very little money can easily be persuaded to part with information."

Luty laughed. "You had to bribe a bank clerk, didn't ya?"

"Yes, as a matter of fact I did. We're running out of time. Tomorrow is the twenty-third."

"How did a clerk here in London know about McConnell's bank account in Southampton?" Mrs. Jeffries asked.

"He found out accidentally. Apparently, McConnell handed over the wrong bankbook when he was making an alms society deposit. Both bankbooks apparently have the same cover. The clerk gave it back but not before he'd noticed the name of the bank. It was the Southampton and Portsmouth Bank."

"Excellent, Hatchet," Mrs. Jeffries said. "Who is next?"

"I'll go," Betsy offered. She told them about her encounter with Mrs. Pillington and how it led to meeting Mrs. Walcott. "She seemed to want to speak to me, so I walked with her to the High Street. I didn't think I could ask her the same questions I was going to ask McConnell's housekeeper, so I brought our conversation around to the night Mrs. Starling was murdered. I wanted to find out if she knew if McConnell was home that night. But she and her husband had gone out and so she didn't know."

"That's a pity," Mrs. Jeffries murmured. "Who would—"

"Wait, I've not finished," Betsy interrupted. "What she did tell me was the reason they'd gone out was because of the cat crying. Mrs. Walcott said that on that Sunday they kept hearing a cat screeching its head off like it was being tortured. They went out and searched the back garden but couldn't find the animal. It wasn't till later in the day that Mrs. Walcott realized the noise was coming from inside the McConnell flat."

"If the animal was making such a nuisance of itself, why didn't she knock on the door and ask the McConnell housekeeper what was wrong?" Ruth asked.

"She did. But it was McConnell who answered the door. He'd given Mrs. Pillington the day off. When she asked about the screeching cat, he insisted the noise must be coming from somewhere else—that there wasn't a cat in the house."

"I take it she didn't believe him," Mrs. Jeffries guessed.

"That's right, but the cat's screeching continued, so she and her husband went out to dinner; and when they arrived home, the place was as dark and silent as the grave."

"What time did they get home?" Mrs. Jeffries asked. She was feeling more confident now, as one more piece of the puzzle in her head had slipped into place.

"She didn't know the exact time, but it was late enough that McConnell could have been asleep." Betsy shrugged. "That's it from me."

"Can I go next?" Wiggins paused, and when no one protested, he told them about following Fanny Herald and their meeting at the edge of the cow field. "You were right, Mrs. Jeffries, it was 'er afternoon out. She calmed down a bit when we got to the café. Poor lass, she's worried sick about not 'aving a roof over 'er head. She didn't make a lot of sense, but from what I could get out of 'er, she thought Graham McConnell was sweet on 'er. 'e'd made a bit of a fuss, walked 'er 'ome from Evensong service, and got 'er chattin' about everything that went on at the Starling house. She thought 'e was serious, but then, after Mrs. Starling died, 'e cut 'er off completely—not just that time the inspector said 'e came to the 'ouse, but she saw 'im twice after that and 'e barely spoke to 'er."

"Where did she see him?" Phyllis asked.

"Once on the street outside the alms society and once in the church," he replied. "She said 'e was in the storage room shovin' 'ymnals into a bookshelf. She claims she wasn't followin' 'im, but I think she was."

"I do, too," Phyllis said. "I was at St. Andrew's today and I had a look a good look around. The only way she could have seen into that room is if she was right up at that tiny little window in the door."

"Wasn't the storage room once a private chapel?" Mrs. Goodge asked.

"It was," Mrs. Jeffries confirmed. "Go on, Wiggins, tell us the rest."

"There's not much more to say. She kept goin' back and forth between bein' angry at McConnell and crying that she'd made a fool of 'erself. The only other bit I could get out of 'er was 'er sayin' she wanted to speak to the police again—that now that she'd 'ad time to think about all them times McConnell walked her 'ome from Evensong, 'e'd not really been askin' about 'er; 'e'd been askin' about the Starling household and Mrs. Starling's comings and goings."

"We'll make it a point to let Constable Barnes know they need to speak to her again," Mrs. Jeffries said.

"May I go next?" Ruth asked. "My report won't take long." She waited a moment and then told them about her visit with Janet Madrigal. "Margaret Starling visited Mrs. Madrigal at the end of November. The two women had never met before, but Mrs. Starling managed to convince her that there was a serious problem with the finances at the Angel Alms Society and that she needed to find out how much Mrs. Madrigal donated. She said she sent them three pounds a month and had been doing so for over ten years."

"That's a lot of money. Three hundred and sixty quid," Smythe muttered.

"It is, but she wanted to continue to donate, because when she lived in Putney, she'd gone to St. Andrew's and was a supporter of the charity," Ruth explained. "But the interesting thing she told me was that the monthly donation was always done with coins, not a check. She sent gold sovereigns every month."

"Gold sovereigns," Luty exclaimed. "Why'd she do that? That's the craziest thing I've ever heard."

"The custom was started by her late husband. He used to drop the sovereigns off at the society office on the first of every month, and when he died, she simply continued doing it."

"How?" Mrs. Goodge looked doubtful. "They'd not fit properly in a paper envelope?"

"She sent them in little boxes."

"And she always sent them to the alms society?" Mrs. Jeffries asked.

"That's what she told me"—Ruth picked up her teacup—"which was confusing to me. Reginald Pontefract admitted that he'd stolen three pounds, and when I found out that's what she sent every month, I assumed that was the money Pontefract had taken. But if the box was mailed directly to the society, I don't see how he could have had access to it."

"He has a key to the office," Phyllis pointed out. "According to Stuart Deeds, the vicar can come and go as he pleases. If Mrs. Madrigal has been sending gold sovereigns for ten years, it's likely he knew about it."

"And he could easily have waited till the office was empty, slipped inside, and taken it." Ruth sighed. "That is so very unbecoming of a man of the cloth."

"Sorry, I didn't mean to interrupt you," Phyllis apologized to Ruth.

"I was finished anyway, and your explanation does make sense."

"Good, then I'll go next," Phyllis laughed. "I've already told you the best bit; now I'll tell you the rest." She reported the details she'd heard from Stuart Deeds. "After the meetings, Stuart always tidied up, which gave him the opportunity to eavesdrop on the board of governors. He said Mrs. Starling always stayed late, and he overheard her talking to the board members. The most important conversation he overheard was Sir Gareth Cleary agreeing they should bring in an outsider to go over the books. I know we already know that much, but—and this is significant—after every meeting since the beginning of November, Graham McConnell made a point of asking Stuart what he'd overheard. Stuart says it took a few times before he realized that McConnell expected him to repeat everything." She continued her narrative, taking her time and making certain they had all the details. "Unfortunately, the inspector and Constable Barnes arrived and I had to make a run for it. Lucky for me, Graham McConnell's office door was unlocked, so I managed to get inside and out the window before the inspector could see me." She told them about her encounter with the verger and how she'd stayed inside St. Andrew's for more than an hour to avoid running into Witherspoon.

"Cor blimey, Phyllis," Wiggins laughed. "I'd have paid to see you climbing out a window."

"Yes, well, I'm not doing it again for your entertainment"— she grinned—"but it was quite exciting. That's all I've got."

Mrs. Jeffries looked at Luty.

The elderly American swallowed the bite of bread she'd just taken. "Nelson Biddlington will be home tomorrow morning. He's comin' in on the night train from Scotland, but the butler—he's the one I spoke to today—he wouldn't tell me if Margaret Starling had been there or if anyone had sent any sort of package there or not." She sniffed disapprovingly. "He flat out said what was or wasn't delivered to Mr. Biddlington wasn't any of my concern. Acted like he had a poker up his bu—" She broke off. "—uh, er, spine."

Everyone laughed. They knew what she'd almost said.

"Really, madam, such language," Hatchet chided.

"I didn't say it; anyway, our little Amanda isn't here. We're all grown-ups and we've all heard words like that before. But let me finish—I'm goin' to see Nelson tomorrow and he'll tell us what we need to know."

"I'll go next," Smythe said. "Merton Nesbitt was at the Three Swans the night Mrs. Starling was killed. No one knew what time 'e arrived, but everyone knew 'e didn't leave until closin' time and that 'e was dead drunk. What's more, no one noticed any blood on 'is clothes. So unless 'e went 'ome and changed before 'e went to the pub, I don't think 'e's the killer." He looked at the housekeeper. "I hope you've really figured it out, Mrs. Jeffries. Tomorrow's the twenty-third."

"I think I know who did it, but I could be wrong." Mrs. Jeffries drummed her fingers on the tabletop. "And if I'm wrong, we're right back where we started."

Witherspoon was in a pensive mood when he arrived home. He handed Mrs. Jeffries his hat and unbuttoned his overcoat. "It's been quite an eventful day, and, to be perfectly honest, I'm tired."

She hung up his hat and took the coat after helping him take it off. "Are you too tired for a sherry, sir?"

"Absolutely not. I've been looking forward to relaxing." He headed down the hallway.

"And I've been looking forward to hearing all about your day, sir." She hurried after him. She got their drinks as he settled into his chair and, a few moments later, took her own seat.

He took a sip and then ran his finger along the rim of the small crystal glass.

"Did you learn much today, sir?" she asked.

"Oh, yes, but I'm not certain what it all means. We started out by interviewing the head of the board of governors, Sir Gareth Cleary." He told her what they'd learned and she listened as carefully as always until he got to the end.

"So Mr. McConnell's explanation as to why there wasn't anything recorded since September was that sometimes this particular donation went to the alms office and sometimes to St. Andrew's?"

Witherspoon nodded. "That's what he said, and he was very sure of his facts. He spoke to Graham McConnell directly."

She was confused now. Her theory about the murder was based on there being two sets of financial records, one for the alms society and a secret one kept by the embezzler. Was she wrong? Or was there some other explanation?

"After we left Sir Gareth, we went to the Angel Alms Society and had a word with the clerk."

She forced herself back to the here and now, listening as he told her the details of that encounter.

"But I must say, I think Mr. Deeds is a tad forgetful." He told her about the missing young woman and his concerns that the clerk wouldn't be a reliable witness. "Luckily, Constable Barnes seemed to feel the fellow simply got confused about the sequence of events this morning. I've done that myself a time or two."

"What did you do after that, sir?" she asked quickly. The less he thought about the "missing young woman," the better.

"We met up with the constables. By the way, pairing the Ladbroke Road lads with the ones from Upper Richmond was a very good idea." He repeated what they'd learned.

Mrs. Jeffries sipped her sherry as she listened. She forced the questions that were now screaming for her attention to the back of her mind and hoped she could remember everything. "And what did you do then, sir?" she asked when he finally finished.

"Well, we went back to the alms society. I had a number of questions for Mr. McConnell. We waited for quite a while, but he never returned. While I waited, Constable Barnes went to St. Andrew's to have a word with the verger."

"About what, sir?"

Witherspoon looked embarrassed. "I'm not sure. He murmured something about finding out about the history of the building. I didn't want to say anything, Mrs. Jeffries; you know I have the highest regard for Constable Barnes. He's an excellent policeman and a cracking detective. But I do fail to see how the history of that building could have anything to do with this murder."

CHAPTER 11

Mrs. Jeffries couldn't sleep. She lay in the darkness staring at the ceiling while her mind raced from one thought to another. She rolled over onto her side and wondered if she was completely mistaken about this case. Perhaps the murder of Margaret Starling wasn't the result of a complicated plot of embezzlement and fraud but the result of simple, ugly hatred.

She rolled back the other way and let her thoughts come willy-nilly as she played with the idea that her recent assumptions were wrong. Edgar Redstone wasn't home the night of the murder and no one knew where he'd really been. His housekeeper had said that he was "in his cups" when the next-door neighbor and the hansom driver helped him into his flat on Sunday night. But the only motive he had had to kill the victim was hatred. On the other hand, he'd only recently learned that the income he depended on from the quarterly trust actually belonged to Margaret Starling and she'd taken it back. Depriving him of his livelihood could have been what drove him over the edge and into murder.

What about Merton Nesbitt? There were witnesses who said he'd been at the Three Swans, but he could have killed Mrs. Starling before he went there that night. But when he arrived, no one noticed blood on his clothing, and smashing someone's skull with a heavy shovel would have resulted in stains.

She frowned. Mrs. Huxton had claimed that without the letter, Margaret Starling had had no slander case against her. But was that true? No, of course not. Reverend Pontefract had shown the letter to the board. If a sample of Mrs. Huxton's handwriting was shown to the board members, surely some of them would be able to testify it was the same as what they'd seen in the letter. Even if it wasn't enough evidence to win a slander case in a court of law, it was surely enough to damage her social reputation. Or was it?

This was getting her nowhere, so she closed her eyes and took long, deep breaths to calm her mind. Her last thought before she drifted off to sleep was that she wasn't wrong. But now she wasn't sure she could prove it.

Constable Barnes arrived early the next morning. "We've a lot to cover," he told the two women as he took his usual spot. "First of all, there's something the inspector doesn't know and it's important. Nivens has one of his lackeys following us about and trying to interfere in the case." He told them about Constable Griffiths meeting with Constable Forman. "After Forman confessed what he'd been up to, Griffiths told him to report it to Chief Superintendent Barrows."

"Will that do any good?" Mrs. Goodge demanded. "Nivens is as slippery as an eel. He'll wiggle out of it some way or other."

"Not this time," Barnes said confidently. "Not if Inspector Witherspoon follows through on his threat to report Nivens. That's why I'm telling you about this." He looked at the housekeeper. "You'll need to keep after him to do it. Otherwise, Nivens will keep coming after him and he'll go after that idiotic Constable Forman. Stupid fool should have known better than to trust Nivens."

"I'll do my best," Mrs. Jeffries promised. "But Inspector Witherspoon is so kindhearted . . ."

"True, but this time Nivens went too far. He tried to hobble a murder investigation," Barnes explained. "You just need to keep reminding him of that. Now, tell me what your lot found out yesterday."

It took less than a quarter of an hour to share the details. When they'd finished, Mrs. Jeffries said, "Now it's your turn, Constable Barnes."

It only took him a few minutes to add to the information Witherspoon had shared with Mrs. Jeffries. "I did go see Tom Lancaster. I wanted to see if he would mention running into Miss Phyllis in the churchyard—you know, just in case the inspector wants to have another word with him—but he didn't. Mind you, now that I know Fanny Herald saw McConnell mucking about with the bookshelf in the storage room, I really wish I had asked him about the history of the church."

"You think McConnell was hiding something there?" Mrs. Goodge asked.

"It's possible. I'll duck in and have a look this morning," Barnes said. "We've some questions for McConnell."

"I think you should send a constable to watch his flat," Mrs. Jeffries suggested. She was on dangerous ground here; she could easily be wrong.

"You think he's the killer?" Barnes asked. "Based on what?"

"I think he's been embezzling from the Angel Alms Society and Margaret Starling found out about it." She took a deep breath. "But I could be wrong. You should know I'm not one hundred percent sure of my conclusions. Nonetheless, I'm going out on a limb here and asking you to watch his movements."

"Do you have any evidence he did it?" Barnes pressed. "You know how much I respect your abilities, Mrs. Jeffries, but there's three other people who hated the victim, and any of them could have done it."

"There is evidence against him," she acknowledged, "and I think I know where it is. If I'm right, we should have it by noon. If I'm wrong, the only mistake you'll have made is sending a constable to watch his flat."

"All right, I'll see if I can talk our inspector into it. But I'm goin' to look a right fool if we get to the Angel Alms Society this morning and Graham McConnell is sitting at his desk."

At the morning meeting, no one was surprised by Mrs. Jeffries' revelation. "I know I generally don't say who I think committed the crime," she admitted, "but I think in this situation I needed to tell you. The truth of the matter is that I'm not a hundred percent sure it's McConnell."

"You're never a hundred percent sure," Mrs. Goodge told her. "Now, what if anything do you want us to do today?"

"Constable Barnes is going to try to get a constable to watch McConnell's flat, but I'd like one of us to keep an eye on it as well."

"I can do that," Wiggins offered. "You think he's goin' to run off?"

"It's possible. If he did return to the office yesterday afternoon, I'm sure Stuart Deeds told him the police had been there; and if Mrs. Pillington, his landlady, tells him a private inquiry agent was at his flat, that might frighten him enough to leave."

"I'll go with ya," Smythe told Wiggins. "Might as well 'ave two of us on the job. If 'e goes, one of us can follow 'im and one of us can get back 'ere."

"Should I still go to Nelson Biddlington's house?" Luty looked confused.

"Yes, that's very important. You need to find out if Mrs. Starling came to see him and if she left the second set of books at his home," Mrs. Jeffries explained.

"But we don't know for certain she was actually there," Ruth reminded her. "We only know that my source *thought* Mrs. Starling was on Porchester Terrace a few days before she was killed."

"I'm aware of that." Mrs. Jeffries looked at Luty. "If I'm wrong, it could be very embarrassing for you."

"I'll be with you, madam," Hatchet said cheerfully. "Then we can both be embarrassed."

"Where is Constable Forman?" Inspector Nivens paced in front of the counter. "He was supposed to report to me half an hour ago."

Sergeant Wylie looked surprised by the question. "I'm sorry, sir, I don't understand. Didn't you send him to Scotland Yard this morning?"

"No, I didn't." Nivens' brows drew together. "Are you saying he's gone to the Yard on his own?"

"Apparently, sir," Wylie replied. "He came in fifteen minutes before his duty shift and said he was going to the Yard. I just assumed he was running an errand for you."

"You shouldn't have made such a stupid assumption, Sergeant," Nivens snapped. "You should have jolly well asked Forman what he was doing and who had authorized him to be absent from duty."

"If he's at the Yard on official business of any kind, sir, he's on duty, not absent," Sergeant Wylie said.

"He can't be on official business!" Nivens yelled. "I didn't send him there."

"Perhaps Inspector Witherspoon did, sir." Wylie smiled as he spoke.

Nivens stared at him for a long moment, then turned on his heel and marched to the duty inspector's office. He stepped inside, slamming the door so hard the building shook.

Witherspoon stepped out of the hansom and waited while Barnes paid the driver. The constable joined him on the pavement in front of the alms society building. "This is the moment of truth, sir. If I'm right, Graham McConnell won't be here."

"You really think he's guilty?" Witherspoon said.

"Yes, sir. I think he's an embezzler and I think he killed Mrs. Starling because she'd found evidence against him." Barnes repeated Mrs. Jeffries' words, but as she'd not mentioned any real evidence against the man, he hoped that when they went into the office, they'd find neither hide nor hair of the fellow. "It's ten past nine, sir, so the place should be open."

When they stepped inside, the foyer was dark. "The gas lamps were lighted the last two times we were here." Barnes moved toward the outer office. "Mr. Deeds, are you here? Mr. Deeds? Where are you?"

"The gas lamps are out here as well," Witherspoon muttered. The two policemen moved into the center of the room. "And the blinds are still drawn. What on earth is going on? Mr. Deeds? Mr. McConnell?"

They heard a groan. "Oh . . . oh . . ."

"It's coming from in there, sir!" Barnes raced toward McConnell's open office door. Witherspoon was right on his heels. They charged inside. Stuart Deeds was on the floor. His head was covered in blood as he struggled to get to his feet. "Help me, uh . . ."

Rushing to him, Barnes gently pushed him back down. "Don't move. We'll get a doctor."

"He hit me," Stuart's whispered. "He hit me hard, two times, and I don't know why . . . I gave him the address but he hit me anyway . . . He ran . . . Oh . . . it hurts."

"Stay with him," Witherspoon ordered. "I'll get help."

"There's a fixed-point constable on the corner," Barnes yelled as the inspector disappeared.

The constable looked around the room for something to cover Deeds with but saw nothing. "Don't move, Stuart. I'm going into the other office to get something to keep you warm."

"All right." Stuart's eyes fluttered shut. "I hurt. My head hurts, uh . . ."

Barnes scrambled to his feet and raced to the first coat

cupboard in the outer office. He flung open the door and grabbed five or six garments, not caring that they were women's coats and cloaks. He hurried back to Stuart Deeds, hoping the lad was still alive.

But Stuart's eyes were closed. Dropping to his knees, Barnes draped a heavy gray mantle over Stuart's legs and then a navy-blue cloak over his chest. Stuart's eyes opened. "Am I dying?"

"Not yet," Barnes said. "Who did this to you?" He knew who it must have been, but as a policeman he needed to hear Stuart say the name.

"Mr. McConnell. He was here when I came in, I came early to do . . ." His voice trailed off.

"Don't try to talk anymore. The doctor's on his way." Barnes saw there was blood all over the lady's shirt and coat. He looked around the room, noticing for the first time that all of desk drawers were wide-open and the chair behind the desk was overturned.

McConnell was either looking for something or was in a miserably bad mood.

"But I must tell you," Stuart struggled to get the words out. "He's insane. He's got a gun. Hit me with it."

"Nelson Biddlington has done very well for himself," Hatchet commented as he and Luty waited in the drawing room.

The walls were painted a pale blue, indigo-and-gray-striped curtains hung at the windows, and ivory-and-sapphire-patterned rugs lay on the polished oak floor. An ivory settee and three matching upholstered wing chairs were grouped in front of the fireplace.

"There's family money here," Luty murmured. "But even if there weren't, Nelson woulda done just fine. That's why I hired him and Ronald."

"Ronald Biddlington is his identical twin, right?" Hatchet knew they were her solicitors, but he'd never met either man.

"That's right. They're both good men and Nelson is a smart as they come."

"Why, thank you, Luty." Nelson stepped into the room. He was a short, thin man with curly gray hair, a prominent nose, and bright blue eyes. "What a nice thing to say. It's so lovely to see you. I'm sowwy I wasn't available when you came yestewday, but I've only just weturned fwom Scotland."

Luty had already warned Hatchet that Nelson had a speech problem and he couldn't say the letter *r*.

"It's good to see you, too, Nelson," she got up from the settee as he advanced across the spacious room. "This is Hatchet, he works for me."

Nelson extended his hand and the two men shook. "I'm vewy pleased to meet you, Hatchet. Please, let's sit down. I've asked Pwingle to bwing tea."

"Please don't go to any trouble on our account." Luty sat down on the settee and Hatchet and Nelson each took a wing chair.

"It's no twouble," Nelson assured her. "It's just Pwingle and me today. The othew sewants won't be coming back until Chwistmas Eve.

"I'm sorry to barge in on you when you've just got back from a trip," Luty said, "but I've got something real important to ask you."

"Is it about Mawgwet Stawling's mudder? She was one of my clients and a fwiend as well. I want the muddewah caught, so I'll do anything I can to assist Inspecto Withah-spoon."

"Thank you, Nelson, I know this must be difficult for you," Luty began. "The first thing I need to know is whether Margaret brought something here to you a few days before she was killed."

"I don't know. I've been in Scotland fow two weeks. Pwingle was heah, so if she bwought anything, he'd have put it in my study." He got up from the chair. "It's this way," he motioned for them to follow him.

"The wound bled copiously"—Dr. Littleham tucked the roll of bandages into his medical bag and snapped it shut—"but there's no indication of any additional damage." He smiled at Stuart, who was sitting up with a huge bandage wrapped around his head. "You'll need to take it easy for a few days, young man. But you'll soon feel better."

"Thank you, Dr. Littleham," Witherspoon said. "We're very grateful you were able to come so quickly."

"Yes, well, my surgery is just up the road. I must get back, I've patients to see." He turned his attention to Stuart. "Be careful for the next day or so, and if the headache gets worse, come see me and we'll try something else for the pain."

"Yes, sir." Stuart still looked dazed. "Feels like my head is foggy."

"That will pass," the doctor assured him. He picked up his bag. "You took a bad blow, but you'll be fine. Good day, everyone."

Witherspoon waited until the door closed behind the doctor before he spoke. "Can you tell us what happened, Mr. Deeds?"

"Mr. McConnell hit me," Stuart said. "You must find him. I just realized, he's gone to hurt someone."

"Gone where?" Barnes asked sharply.

"To Mrs. Starling's solicitor. That's why he came into the office today. He needed the address from my files. He'd donated to us, so I wrote it down and took it to him, but he hit me anyway. He's going to do something bad. I saw him put more bullets in his pocket."

"Do you remember the address?" Witherspoon demanded.

"Uh . . . uh . . . let me think . . ." Stuart squeezed his eyes shut in concentration. "Bayswater. Porchester Terrace . . . I think it was number three."

"Stay with him," Witherspoon ordered Constable Quinn. "Griffiths, Evans, you're with us!" he yelled as they raced for the door.

Wiggins hurried into the kitchen. "We've got a problem. McConnell's gone. 'e left his flat this mornin' before we got there. He was carryin' a carpetbag with 'im. Smythe's gone to the alms office to see if McConnell went there."

Betsy looked at Mrs. Jeffries. "You were right: His landlady must have told him I was there yesterday asking questions."

"Is he trying to run away from the police?" Ruth asked. "Is that what's happening?"

"I don't know what is going on," Mrs. Jeffries admitted, "but I've a feeling something awful is going to happen. Oh, dear, I do wish I hadn't sent Luty and Hatchet to see Nelson Biddlington."

"You think McConnell is going there?" Wiggins exclaimed. "How would he know that Mrs. Starling went there?"

"From Fanny Herald," Mrs. Jeffries said. "That's why

she's been crying and carrying on. She feels guilty about passing along so much information about Mrs. Starling. But that's not important now. Wiggins, take a hansom and get to Porchester Terrace."

"What's the 'ouse number?" He headed for the back door.

"I don't know, but you can find it. Luty's carriage will be out front."

Nelson ushered them into his spacious study. The curtains were pulled back and they could see the garden through the French doors. A fire screen stood in front of the green marble fireplace; next to that was a set of brass fireplace tools. The mantelpiece was cluttered with magazines, puzzle boxes, a stack of novels, and a huge glass globe, inside of which was a mountain village complete with snow. Shelves filled with books covered two of the four walls. A globe of the earth was next to the desk, and the floor was covered with a colorful oriental rug.

"If she left something fow me, it would be on my desk," he said as he crossed the room. They trailed after him.

The package was sitting in the center next to a black file box. It was wrapped in brown paper.

"I'll bet that's it." Luty grinned.

Nelson stopped and stared at the package with a sad expression on his face. "She did bwing me something. I wish I'd been home."

There was a loud crash from outside the room. All three of them jerked in surprise.

"Oh, deah, I think Pwingle must have dwopped the tea tway. He's been having pwoblems with his balance lately. I'll go check." Nelson hurried out of the study, pulling the door shut behind him.

Nelson's voice came through the study door loud and clear: "What do you want? Stop that wight now!"

A second later they heard Pringle yell, "Run, Mr. Biddlington, run! This man's got a gun." There was the sound of breaking china; metal clanged and footsteps pounded against the floor. Someone screamed.

"Get out to the garden." Hatchet pushed Luty toward the French doors.

"Don't be dumb." Luty jerked away from him and raced to the fireplace. She grabbed the snow globe and started for the door.

"Not that." Hatchet picked up the heavy poker. "Madam, I must insist you stay behind me."

From the foyer they heard a high-pitched, hysterical male voice. "Where is it? Tell me where it is or I'll kill him!"

Hatchet, with Luty on his heels, cracked open the study door and peeked outside. He saw a man with graying hair standing over the butler. His back was to them but they could clearly see he had a gun pointed at Pringle's chest.

"I want the package," he said to Nelson. "I know she brought it here and I want it. Get it now."

Nelson tried to bluff it out. "What package?"

"The one Margaret Starling brought here. Stop trying to play me for a fool." He kicked Pringle in the leg. The butler winced but didn't cry out. "I can do worse than this. The next time it'll be a bullet in his knee."

"Don't shoot; I'll get it," Nelson said. "You don't have to kill anyone. You can have the package."

Hatchet shoved Luty back, opened the door wide, and crept out into the foyer, holding the poker high over his head. McConnell's back was to him but both Nelson and Pringle could see him. The butler's eyes widened in surprise, but Nelson kept calm.

"Put the gun down, suww, and let my butlew up," he said in a loud, strong voice as Hatchet moved closer and closer.

"Get the package first," McConnell yelled, "and be quick about it if you don't want this man to die! I don't have all day and my patience is wearing thin!"

Hatchet was close enough to strike a blow, but suddenly McConnell sensed his presence and turned his head. Hatchet brought the poker down just as McConnell ducked to one side. The blow landed on the side of his head.

McConnell stumbled but managed to bring the gun up. He stared at Hatchet in disbelief, aimed the weapon, and then collapsed completely, dropping the gun, which mercifully didn't go off. Pringle scrambled away as McConnell fell to the floor.

"Is he dead?" Nelson dropped to his knees and grabbed McConnell's wrist, feeling for a pulse.

"Oh, deah, what a mess." Pringle looked around the foyer. A table was overturned; the tea tray had landed against the wall; cutlery, sugar and cream, and cups and saucers were scattered everywhere; and the teapot had broken in half and now sat in an ever-increasing brown puddle.

There was a furious pounding on the front door. "Mr. Biddlington, Mr. Biddlington, are you all right? It's the police."

Hatchet yanked Nelson to his feet and shoved the poker into his hand. "We can't be found here."

"Go out the Fwench doowahs, I'll stall them," Nelson replied. "Huwwy, get out now. I know what to do."

Hatchet raced into the study just as Witherspoon and the constables burst through the front doors.

Luty was already outside, motioning for him to hurry. He ran across the room and into the garden, closing the doors behind him. He grabbed Luty's elbow and they ran as fast as they could toward the far end of the property.

"Are you all right, Mr. Biddlington?" Witherspoon shouted as he rushed toward them. "We could hear screaming."

The constables surrounded Graham McConnell as he struggled to get up.

"I'm fine, suww. This man"—he pointed to McConnell—"bwoke into my home and assaulted me and my butlew. I defended myself with a pokuh."

Griffiths and Evans pulled McConnell to his feet. Blood dripped from the side of his head and ran down his neck.

"I'm Inspector Gerald Witherspoon." The inspector introduced himself. "I take it you are Mr. Nelson Biddlington?"

"I am, Inspectuh, but I've no idea what's going on heuh."

"I'll explain in just one moment, sir." He turned to McConnell. "Graham McConnell, you're under arrest for the murder of Margaret Starling and the attempted murder of Stuart Deeds. Take him to the station, Constables, and be sure to put a bandage on his wound. Constable Barnes and I will be there shortly."

"Who hit me?" McConnell muttered as they led him toward the door. "What happened to that other man? Where'd he . . . oh, God, my head hurts."

Pringle turned to his employer. "If it's all the same to you, sir, I'll put a poultice on my leg before I clear up."

Biddlington smiled at his butler. "Don't wowwy about tidying up; we'll do that when the police aah gone. I'm so sowwy you wuh huwt."

"Not your fault, sir," Pringle said as he disappeared up the corridor.

"This must be very confusing for you," Witherspoon said to Nelson.

"It is quite stawtling, suh, but I think I unduhstand some of it. Margaret Stawling was my client and my fwiend. She bwought a package and left it faw me but I haven't opened it as yet."

"Can we open it now, Mr. Biddlington? I think that package may contain vital evidence."

Mrs. Jeffries resumed pacing. "Are you certain that Luty and Hatchet weren't harmed?"

"They're fine," Smythe assured her for the third time. "Wiggins saw them coming out of Biddlington's back garden."

"They're on the way 'ere," Wiggins added. "I just got 'ere quicker; they'll be 'ere any minute."

"I'll do a fresh pot of tea, and when they arrive, Mrs. Jeffries can tell us how she figured it out," Phyllis got up and grabbed the teakettle.

By the time the tea was made, Luty and Hatchet were at the table. They took turns telling the others about the events at the Biddlington house. "You shoulda seen Hatchet." Luty grinned at him. "He snuck right up behind McConnell and whacked him with a poker."

"Madam had grabbed a glass globe, but I was concerned

it was too unwieldy to be effective as a weapon. The poker was far more useful in stopping Mr. McConnell's rampage."

"I'm glad he isn't dead," Ruth added. "Justice needs to run its course and I've a feeling that it would have haunted you to take a human life."

"That's true," Hatchet agreed. "Now, Mrs. Jeffries, tell us how you figured it out."

"There were two things that kept bothering me. One was the note of warning found in Mrs. Starling's letterbox—it was written on a typewriter—and the other thing was the handwriting. I couldn't account for either of those factors when I was considering Nesbitt's, Redstone's, or even Mrs. Huxton's motives."

"Whose handwriting?" Phyllis asked, her expression curious. "The only mention of handwriting was Mrs. Huxton claiming hers was so ordinary that even if she'd not destroyed that nasty letter she wrote, it wouldn't have mattered."

"True, but remember what else she said. She told the inspector that Graham McConnell's penmanship was so elaborate, it was unreadable. That fact simply wouldn't go away. I kept asking myself why someone would use a typewriter to write a short note; we've all played about with one of them—"

"I haven't," Mrs. Goodge muttered. "Sorry, go on."

"As I was saying, most of us have played about with one, and they're very difficult to operate. So why would anyone type rather than write?"

"Because their handwriting was distinctive." Phyllis nodded. "That makes sense." She looked at Mrs. Jeffries. "That was the only thing that made you realize who had killed her?"

"That is what got me to take a closer look at him. It was

a very confusing case, but there were several things that kept bothering me. From the very beginning, we knew Margaret Starling was concerned with the society's finances. But that fact was overshadowed by her conflicts with so many people. It suddenly occurred to me that someone might have wanted to take advantage of that situation—someone who didn't want the police looking in their direction."

"By 'someone,' you mean Graham McConnell," Hatchet said. "How did he do it?"

"I think he was the one who typed the note to her—the one that told her the vicar had betrayed her confidence."

"Is that why you had me ask Stuart Deeds all those questions?" Phyllis asked. "Because he'd already told me that he thought someone had been messing up his desk."

"That's right, and once you got him talking, he told you about McConnell essentially using him as a spy. He told McConnell everything he overheard."

"But it was the note that caused the quarrel with Pontefract," Mrs. Goodge observed. "One loud enough so that everyone heard it."

"That's right. Pontefract had only shown the note to the board, and he was certain that none of the members had told Margaret they'd seen it. None of them wanted to agitate her any more than she already was." Mrs. Jeffries took a quick sip of tea. "He made sure Pontefract's own behavior made him a suspect."

"He's an embezzler, isn't he?" Ruth said.

"I'm sure that was his motive," Mrs. Jeffries agreed. "I think once the inspector sees the second ledger, the one Mrs. Starling took to Nelson Biddlington, we'll find that he's been stealing from the moment he arrived at the Angel Alms Society."

"They made it dead easy for 'im," Wiggins muttered. "One of the board members told Mrs. Starling that thirty percent of their donations was notes or coin."

"Yes, and because Stuart was passing along the information he overheard after the meetings, McConnell began to suspect that Margaret was aware of his scheme."

"He also had Fanny Herald," Wiggins pointed out. "That's why 'e was so keen to walk 'er 'ome after Evensong services."

"I believe that's one of the reasons she's been so upset," Mrs. Jeffries said.

"You think she'd started to suspect him?"

"Yes, and that, paired with the worry about being unemployed, probably sent the poor girl half-mad." She took another sip. "McConnell had been to the Starling house many times. He knew where the back door key was kept. He stole it one of those times when he walked Fanny home. She was quite useful to him. He also would have known the shovel was kept in the garden shed. It was dark when the murder was committed, and I think he was the one who struck a match, grabbed the shovel, and, without thinking, dropped the match on the floor. Another thing that bothered me was the clothes. First of all, only McConnell had seen the three bags of clothing that he wanted Mrs. Starling's committee to go through. But the clothes were never there. No one else—not the verger, the vicar, or the clerk—saw those items. McConnell mentioned them because he needed an excuse for speaking to Mrs. Starling as she hurried to confront the vicar the day after he'd dropped off the note in her mailbox and he used them as an excuse for going to the Starling house on the morning her body was found."

"Why did he do that?" Luty asked. "Seems to me he shoulda stayed as far away as he could."

"I think he was desperate to know what was happening," Mrs. Jeffries replied. "He's one of those people that likes to keep control over everything. What's more, I'm sure he took the coat out of the closet, the one that Stuart said the vicar wanted to give to a street person. I think McConnell took it to wear when he committed the murder to keep the blood off his own clothes."

"He thought of everything, didn't he," Phyllis murmured.

"What I don't understand is how he got Mrs. Starling to come out of the house that night," Betsy said.

"The cat. It had been missing all day. He took it to lure Mrs. Starling out that night—a night he knew the servants were gone."

"That's what Mr. and Mrs. Walcott heard all day: He had the cat in his flat and it kept crying," Betsy realized. "That's why he gave his housekeeper the day off. He didn't want her to know."

"My theory is that he took the cat back, did something to make it cry, and when she came out, he killed her. McConnell then put the cat back in the house, locked the door, and walked away."

"Why put the cat back inside?" Luty asked. "I don't git that."

"He did it to keep the servants from going out and looking for it. Mrs. Starling loved the cat, and if it hadn't been in when they came back from the theater, he was afraid one of them might go outside to look for it. But his stealing the key had two purposes: one, to lock the door from the outside, and two, to make sure the servants had to come in the front door, not the back. He didn't want her found too quickly. Of course, what he didn't realize was that there were consequences to kicking the cat. According to what Stuart told the inspector, McConnell's arm was so badly scratched he had to go to a doctor for treatment."

"Good. I'm glad that Gladstone defended his mistress." Mrs. Goodge smiled at Samson, who was sitting in the doorway.

They discussed the case for another hour, going over all the details and seeing how neatly they fit.

Ruth got to her feet. "I do wish I could be here when Gerald comes home, but I've some guests coming tonight for supper, so I'll have to wait until tomorrow to hear what he has to say about it."

"Tomorrow's Christmas Eve," Luty reminded her. "You're all comin' to my place for afternoon tea. We'll get an earful then."

"Then it's here for Christmas Eve dinner. We've a lot of celebratin' to do," Mrs. Goodge announced. "And as I predicted"—she poked Mrs. Jeffries lightly on the arm—"my feelings were right and you did solve it just in time."

The inspector arrived home just before five o'clock. "We did it, Mrs. Jeffries." He handed her his bowler. "We arrested Margaret Starling's killer."

"Who was it, sir?" she asked as she hung up his garments.

"I'll tell you over a glass of sherry. Come along, I want to celebrate. This has been a very, very hard case."

A few minutes later she handed him his glass and took her seat. "Now, you mustn't keep me in suspense, sir. Who did you arrest?"

"Graham McConnell. We arrested him at the home of Margaret Starling's solicitor, Nelson Biddlington. He'd gone there to retrieve a package she'd taken to Biddlington for safekeeping. He confessed to murdering her."

"Why did he do it?"

"She found out he'd been embezzling from the Angel Alms Society. That's why he went to the Biddlington house: He wanted to get back the items Margaret Starling found hidden in the storage room. He used it as a hiding place and she must have seen him."

"Was it evidence of his embezzling?" She knew it had to be the second set of books.

"It was evidence of a sort. It was a box of money, five-pound notes and gold sovereigns."

She couldn't believe it. "Only money? That was all?"

"Isn't that enough?" He looked at her curiously.

"Of course, sir. I'm just surprised there wasn't a ledger or something like that. Why would Margaret Starling take a box of money to her solicitor? Doesn't there have to be something in it that links McConnell to the embezzlement in order for it to be evidence?"

"There were the gold sovereigns, which we found out were sent by Mrs. Madrigal, but we don't really even need her to testify when the case goes to court. He confessed." He told her everything that happened. She listened carefully, occasionally asking a question or making a comment. But basically he covered very much the same ground as she had only a few hours earlier. Knowing that Constable Barnes was responsible for nudging the inspector down the right path, she made a mental note to thank him for his efforts.

When he finished, she said, "Gracious, sir, this was such a complicated case, but you solved it in the end. I knew you could." She was starting to have doubts about her own abilities. How could she have been so wrong about the second ledger? Still, she'd been right about most of it.

He smiled proudly. "Thank you, Mrs. Jeffries. I'm just happy that we'll be able to celebrate Christmas properly. Is the tree still coming tomorrow?"

"Yes, and everyone is very excited about that and the tea party at Luty's house. Would you care for another sherry, sir?"

"Not tonight, I think I'll take Fred for a walk and enjoy a bit of peace and quiet. I think I've earned it."

January Tenth
Chief Superintendent Barrows' office

"Good morning, sir." Inspector Nivens greeted his superior with a polite nod and a smile.

The chief didn't return his greeting or his smile. "Inspector Nivens, have you any idea why I've asked to see you?"

Nivens knew but he wasn't going admit to it. "None whatsoever, sir."

Barrows pointed to an open file on his desk. "This is a complaint against you. It was filed by another officer and it accuses you of deliberately interfering in a homicide investigation."

"I take it the charge was filed by Inspector Gerald Witherspoon."

"That's correct. You understand that in all his years on the force, Witherspoon has never filed a complaint against a fellow officer?"

"I have a right to challenge the accusations," Nivens said. "And I intend to do so."

"You have that right." Barrows pulled a thin stack of papers from beneath the folder. "But before you consider that course of action I must tell you that we've verified Witherspoon's charges with six officers from the Upper Richmond Road. These are their statements."

"So taking this any further would be pointless," Nivens snorted faintly. "So even though I've been an exemplary officer, I'm to be sacked?"

"You deliberately tried to hobble a murder case," Barrows snapped. "What did you think was going to happen if you got caught?"

"I didn't expect my own men to be such turncoats."

"Your men neither like you nor do they respect you. Don't you understand that?" Barrows caught himself. "In the normal course of events, yes, you'd be sacked. But we both know you have some powerful friends, or at least your mother has powerful friends. Apparently she's prevailed upon some of them to intervene in this matter on your behalf. You'll still be a member of Metropolitan Police Force."

"Will I be able to keep my rank?"

"You'll still be an inspector, but you'll no longer be assigned to the Upper Richmond Road Police Station." Barrows allowed himself a smile. "I'm sending you to the East End."

"Where in the East End?" Nivens asked, but he already

knew Barrows was going to send him to the nastiest and most miserable part of town he could find.

"Whitechapel. I think you'll do very well there. Think of it as a late Christmas gift."